# PRAISE FOR GRAY HORIZON

**2019 Bronze Award winner Readers' Favorite Awards in thriller genre**

"[*Gray Horizon*] is a thrilling ride from start to finish. Grabbing me from page one, I was taken on a rollercoaster journey in a story that I didn't want to put down.... The characters were developed very well and the entire story was full of suspense with a little humor thrown in to lighten the mood a bit. It has made me want to read the other Dr. Whyte books as I thoroughly enjoyed this one. I would recommend this for any reader who is looking for a gripping story, keen to get their teeth into something solid."

— READERS' FAVORITE REVIEWER (FIVE STARS)

"C.B. Samet has a strong voice in this book, perfect for a thriller. She's an EVVY award winner for her fantasy books, and the bold, confident prose and propulsive plot make it easy to see why she's won the award.... Samet's book is a joy to read."

— PAUL ARDOIN (USA TODAY BESTSELLING AUTHOR)

"I thoroughly enjoyed this book! Excellent plot, fast-paced, well-drawn characters, and a storyline that grabs you from the start."

— JANE F., NET GALLEY REVIEWER (FIVE STARS)

"This is the first book I have read by this author and it was engrossing and captivating. *Gray Horizon* finds Dr Lillian learning that a nuclear weapon is on the loose in Europe. As she tracks down the weapon she is drawn into a chase that keeps her one step behind the criminals. This is definitely the kind of book that will keep you on the edge of your seat. Kudos to the author!!"

— NET GALLEY REVIEWER (FIVE STARS)

# GRAY HORIZON

A DR. WHYTE ADVENTURE

CB SAMET

AVANTSTAR
PUBLISHING

ISBN ebook: 978-1-7324525-8-9

ISBN print: 978-1-7324525-9-6

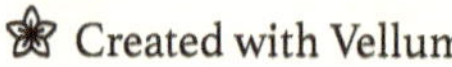 Created with Vellum

# CHAPTER 1

L illian heard shouting from across the hallway and looked up from the imaging screen. A red-cheeked, burly man jabbed a finger toward one of her residents in irritation. A bulge in his jacket pocket suggested the presence of a gun. She had seen too much violence in her lifetime to think it could be anything other than a weapon. Too bad the emergency room didn't have metal detectors at the entrance. The slight sway of the man's rotund body indicated some degree of intoxication.

He was trying to force his way to the bedside of a woman who had been brought in earlier after a car accident. She had multiple injuries, old and new, none of which matched a low-impact fender bender.

Lillian's gaze roamed the emergency room to gauge the level of the threat. The bustle of activity was fairly standard for evening traffic. The waiting room was twenty people deep. Resident physicians, respiratory therapists, phlebotomists, and nurses bustled to and fro, while paramedics wheeled in a stretcher with the newest emergency arrival. In one corner, two policemen were helping subdue a psychotic patient until chemical restraints could be implemented.

This was a normal day at the office, except that this woman's inebriated husband might reach for his gun and open fire at any moment.

Lillian leaned over to Mary, one of the nurses. "Please ask security to meet me at bed four. *Discretely.*"

Mary looked up from her computer screen and stared at Lillian. Her mouth fell open in alarm. "Bed four. Yes, Dr. Whyte."

The escalating situation couldn't wait for security to finish with the psychotic patient. Lillian needed to intervene, especially since the man was armed. The hair on the back of her neck stood on end as she approached the shouting. She steeled herself for the confrontation.

The young resident looked terrified, but stood his ground to protect his patient.

"Let me see my wife, you damn punk!"

Lillian stepped into his direct view. "Hello. I'm Dr. Whyte. Can I help you with something?"

The man scrutinized her black scrubs and red hair. "You can get this kid out of my way, so I can see my wife," he snarled. He gestured to the closed curtain.

Lillian could smell the schnapps on his breath and see his blood-shot sclera. She positioned herself between her resident and the man.

Although her heart thudded in her chest, she kept her voice calm. "She's resting. If you want to wait in the lobby, we can let you know when visitors are permitted." Her senses were on high alert, watching his every twitch and shift.

"I'm not a goddamn visitor! I'm her husband!"

In a quiet but sharp tone, Lillian said, "Then would you also be the man who broke her wrist, cracked three ribs, and bruised her neck?"

A deep scowl settled on his face causing his bushy eyebrows to nearly touch over the bridge of his beefy nose. His eyes became obsidian. Lillian imagined she was seeing what this man's poor wife had seen time and time again.

Despite sensitivity and leadership training, Lillian's mouth seemed to land her in hot water. She had angered him and was now the object of his wrath. Better her than his wife or her resident.

Events in her Lillian's life over the last decade had propelled her into learning advanced self-defense. She had more training for combat than most people, yet her previous experiences did nothing to dull the adrenaline coursing through her.

The man's knuckles cracked under the force of restrained fury as he balled his fists. "She tell you that?"

Lillian looked him directly in the eyes. "She didn't have to."

The man snapped. He roared and lunged at Lillian.

Time seemed to slow as she watched every motion and took evasive measures. She twisted her torso to the right and dodged him, letting him collide with one of the beams holding the curtains partitioning the room.

He swore and spun around to find her.

Several nurses and emergency room technicians turned to stare. The police were still on the opposite side of the emergency room.

Lillian knew what would come next—the gun. Multiple homicides would be followed by either suicide or the police taking him down when he ran out of bullets. She needed to end the fight before anyone conjured the idiotic idea of coming to her rescue.

The man drove his hand into his pocket and jerked out the gun. The flash of metal glinted in the fluorescent light of the emergency room.

Lillian was already moving closer. She grasped the revolver and launched a knee into the man's upper abdomen. As he bent over with a grunt, she twisted the gun out of his hand.

He took an enraged swing. His tree trunk of an arm barreled toward her. Stepping back, she avoided the blow then kicked at his knee hard enough to shred ligaments.

He unleashed a howl of pain and crumpled to the linoleum floor. If he knew what horrendous germs and bodily fluids lurked on the floor, he might not linger there.

She looked down at the revolver in her hand. It was loaded. She opened the cylinder, swung it out, and dropped the bullets on the counter. With her heart pounding, she laid the gun beside the bullets and stepped back from the counter.

Two police officers scurried over and began restraining the man even as he complained about the assault and the pain in his stomach and leg.

Lillian sighed. Now she had created an extra patient in the already crowded ER. At least nobody got shot.

———

IVAN KLEIST SPLASHED water onto his face from the public restroom sink before inspecting his bruised, swollen jaw. He ran his tongue over his chipped molar. He had spit out the bloody tooth fragment during the fight two days ago. If only the German tooth fairy —*Zahnfee*—still paid in gold coins, Ivan wouldn't have to work so hard for fifty thousand Euros.

*Verdammt.*

He had retrieved the file, no easy feat. But the beating he'd taken would ache for days. Maybe he was getting too old, too slow. Crime had many financial advantages, but sometimes the physical cost seemed steep.

"*Tu va bien?*" Renni asked.

Ivan looked in the mirror at the Frenchman standing behind him. "*Ja.*"

Renni Durand hadn't escaped unscathed either. Ivan wouldn't be surprised if his colleague peed blood for the next week from the punches his flank had sustained. He had a cut on his cheek above his stubbled jaw. One brown iris was encircled with blood.

Renni wiped his face with a damp paper towel. "Ze exchange is in one hour. We've got to move."

As they left the bathroom, Renni lit a Gauloises and took a drag. "Somezing felt off about zis job." A wisp of smoke twisted into the air.

Ivan had no interest in smoking, but at least the smell of the French tobacco was more reminiscent of a cigar than bleached American and Canadian cigarettes. German smokers often smoked American brands unless they enjoyed the German F6. Just like his country to pick a practical name—nothing sexy or luring.

"You say that about every job." Ivan ran a hand through his short, spiked, pale blond hair.

"This one is different."

"You say that too."

"*Zut*," Renni swore.

"So don't go to the exchange," Ivan offered as they walked the Ring Road away from the Beijing Railway Station. The enticing aroma of chuan'r—roasted meat, charcoal, cumin, and pepper—from street vendors filled the air.

"If I don't go, who has your back?"

Ivan couldn't argue with Renni's logic. They knew little of the individuals who had hired them except that they wanted this flash drive and its contents in mint condition, and they wanted the previous owners of the USB in the grave. The previous owners put forth a stronger fight than expected. They had been surprisingly averse to dying. As a result, Ivan's jaw still ached.

The men they fought had claimed the attack was a double-cross. Ivan and Renni had done the job they'd been hired to do. They were not told of the contents of the USB drive, so they couldn't possibly be double-crossing anyone. The men went to their graves thinking someone had betrayed them.

Perhaps someone had, but Ivan had no way of knowing the details. It wouldn't be the first time he had been hired to eliminate someone previously in cahoots with whomever had hired him. Business was business. If nothing was fundamentally different in this job compared to others, why did he feel the need to be hyperalert? Now that they had the USB, the job was almost finished. They would make the exchange.

After that, Ivan planned to take the week off and go back home to Germany to recuperate.

. . .

Ivan and Renni took the stairs to the third floor of the office building under renovation. The steps creaked under their weight.

Ivan was accustomed to secretive meetings in secretive places. This particular exchange was no different. Except that it *felt* different.

Renni Durand—the cavalier, nicotine-addicted Frenchman—seemed on edge as well. Or was Ivan projecting his own emotions? No matter. They weren't a couple of amateurs. They could outmaneuver any opponent.

Ivan and Renni exited the stairwell on the third floor. Battery-powered LED lanterns dimly lit the room at the end of the hall.

"Are you the cook?" Ivan asked a tall, bearded man sporting a CZ 75.

The sleek, 9mm semiautomatic pistol had been made in the Czech Republic. It was a respectable weapon, but it appeared out of place in the hands of a man whose ridged brow and jutting jaw made him look like he belonged in the Paleolithic era. He needed a club, not a gun. Another man who could have been his twin stood a few feet to the right of him.

The first caveman grunted in amusement. He stepped aside to reveal a petite Asian woman.

"*Annyeong hashimnikka.*" The woman bowed.

Ivan mimicked her bow but was at a loss on how to acknowledge her greeting. He was fluent in German, French, English, Dutch, and Russian, but he knew scant Korean.

"I am the cook," the woman said in English.

Ivan straightened. "I—" he began, but she turned and walked away from him.

*—am insignificant, apparently.*

This was not his first encounter with arrogance. The people he worked for often thought they were better than him. Ivan knew the truth. The contractor of a thief was no different than the thief himself —or herself. He didn't discriminate as long as he was paid well. And he didn't feel the need to explain the lack of distinction to those who employed him. They could stare down their nose at him as long as he walked away with a bigger bank account.

His gaze followed the cook as she walked to a tiny metal desk with an open laptop.

She extended an open palm. "The package?"

Ivan withdrew the flash drive from his pocket and handed it to the cook. His eyes caught a glimpse of burn scars on her hand. After turning and sitting at the desk, she plugged it into the laptop.

One of the men stepped between Ivan and the cook, blocking his view of the computer screen. He could hear her small fingers as they moved over the keyboard rapidly. She would be opening file after file skimming through document after document long enough to confirm he had provided the stolen information she sought. Ivan had already examined the flash drive and knew what terrible secrets it held, but he kept his expression neutral.

Ivan glanced at his partner Renni, who kept his position, standing back far enough that he was near the exit and could see the cook and her two guards clearly. Ivan had no doubt his partner would ensure their safe escape should the cook intend a double-cross.

The woman nodded in satisfaction. "*Joh-eun.*"

Although none of the gunmen had drawn their weapons, a window shattered. Behind Ivan, Renni collapsed with a grunt.

*Sniper.*

Ivan dove to the floor and rolled. He didn't hear a second sniper shot. Of course the shooter wouldn't want to risk hitting the computer and drive.

With the rustling of fabric, the cook's men drew their guns.

Ivan lurched behind a metal rolling cart with construction supplies as bullets erupted around him. When he drew himself into a tight ball, his joints protested with pain. He positioned his fingers to draw his weapon.

The noise of gunfire and ricocheting bullets filled the room. His ears rang from the deafening roar as his heart, amped up on adrenaline, thudded in his chest. His opponents had the clear advantage. Three against one. Ivan planned to at least put up a good fight.

The hair on his neck stood on end as a trickle of icy sweat ran down his spine. He was accustomed to fear and danger in his work—

dark people doing dark deeds—but the contents of the encrypted documents they had stolen for the cook sealed his death warrant. After they had stolen it and before this delivery, Ivan had seen what terrible information was on that flash drive. He had debated the consequences of not making the delivery at all, but that would have certainly made him a target.

Now he understood he had indeed been hired to double-cross the men from whom they had stolen this information. The men he had killed. Just as he would be killed.

When the cook's men had emptied their semiautomatics, Ivan came up shooting.

The cook was already exiting via the stairwell, laptop tucked under one arm. Ivan didn't have much time. Once she was out of harm's way, the sniper could open fire. In fact, when she was out of the building, the whole place could be incinerated if they felt so inclined. He needed to get outside.

He darted across the room. A sniper's bullet grazed his arm.

"*Verdammt*," he growled.

Judging by the timing of fire, he was up against a bolt-action sniper rifle. At least it wasn't an automatic weapon. At fifty, he wasn't as agile and fast as he used to be. He suspected the sniper was positioned in the building adjacent to this one.

One of the cook's guards stayed behind, and Ivan heard him reloading his gun. Ivan faced bullets from two sides. He slid under a vinyl curtain tacked to an unfinished wall, partitioning the room.

Glass rained down as the sniper continued to fire through the windows.

Ivan crawled along the floor, ignoring the shards of glass biting into his bare forearms. He reached a gaping hole in the floor where wires and pipes crisscrossed haphazardly. He squeezed his battered body through the opening, slipping on his own blood before falling into the darkness of the room below him.

Pain shot through his back as he struck a metal beam lying across the floor. He grunted and rolled over, listening for motion as his vision adjusted to the darkness.

The gunfire had ceased, but it was only a matter of time before they found him. His escape routes were limited. The stairwells were not an option; they would be watched. The elevator shaft would be the next logical place for them to lie in wait to execute him. He was too high up to jump without breaking a leg—or worse.

Ivan recalled the construction waste chute on the side of the building. He had spotted it when he and Renni arrived and first inspected the building. Since the chute was on the other side of the building, it would not be visible from the sniper's vantage point.

Gritting his teeth through the pain in his back, Ivan pushed himself to his feet. He wound his way out of the room, down the hall, and toward the rear stairs. As he pressed his face to the glass, he looked outside the building. Streetlights faintly illuminated the forklifts and cranes outside the window. He looked up and noted the chute's opening was two stories above him. It ended in a large, rectangular trash bin. No doubt it would be filled with jagged chunks of concrete, shards of fiberglass, and twisted rebar, because that was the sort of day he was having.

He cringed when the door to the stairwell moaned. Straining to listen over the sound of his own thudding heart and panting breath, he heard no footsteps or voices. He took the stairs two steps at a time up two stories.

He found the chute.

Judging from what he had seen from the stolen drive on the laptop, he would have a permanent target on his back. He needed to go into hiding. He could trust no one, because the bounty the cook would put on his head would be high.

Such a thought made him remember Renni was dead. With a pang of guilt, he softly apologized to his friend. *We should have been more careful.*

Ivan hoped he wasn't such a bastard that he would have ever betrayed Renni. Perhaps he would never know.

His only hope of survival was to hide and change his identity. He had the money and resources for both. Except he couldn't hide.

Based on what he had seen in those files, he couldn't cower and let events unfold. With that thought, he leaped into the chute and hoped to hell it could withstand the weight of an eighty-five kilogram man.

———

LILLIAN SHOWERED and crawled into bed. The adrenaline rush of her ER confrontation had long since worn off. Now she needed rest.

Warm arms enveloped her. The comfort of them eased the tension in her body.

"You're home late," Sean said, scooting close behind her and burying his face in her hair and into her neck.

She had called him to let him know she'd be late, but one hour late turned into three.

"I had to give a statement to the police. And then there was the documentation." The paperwork was never-ending for a physician. Since she had gotten into an altercation, more paperwork presented itself.

"What'd you do this time?"

"Hey." She rolled toward him. "Why would you assume it's my fault?"

He chuckled as he repositioned to keep her close.

She looked into his warm, brown eyes. Small crow's feet crinkled at the edges. She liked to think all of their laughs and fun times together over the years had created those character lines.

"Okay," she conceded, running a hand through his brown hair and along his firm jawline. "Yes. It was my fault. I turned a wife-beater into a patient."

Sean arched an eyebrow at her. "You think a taste of his own medicine will make him repent and turn over a new leaf?"

"No. But he was harassing my resident, and I wasn't going to stand for that."

He pursed his lips. "Is this something we're going to need legal representation for later?"

"No. It's all on video. He attacked me, and then he drew a gun."

She tapered the last few words into a quiet tone as she cringed, waiting for Sean's response.

She felt his body tense around her.

"A gun?"

"A little snub-nose Colt."

"Probably a Cobra."

"Which I identified on him early and was prepared for the draw."

Sean sucked in a deep breath, but kept his voice calm. "I didn't give you combat and weapons training so you could pick fights with belligerent wife-beaters. You should let the police and hospital security handle trouble in the ER."

"I would have, but they had their hands full. If I hadn't intervened, I would have been on the other side of the ER when he opened fire on my resident."

Sean squeezed her tight. She could feel the strong and steady thump of his heart. Her cheek rested against his warm neck.

"I would prefer you on the other side of the room when violence erupts."

"That's not who we are."

He didn't reply, but she felt his throat bob in a swallow. She hadn't meant to make the events of Montreal resurface, yet she knew Sean would be thinking of the day she had been shot. The day she nearly died in his arms.

"You're okay?" he asked.

"I'm okay." She nuzzled her nose into his neck.

"Do you want to talk about it?"

She kissed his neck and the stubble along his jaw brushed her cheek. "Done talking."

He massaged a thumb along her back in small circular motions. "You're still tense."

"What does my secret spy suggest I do about that?" She nipped at his ear.

He sucked in a sharp breath as he pressed his firm body against her. "*Former* spy."

"Sure. Whatever you say."

"I suppose I could share my top secret, for-your-body-only techniques for tension reduction."

She wriggled out of her nightgown. "Show me."

———

DEPARTMENT OF DEFENSE
TOP SECRET
NUCLEAR THREAT INVESTIGATION

CASE FILE: 8966B20
Deputy Director: William Austin
Re: Dr. Lillian Whyte and Agent Sean Jennings

TRANSCRIPT:
DEPARTMENT OF DEFENSE INQUIRY

DOD: You've been involved in quite a few violent altercations in the last several years.
DR. WHYTE: Being an emergency room physician isn't for the faint of heart.

DOD: Do most emergency room physicians disarm gunmen?
DR. WHYTE: Not that I'm aware of.

DOD: But you do.
DR. WHYTE: I've had training.

DOD: After Kenya?
DR. WHYTE: Kenya and Montreal.

DOD: Much like those events, you were face-to-face with international criminals again in this most recent incident.
DR. WHYTE: Was there a question in there?

DOD: It is intriguing and confounding that a civilian with no known ties to the criminal underworld would be entangled on three separate events in international crises.
DR. WHYTE: Agreed.

DOD: Would you say there were any abnormal events prior to your trip to Iceland?
DR. WHYTE: None.

DOD: Not even the detonation of a nuclear weapon out to sea by North Korea?
DR. WHYTE: I wouldn't categorize that as abnormal, no.

# CHAPTER 2

Dmitry stretched in his chair and cracked his neck as he watched the satellite images and listened to Kino playing through his speakers. The same trees, buildings, cars, and trucks stared back at him day after day.

He stood, poured a cup of coffee, and returned to his screens. He needed better coffee, a Raf perhaps—expresso, cream, and the perfect amount of sugar. But he couldn't leave the screens. And for the amount of money he was making to watch them, he wouldn't dare risk distraction. He shoved some papers aside to make room for his coffee. He also needed to clean his desk. His sniffed his armpit ... and he needed a shower.

When he first launched his satellites five years ago, investors balked at the price. Sending two dozen small, solar powered reconnaissance satellites into orbit wasn't cheap. He'd had to explain to the ignorant investors that one satellite would be insufficient for spying since satellites moved in orbit. They did not remain stationary over a single location, and even if such a thing were designed, it would burn through costly fuel to stay there. With two dozen birds, he could watch one location with multiple satellites. There were still gaps, but the reconnaissance was impressive.

His investors had made their money back five-fold and didn't care on who or what their expensive lenses were focused. Politicians wanted to spy on other politicians; smugglers wanted to know the locations of convoys or military patrols; spouses of multi-millionaires wanted to know to where their significant others were taking the private jet or yacht.

Dmitry took off his glasses and cleaned the lenses on his shirt. When he replaced them, he admired the high-resolution—1.5 meters per pixel. It wasn't military grade, but it was respectable. Russian made. Since Russians were the first to launch a satellite into space—Sputnik in 1957—why shouldn't his little *sputniks* be top of the line? There were over eleven hundred functioning satellites circling Earth, but his system was ideal for private, non-government funded spying.

And what was he doing with his state-of-the-art reconnaissance equipment? Staring at a building. He sighed, blinked, and sipped his coffee.

Movement caught his eye. He pushed his glasses back up on his nose as he leaned closer to the screen. The increase in vehicles in and out of the compound in a rushed manner were a break from the daily routine. Something had happened.

*Evrika!*

He would need to go back through the footage and see precise events leading to the sudden flurry of activity. Once he isolated what had happened, he could focus other satellites to follow the source of the disruption.

*Watch for unusual activity and track it*, had been his instructions.

He reached for his phone to alert his client.

---

Yu poured a cup of tea and watched the wisps of steam float from the porcelain cup. The plane shimmied slightly from turbulence. She looked out the window, knowing she'd be over Europe soon.

The scheme had taken months of planning, though truthfully, she had been thinking of how to accomplish such a feat for years. Her team was completing the first phase of the mission. She would dispose of this team as she had the last, and the fresh team would be ignorant of her future plans. The same way Ivan was supposed to be ignorant up until his death. Except, he hadn't died.

Thus far he was the one misstep in her plans. She had made a mistake, and she despised mistakes. Sun Tzu wrote in *The Art of War*, "*If you know the enemy and know yourself, you need not fear the result of a hundred battles. If you know yourself but not the enemy, for every victory gained you will also suffer a defeat.*"

Did she not know this enemy?

She had researched Ivan Kleist well, as she did her many other pawns. They were all the same—kill anyone for a price. This pawn happened to be a little more slippery, that was all. She still knew him well. He would go into hiding—a fox to his hole. And she knew his holes.

He knew Africa intimately from his many years helping an oil profiteer. He knew Eastern Europe well, having done his share of crime in France, Poland, and Austria. But never Germany. He didn't violate the law within his home country. However, he did visit often. His sister had an isolated cabin in Germany somewhere.

Yu would need to plant moles to find the fox since he was the only person who could surmise her plans. She would be more thorough this time. A team larger than a single sniper and two men would be needed to eliminate Ivan Kleist.

---

Lillian sat in Kelly's kitchen, sipping iced tea. In typical Southern style, the sugary drink coated her esophagus as it went down.

"So, Iceland's next?" Kelly asked.

"Yeah. I'm excited."

"At the rate you and Sean travel, you'll have been to every country before you die."

Lillian shook her head. "Not every country. No other African countries."

Lillian watched as Kelly leaned on the counter. The petite blond woman had been her friend since grade school. They had gone to college together and later both moved to Atlanta—Lillian to medical school and Kelly for work.

Lillian heard a cry from the upstairs bedroom.

"Katie's up," Kelly announced.

She left and returned to the kitchen a few minutes later carrying her eighteen-month-old daughter.

Lillian swiveled in her chair, watching the toddler wriggle free of her mother's grasp.

"Can you watch her a sec?" Kelly walked to the fridge and pulled out a bag of chilled fruit.

Lillian stood and looked down at the child. With a series of grunting noises that resembled "Lily" but sounded perhaps like "Wily," the small child toddled unsteadily toward Lillian.

Lillian eyed Katie skeptically, as the toddler clutched her pant leg. "Are they supposed to be so mobile at this age? Seems hazardous."

Kelly snorted. "It is hazardous." She cut the peel off a mango. "Didn't you learn the developmental stages in medical school?"

Katie began scaling her way up Lillian's blue jeans.

"Sure. But that was fifteen years ago." She picked up the child and held her at a distance. Her blue eyes were wide and curious. Her wispy hair was blonde, like her mother's. She wore some type of pink jumpsuit with a tutu.

"You dress her like something out of a Disney movie."

"You should see her when she wears her tiara."

Katie started to squirm. Lillian flipped her over and dangled her by one foot, still holding her at a distance.

Katie laughed.

Kelly gave Lillian a sour look. "You don't have to hold her like she's some alien life-form with a communicable disease." She quickly sliced through the mangos and set the plate on the table. After wiping her hands on the dishtowel, she reached for Katie. "Honestly,

Lily. You act like you've never held a child." Kelly turned her daughter back upright and sat her in her high chair before the mangos.

Lillian sat back down at the counter by her tea. "You remember how many times I babysat in high school?"

Kelly looked contemplative.

"Once," Lillian said. "One time was enough crying, fussing, and chaos to last a lifetime."

With parental pride, Kelly watched Katie devour the mango. "So you and Sean—"

"Nope."

Kelly gave her a doleful look. "It isn't easy, but it has its rewarding moments."

"I admire you for the self-sacrifice, loss of sleep, loss of independence, and all those dirty diapers. It's not for me."

"Sean's never expressed an interest?"

The question saddened Lillian. She had told him she didn't have a strong desire for motherhood. He had told her that even if he wanted children, he wouldn't have them for fear his past would seek vengeance on his children.

"He doesn't think it's safe for children."

"*It* being the world in general—because every parent feels that way—or is he referring to his military past?"

Lillian felt a twinge of guilt at the secrets she had kept from her friend. Kelly didn't know Sean was former CIA. She only knew him as the former Navy Seal turned history teacher whom Lillian had met in Africa nine years ago when he was a Swahili translator. Her best friend didn't know the truth about everything that had happened in Africa, and she didn't know anything about the biological weapon in Montreal three years ago.

"His past," Lillian replied.

*And his present.*

Sean was still CIA, part-time. He worried about his past and present endangering Lillian.

Kelly poured Katie a sippy cup of watered-down juice and passed it to the excited toddler. "Well he may be former military, but it's still in him—the way he watches his surroundings with casual scrutiny and the way he's protective of you."

Lillian wondered about Kelly's powers of observation.

Kelly continued. "I bet he'd make a great dad—loving and protective. He'd probably install some high-tech baby monitor and a nanny cam in every room."

Lillian smiled. Kelly wasn't wrong about him. Add bulletproof windows and a panic room.

Because of his protective nature, Sean had taught Lillian to know her way around different guns as well as some martial arts maneuvers.

"He might make a good dad, but I lack the motherly tendencies that seem innate to most women."

Kelly arched an eyebrow at her. "When it's your own child, you discover your innate abilities."

Lillian looked skeptically at Katie. Her cheek was smeared with orange mango, which she had managed to clump in her hair as well. The highchair was dripping with mango juice. She beat her pink cup on the plastic chair, demanding attention.

Nothing about the scene stirred Lillian's womb or created any desire to alter her life for such a creature.

---

DEPARTMENT OF DEFENSE
TOP SECRET
NUCLEAR THREAT INVESTIGATION


CASE FILE: 8966B20
Deputy Director: William Austin
Re: Dr. Lillian Whyte and Agent Sean Jennings


TRANSCRIPT:
DEPARTMENT OF DEFENSE INQUIRY

DOD: Your current position is chair of the emergency room at your hospital?
DR. WHYTE: That's correct.

DOD: And your former boss retired, leaving the position vacant?
DR. WHYTE: George McClellan retired. I took his position as interim chair until they find a replacement.

DOD: How many hours a week do you work?
DR. WHYTE: Fifty to sixty.

DOD: What do you know about your husband's employment?
DR. WHYTE: He teaches history and writes history books.

DOD: What do you know about his CIA involvement?
DR. WHYTE: When they ask him to help, he helps.

DOD: How often would you say they required his help?
DR. WHYTE: I don't ask.

DOD: So you don't know about any of his CIA activities?
DR. WHYTE: We take a trip. It could be all vacation for him or he might be working for the CIA.

DOD: Did he have any CIA work planned in Iceland?
DR. WHYTE: I didn't ask.

# CHAPTER 3

Lillian sat at her computer desk fulfilling a day of administrative responsibilities. She had made the mistake of completing several courses on leadership a few years ago. Subsequently, when her boss stepped down as department chair, someone mistook Lillian as a suitable replacement. She was six months into her new position as interim chair of Emergency Medicine. She would be in this role until the hospital completed a nation-wide search, performed interviews, and found a suitable replacement.

Meanwhile, her former boss and mentor, George McClellan, was enjoying retirement. The last time she spoke with him, he was still touring Europe.

While she waited for her email to open, she stretched in her chair. Her body, personality, and attention span were not meant to be stationary.

She decided to re-read a specific message in her inbox from six months ago that she had kept, if only for amusement purposes. The long email chain had been initiated by the chief medical officer to gauge opinions about granting the position of department chair to

Lillian—though she didn't aspire to the role. She was never supposed to see the email, but someone had accidentally not read it in its entirety and forwarded it to her. She reread it in chronological order.


> FROM: Bob Goldberg, MD, MBA
> 8:32 AM
>
> As you know, George is retiring from his position as department chair of the emergency room. While we are conducting a national search for his replacement, we will need a suitable interim chair. Dr. Lillian Whyte has been recommended. Please send any comments or concerns about this physician fulfilling the duties of this position.
>
> Bob
> Chief Medical Officer

Lillian wondered if CMO-Bob even knew what those duties were. She had little interaction with the man other than to know he was another suit who cut already lean budgets while expecting revenue to continue and patient satisfaction to miraculously increase.

> FROM: Katherine Wayward, RN, MBA
> TO: reply all
> 8:53 AM
>
> Dear group,
> I have no reservations in recommending Dr. Whyte. She provides exemplary care and works well with nursing staff.
>
> Kate
> Vice President for Nursing

*Very sweet. Thanks Kate.*

> FROM: Gregg Shoup, RRT
> TO: reply all
> 9:02 AM
>
> I have worked with Lillian for ten years. I think she
>     will do well in this position, and it will allow for
>     continued personal and professional growth.
>
> Gregg
> Director of Respiratory Therapy

Nice of Gregg to give a positive vote. She still felt a pang of frustration. If Gregg were sending such a message on behalf of a male physician, he would have used his physician title and not his first name. Instead, he called her Lillian rather than Dr. Whyte. When they interacted in meetings and talked about patient care, she preferred "Lillian," but an email to hospital leadership should have shown respect and professionalism.

> FROM: Kamaran Awabdy
> TO: reply all
> 9:37 AM
>
> I think you should take into consideration the multiple
>     patient complaints over the years. We are in an era
>     of being judged by patient satisfaction. I have
>     concerns about Dr. Whyte's confrontational nature
>     and the challenges that may arise with her in a
>     leadership position.
>
> Kamaran
> Clinical Manager

A sound voice of reason. Why did no one take his advice? If they had, Lillian might not be inundated with ER physician resumes, resident requests for letters of recommendation, new product request permission forms, appointments with product representatives to sell her the latest technological diagnostic toys, and protocol development committee meetings.

> FROM: Chad Brunwick, MD
> TO: reply all
> 9:59 AM
>
> Bob,
> I think you should use Lillian as the interim then
>     everyone will be incredibly relieved with whoever
>     you hire next.
>
> Chad
> Assistant Medical Director

This one Lillian was sure Chad meant to send only to the CMO. Bob and Chad were golfing buddies. The dunce hit "reply all" instead. Chad couldn't even email correctly and in proper English, and he was passing judgment on her.

> FROM: Diana Turner, MBA
> TO: reply all
> 10:05 AM
>
> Dr. Whyte has twice as many accolades for efficiency,
>     saving lives, and teaching residents as she does
>     complaints from patients with unrealistic expecta-
>     tions and drug abuse. She would make an excellent
>     departmental chair, not just interim.
>
> Diana

Director of Patient Access Services

True. But Diana might have asked Lillian if she was interested in the position before she praised her. Diana's comments probably overrode Kamaran's. Darn it. Lillian appreciated the compliment, but not the work it created.

> FROM: Ruth Sanders, RN, MPH
> TO: Lillian Whyte, MD
> 10:44 AM
>
> Lillian,
> Congratulations. I hope you get the position.
>
> Ruth
> Admitting Director

Oops. Ruth had apparently only read Diane's email and not read Chad's.

Lillian had archived the emails and looked at them from time to time to find the humor of it all. Little did her allies know they had done her no favors by supporting her for the position. Oh, well. She liked them anyway. She could do this job for a year until a replacement was installed.

Lillian returned her attention to reviewing the details of upcoming events that would happen during her absence. She was making a long list for her assistant, Tonya. The ultrasound probes would be delivered and would need to be programmed as well as tagged, so they could be located if missing. The updates to the sepsis order set would go live in three days.

After emailing the list to Tonya, Lillian walked down to the woman's desk and reviewed the items with her.

"Don't forget to schedule the meeting with Dr. Sumner for when I get back."

Tonya gave her a blank stare.

"The cardiologist."

"Oh, right." Tonya bobbed her head, the mass of auburn hair, stiff with hairspray, remained unmoving. She wrote down a reminder on a sticky note.

The woman's desk was littered with them. Lillian wasn't sure if there was a highly organized color-coded system to them or a rainbow potpourri. In any case, if any top-secret information were buried there, it would remain forever indecipherable.

Tonya scribbled, *Dr. Sumner—cardiology meeting.*

Lillian felt rising irritation seeing the man's name. Meeting with him was going to be headache-inducing, but she needed to address changes to heart failure management in the ER. They had a code STEMI team for when a patient was having a heart attack. It worked fairly quickly and effectively to get patients to cardiac catheterization. However, the responsiveness of some cardiologists to patients in heart failure was atrocious. Apparently cardiac catheterization and reperfusion were cool and sexy and worthy of their attention, whereas heart failure conjured images of a big, beefy, overloaded heart, and giving diuretics induced a feeling of blasé.

Lillian could care less what lay behind their motivation. They were heart doctors. That was their organ. Deal with it. Get the patient to the cardiac care unit with the same efficiency as a heart attack and stop forcing her ER doctors to be referees between the cardiologist and the pulmonologists.

"Anything else, Dr. Whyte?" Tonya asked.

"No, but you have my mobile phone number if you need anything. I've already alerted my carrier that I'll be international."

---

JONATHAN ROSE UP from behind the pair of steel drums and took aim with his weapon. He squeezed the trigger.

*Bull's eye.*

The man he shot unleashed a stream of curses as he looked down in surprise at the color soaking his chest.

*Three remaining.*

He heard the chink of shots hitting metal and missing him as he ducked back behind the drums.

*Good. Waste all your ammo.*

Perry signaled to him. Perry and Steve would lay down cover fire as Jonathan took the hill. Well, Perry was a decent shot, so maybe he would have a chance. Steve was an overweight accountant who couldn't hit the broad side of a barn.

Jonathan dashed out from the drums. His legs pumped ferociously beneath him. With his heart pounding, he leaped over a pair of strewn tires, his feet landing in thick mud. He kept moving. With two giant strides, he leaped onto a stack of tin and over a wooden barricade. He fired at the squatter on the other side.

*Another man bites the dust.*

Jonathan curled into a roll before getting back to his feet. His muscles surged with adrenaline. The next dash was a hundred yards to the top of the hill. He felt something sting his arm. He looked down and over, seeing where he'd been hit.

*Damn it, Perry, do your job.*

The strike didn't slow him down. He reached the top of the hill and claimed the flag.

A victorious shout escaped his lips. "Oorah!"

Looking back down at his shirtsleeve, he inspected the fluorescent pink paint. His only hit today. His team gave him cheers between ragged breaths. Jonathan beamed, basking in his glory.

Arnold shook his head. "Seriously man, it's paintball. You don't have to act like you just saved the president."

Jonathan stared at his competitor through his protective eyewear. Arnold was covered in pink, blue, and yellow paint. Was there anyone who hadn't shot him? Or anywhere he hadn't been hit? No wonder he was a sore loser.

Perry laughed at the sight of Arnold. "You're the one who invited the former marine to play."

Jonathan had enjoyed playing paintball for nine months now. He felt young and alive feeding his competitive nature. He hadn't seen much combat during his marine days. Perhaps the most direct confrontation he'd had was nine years ago when his sister, Lillian, had a crazed attacker who decided to put a hit out on him. He'd barely escaped his house alive. Then the same group attacked him when he was in the hospital.

Since then, his life had settled into a routine of domesticated farm work. Not so for his little sister. He didn't know how many harrowing adventures she'd been on since marrying a CIA agent. Jonathan knew of at least one escapade where she had been shot during events involving terrorists in Montreal.

He struggled between wanting to be the protective older brother and acknowledging the absurdity that her life with Sean seemed to make her infinitely happy. They were two peas in a pod soaring full speed through an asteroid belt.

Jonathan seldom entertained romantic notions of life in general, but the two of them together made him wonder if people truly did have soul mates. Although he would never admit it to his arrogant brother-in-law, Jonathan felt Sean was the right man for his sister.

"Beer at Willies?" Perry asked the group.

Arnold nodded with his fists on his hips. "Winner buys."

Jonathan scowled.

---

DEPARTMENT OF DEFENSE
TOP SECRET
NUCLEAR THREAT INVESTIGATION

CASE FILE: 8966B20
Deputy Director: William Austin
Re: Dr. Lillian Whyte and Agent Sean Jennings

TRANSCRIPT:
DEPARTMENT OF DEFENSE INQUIRY

DOD: Mr. Jonathan Whyte, can you please remove your cowboy hat?
Thank you. What do you know of your sister's involvement with
the CIA?
JONATHAN WHYTE: She's married to a CIA agent.

DOD: Does your sister work for any covert government agencies,
nationally or abroad?
JONATHAN WHYTE: (snorts) Have you met my sister?
DOD: Please answer the question.
JONATHAN WHYTE: Lily does not work for any government
agencies.

DOD: Were you aware of her dealings with international criminals in
Kenya?
JONATHAN WHYTE: If by dealings you mean how she destroyed the
infrastructure of an oil thief and stabbed the asshole, then yes, I am
aware.
DOD: Just the facts, Mr. Whyte
JONATHAN WHYTE: The fact is, that Frenchman sent assassins
after me, so I'm allowed to call him an asshole.

DOD: Were you aware of her dealings with terrorists in Montreal?
JONATHAN WHYTE: If by dealings you mean how she prevented
the release of a biomedical weapon and killed an asshole terrorist in
the process, then yes, I'm aware. And since the terrorist shot her, I'm
allowed to call him an asshole too. Just the facts, sir.

# CHAPTER 4

---

Lillian arrived home at her apartment in Dunwoody to find Sean working at his desk in his office. His broad shoulders filled the chair. His brown hair was sprinkled with gray but still full and soft.

She sunk her fingers through his hair and along his scalp.

"Hey, *mpenzi wangu.*" He called her his darling in Swahili from time to time.

His term of endearment always reminded her of how they had met in Kenya. She was on a medical mission and trying to save herself from physician burnout. He was a CIA operative posing as a Swahili translator trying to catch an oil thief. Nine years later she was still madly in love with him. He had forfeited a life of espionage and moved to Atlanta to be with her.

She kicked off her shoes as she moved her hands down to his shoulders.

He groaned softly.

"How's the book coming?" she asked.

"No book writing today."

The hairs on her neck stood at the intensity of his tone, and her hands froze.

"North Korea tested another nuclear weapon."

"They've been doing that for over ten years. What's different?" she asked.

"The difference is now they have two Magnox reactors."

"Those are bad?" Lillian knew nothing about nuclear weapons or nuclear reactors. Such topics did not arise in her ER.

"They can produce sixty kilograms of plutonium per year."

"That sounds like a lot. Is that a lot?" She sat down in his office lounge chair and pulled his foot into her lap. She started to massage his calloused foot. Her rough day at the office had been business meetings. His rough day had been worrying about nuclear threats.

"That's enough plutonium to make ten bombs."

"Yearly?"

"Yearly." He leaned back in his chair and closed his eyes.

"And the US has how many nuclear weapons? Ten times what they have? A hundred times? Aren't we hypocritical?"

Sean answered her question with his most neutral you-don't-have-clearance-to-know-that look. "But, honey, we're responsible with our nuclear weapons."

Lillian laughed. His statement was as humorous as his ability to keep a straight face while saying it.

He grinned and winked at her. Even after eight years of marriage together that heavy-lidded look from him melted her insides. If it was possible, he grew even more handsome with crow's feet and a few gray hairs.

"What's being done about North Korea's less-than-shocking nuclear stockpiles?"

"Sanctions and economic pressure."

"So, no different than the last ten years."

He sucked in a deep breath. "And a convening of the CIA and Pentagon to explore other options."

Lillian stopped massaging but kept her grip vice-like on his foot.

"Good thing your specialty is Africa, so they don't need you for this one."

Sean frowned. "It's a nuclear threat. They need everyone."

"Except *you,* because we're going to Iceland." Her voice grew frostier. Perhaps it was selfish to think their eight-year anniversary trip should take precedence over the threat of nuclear warfare, but honestly, North Korea had been pulling these shenanigans for over a decade. Besides, the CIA was filled with young, eager, qualified operatives to handle this.

Her husband gave her an apologetic look. "We are going to have a wonderful time in Iceland. I promise. We need to delay our trip by three days."

Lillian set his foot down and stood. "You can delay *your* trip by three days. I've already taken the time off work, and I need a vacation. You can join me when you're done with North Korea."

Sean pushed to his feet and wrapped his arms around her. "You know I don't like you traveling internationally without me."

She remained stiff in his embrace without surrendering. "Your ghosts are in Africa. I'm going to Iceland. If you don't like it, join me." She knew she was being stubborn, but dammit, it was their anniversary.

She didn't hold grudges and wouldn't stay mad, but Sean needed to know when he crossed the line into unacceptable behavior. Letting his part-time consulting job infringe on the anniversary vacation was unacceptable—even if they both knew she would reluctantly accept it.

"I'm sorry," he said softly into her ear.

His warm breath and gentle embrace relaxed her posture. She turned to leave, but he kept her in his arms.

He kissed her neck. "I'll make it up to you in Iceland."

"Fine."

Strong hands moved down her back and slid up under her shirt. He nibbled her ear. "I'll make it up to you now."

He unsnapped her bra and slid his hands around to release her breasts.

She groaned under the pleasure of his touch. "No fair. You're cheating."

He knew exactly the spots to caress to seduce her. She felt the satisfactory smile on his lips as he kissed her neck.

She tilted her head back, enjoying his affection. "I'm still going to Iceland tomorrow." Her voice managed to convey some measure of conviction within its husky breathlessness.

"I know," he said before claiming her mouth in a kiss so heated she forgot about nuclear weapons.

———

JONATHAN LICKED the last of the spicy wing sauce off his fingers as the football game hit halftime. He deposited his empty water glass into the sink, tossed the Styrofoam box in the trash, and grabbed a cold beer from the fridge.

He called Lillian.

"Hey, Jonathan."

"How are ya, Lily?"

"I'm packing for Iceland."

"Ah. That must be the next vacation destination."

"It is."

"Because who wouldn't want to go to an island teeming with active volcanoes?"

"Exactly."

He took a swig of his beer as he plopped into his cushioned recliner. He muted the television. "I'm not going to see you in the five o'clock news, am I? Like Montreal?"

He had been casually relaxing in the comfort of his home—much like this moment—watching news about a hostage situation in Montreal only to see his sister appear in the background screenshot. Except it wasn't just any hostage situation—terrorists had kidnapped an Egyptian ambassador. And Lillian didn't appear in the footage by happenstance. She was providing medical care to hostages. Why?

Was there a shortage of doctors in Canada? No. It was because of that damn CIA husband of hers.

Jonathan didn't know any details about Montreal because Lillian refused to share, but he didn't have to be a rocket scientist to surmise that Lillian had somehow been dragged into another one of Sean's agency dangers.

"It's a vacation, Jonathan."

"Sure it is."

"Besides, I'll be on my own the first few days."

Jonathan sat up straighter. "Sean won't be there?" He instantly hated the sound of worry in his tone. Worrying about Sean's absence implied that Jonathan felt reassurance Lillian was safer with Sean than without him. That wasn't true. Was it?

"I thought you two went everywhere together." He couldn't recall her going on a trip without her husband; although he didn't keep meticulous tabs on her, Jonathan was certain international trips were always together.

"He'll join me when he can." The doubtful tone in her voice made the statement sound more like "*if* he can" rather than "*when* he can."

"Is his delay due to his history teacher front or the other thing you can't talk about?"

"Jonathan..."

"Right. The other thing." His mind rummaged through the last few days of current events on the news. A few peacekeepers killed in Nigeria. Fighting along the Pakistan border. North Korea testing nukes. South American drug traffickers. The president and his family back from Camp David. Nothing was out of the ordinary.

Yet the scariest of events could be the ones that were kept from the public.

Jonathan felt his sister's melancholy through the silence on the phone. He decided to move the subject away from vacationing alone. "How's work?"

"I'm not loving my administrative role."

"It's only temporary, right?"

"Thanks for that miracle."

Jonathan leaned back and reclined in his chair. "When you relinquish it, you'll have newfound respect for the next sucker who takes the position."

Lillian chuckled. "Meanwhile the man whose position was passed down to me is leisurely enjoying a three-month European tour to seal his retirement."

"You liked him though, right?"

"Yeah, George was a good mentor. It will be hard to have the same relationship with my replacement."

"Perhaps it is time, young *padawan*, for the mentee to become the mentor."

"Me? I already suffered through leadership training."

"And look at the doors it opened. Imagine what other adventure awaits with a mentee."

Lillian groaned.

Jonathan chuckled.

YU HUNG up the phone and stared at the candle flame, while absentmindedly running her scarred hand over the heat. She had updated the contractor concerning to the progress of the mission.

Soft American.

*Byeong-shin.*

The greedy *waegukin* saw dollar signs—a spike in sales. She knew differently. When the bomb reached its final destination, it would be detonated in an enormous city. The detonation of the nuclear weapon would rope North America into a major war. The United States of America would see nuclear weapons on its land before the war was over. There would be no stocks and bonds left to boost the contractor's millions.

She smiled. She had successfully orchestrated the theft of a nuclear weapon from North Korea. She liked to imagine the leaders of her country—the country that had abandoned her—scurrying like rats to figure out how someone had stolen one of their weapons.

Wouldn't it have been fun to see their expressions when they discovered it missing? The absolute astonishment as they wet their pants.

She would have liked to detonate the bomb in North Korea, but the funds for this mission came from the contractor. He wanted the bomb on European soil, since he needed to threaten the stability of the industrialized world. She knew the perfect place.

She would give Europe flames and the gift of post-apocalyptic life. Only the strong would survive—something her assassin training appreciated. The contractor would not be one of them, despite his desire to rise from the global crisis as a savior and leader.

She knew his background; he had military training but was more politician than soldier now. He overcompensated by surrounding himself with ex-military. Interestingly, most of his thugs had questionable records and some dishonorable discharges. A band of men like that might lose their loyalty to a weak leader in a world where strength was more valuable than wealth. For now, she would continue to use his resources.

When she smelled burning flesh, she pulled her hand away from the fire. She felt no pain from the charred flesh. The world would know that scent when her work was done. They would know true suffering.


THE CONTRACTOR STUFFED his mobile phone in his suit jacket.

*Crazy Korean woman.*

Cold and calculating type of crazy, but certifiable nonetheless. The cook was a means to an end. And, thankfully, he would never have to meet her in person. They would remain continents apart throughout their entire arrangement. For some deranged reason, she wanted to personally see the bomb through to its detonation.

He poured a glass of scotch and paced near the window of his office. Pedestrians busily walked the concrete sidewalks. Ignorant people living ignorant lives.

Fine by him if the cook was suicidal. That was one less person to pay later. Besides, once the deed was done, the world didn't need her sort of intelligent fanaticism lurking in dark corners. Her derangements had been born from an abused, orphaned girl morphed into an abused government assassin. When the North Korean government decided her age and appearance no longer served their purpose, she had been orphaned once again.

Little did her makers know she was driven to assassinate more people than North Korea had ever commissioned her to do.

———————

LILLIAN DEPOSITED her luggage inside her art deco room at Hotel Borg and left to walk the square of Austurvöllur. The long Atlantic flight to Iceland had left her simultaneously exhausted and antsy to move her legs.

She quickly plugged in all of her electronics—tablet, smart phone, smart watch—so they could recharge. Over the years, Sean had replaced her simple mobile phone with a collection of technologically advanced devices. With her tablet she could connect to email and read the news on the go. As long as she had phone service, she had internet access, and it could act as a hot spot for her tablet. Lastly her watch connected her to all forms of communication, although she rarely used it for more than a step-counter and, well, telling time.

She left her room to explore the city. The square was speckled with people enjoying the August weather. They walked or congregated on blankets in the grass, basking in the sun. Lillian grinned. In Atlanta, everyone was hiding from the scorching August sun, waiting for cooler September weather to arrive.

She pulled her sweater tightly around her. Since she had come from highs of ninety-nine degrees, fifty-five was comparatively chilly. Chilly, but perfect. She would run in the mornings through the crisp air without heat and humidity weighing her down.

She stopped before a cathedral—*the* cathedral—of Iceland, Hallgrímskikja. She walked around the statue of Leif Ericsson, early Icelandic explorer, to stare at the tall, structured white church. Its expressionist architecture was breathtaking. The narrow tower looked like a bishop extending his arms; the white stone on either side of him were draping robes. The rest of the church extending back couldn't be seen behind the tower—behind the robes. She anticipated coming back and seeing it lit up with a deep blue-gray night sky behind it.

As she entered the cathedral, the luminous interior stole her breath. White stone stretched heavenward in a series of arches. The long walkway terminated at a pristine alabaster altar devoid of any elaborate or sacrificial sculptures. Pure white light poured in from the many windows. The bright, crisp glow of the church made her feel as though she stood inside Heaven itself, blinking her eyes against a holy radiance.

She turned to see an enormous organ with gleaming silver pipes above the entryway.

Lillian sat on one of the benches. How long since she'd been to church? Too long. Holiday visits were probably insufficient. At least she was going more since her trip to Africa. Before the medical mission trip, she had only worked and slept. In the last nine years she had made exponentially more personal time. Maybe she should make more church time.

Well, she was here now.

This was a Lutheran church, but what did God care about man-made delineations?

Lillian took several minutes to give thanks for the many gifts in her life—Sean, her career, her brother, her friends, and her health.

When she was done, she exited and roamed the streets in search of a place to eat. She wandered into Cafe Loki off Njarðargata. She certainly couldn't pass up traditional Icelandic food, especially since she'd never tasted it.

While waiting for her order of a salted meat and potato dish in yellow lentil soup, she stared at a strange mural on the wall. On the righthand side, the painting showed a terrified man and woman crawling across a sea of dead bodies as they tried to escape a wolf and a snake. Active volcanoes spewed smoke and ash behind them.

Further in the background were snow-capped mountains. A stream cut through the center of the painting. A salmon swam through its waters as two horses, one black and one white, glided over the grass. To the left, a pale man and a woman fought a blond giant under two enormous and vibrant rainbows stretching across the sky.

Cafe Loki. She realized this mural depicted the many creatures of Loki—shape-shifter and trickster—transformed into Norse mythology: a salmon, a mare, and a man. At times he helped the other gods, and at times he worked against them, always serving himself.

Behind the battling trio was a city of gold—Asgard perhaps. City of Norse gods. If it was Asgard, Valhalla, the celebratory hall of the slain, would lie somewhere within its majestic walls. The rainbows must represent Bifröst—the colorful passageway into and out of Asgard.

Lillian ate and enjoyed the ambiance.

———

DEPARTMENT OF DEFENSE
TOP SECRET
NUCLEAR THREAT INVESTIGATION

CASE FILE: 8966B20
Deputy Director: William Austin
Re: Dr. Lillian Whyte and Agent Sean Jennings

TRANSCRIPT:
DEPARTMENT OF DEFENSE INQUIRY

DOD: When did you learn about the nuclear threat?
JENNINGS: The Friday it was announced at a meeting with the president, CIA, and Joint Chiefs.

DOD: And by that time your wife had already departed on vacation without you?

JENNINGS: That's correct.

DOD: And this trip was important enough for her to leave without you, even though it represented an anniversary celebration?
JENNINGS: She works long hours. She needed a vacation.

DOD: Were you aware of any correspondence between your wife and any of the parties involved in the stolen nuclear weapon?
JENNINGS: She had no involvement until Saturday night.

DOD: Have you ever suspected your wife of being a foreign agent?
JENNINGS: No one who knows Lillian would accuse her of being capable of taking orders from any government agency.

DOD: So you've never suspected her of being a foreign agent?
JENNINGS: No, I have not because she is not.

DOD: Yet she claimed she's had training—training enough to have survived many harrowing encounters involving weapons, terrorists, and deadly criminals.
JENNINGS: I trained her.

# CHAPTER 5

---

Sean exited the elevator and walked to the conference room. He tried to decide what worried him more—his wife traveling internationally without him or the threat of nuclear warfare. The threat of a world war was not new, whereas Lillian hadn't traveled across the ocean without him since Kenya.

He tried to shake the nagging concern. She was in *Iceland*. She wouldn't be in danger on a remote island with low crime and modern amenities. He would join her in two days. Besides, she was no longer without training. He had taught her self-defense, gun safety and handling, and disguise.

He had flown from Atlanta to Washington, DC yesterday, rented a car, and stayed at a hotel last night. He drove to Langley that morning for the CIA meeting.

Lillian was correct about the oddity of his being invited to a meeting about nuclear weapons. He had no particular expertise in either North Korea or nuclear weapons. The direct order from Deputy Director William Austin to attend this meeting puzzled Sean. Since receiving the invitation two days ago, Sean had halted his book writing and focused on expanding what he knew of North Korea.

"Sean." Bill greeted him briskly as he entered the conference room. The deputy director looked thin and pale with bags under his eyes.

"Bill." He nodded.

As he poured himself a glass of chilled water and drank, his eyes scanned the room. Barbara, who worked Internet Ops, and Zoey, profiler of terrorists and lords of the underworld, were present. Zoey smiled at him as she pushed her red-rimmed glasses further up the bridge of her nose.

Richard Corrigan, assistant deputy director, approached and shook his hand. "Good to see you, Sean." He had developed graying patches of hair above his ears, but still looked like a rosy-cheeked boy scout compared to the rest of the aged room.

"Thanks, Richard."

"I know this isn't your specialty. President Lawson requested your presence."

Sean stiffened. If the president was involved in this meeting, he knew the situation was bigger than Korea testing nukes again.

Furthermore, if President Lawson requested Sean's presence, then he was here for moral support as much as an advisory role. Cole Lawson and Sean had a friendship stretching back to their early military days and their Navy SEAL missions. After an injury during an extraction, Cole's path took him into politics. Sean's path led to the shadows of covert operations.

Despite Cole's impressive political wins, he was still a relatively young and new president. Having a familiar face present when discussing nuclear warfare would probably be of some comfort.

After greetings, everyone found their way to a seat at the table for the conference. When the audiovisual link connected, Sean could see the president, the defense secretary, the deputy secretary, and the members of the Joint Chiefs of Staff, all seated around a table on the screen. The Pentagon's finest.

*Yep, more than bomb tests.*

In addition, the commander of the National Air and Space Intelligence Center was joining the conference from their Dayton, Ohio facility.

Sean shot a look at William Austin. The man's face remained impassive. He might have had the decency to debrief Sean on events leading to this meeting. Then again, Bill was probably bitter at having to invite Sean at all.

Sean thought about Hwasong—North Korea's monstrosity of a nuclear weapon. Was everyone worried that Hwasong—Mars, God of War—would be launched at the US?

Austin spoke. "As most of you know, we learned two days ago from intercepted communications that a nuclear warhead was stolen from North Korea. We think the theft took place five days before our intel confirmed it. North Korea hasn't publicly acknowledged the theft."

Sean interpreted that to mean everything they had learned about the theft had been garnered through spying, which was status quo when it came to North Korea.

Nuclear weapons *stolen*. He felt like a lump of caustic plutonium had settled in his stomach.

"We have been trying to pinpoint where they may be or who may have taken them," Austin continued.

*Where was the bomb now? What if Europe is a target?*

Sean's mind raced. Irrationally, Sean feared for Lillian's safety. Surely Iceland was too far away to be affected by a detonation anywhere other than the island itself. The nearest populated landmass—the UK—was over a thousand miles away from Iceland. He recalled Lillian reading internet sites about Iceland and sharing her discoveries. When the volcano, Eyjafjnallajökull, erupted in 2010, spewed ash disrupted air travel across Europe. The natural jet stream of wind would blow a European detonation east and away from Iceland.

*Lillian will be fine, and no one is going to start detonating bombs on European soil,* Sean reassured himself.

President Cole shifted in his chair. "Do we have any information

—even a speculative list—of who would want to steal a nuclear weapon and who would have the ability to do so?"

Sean vaguely knew some of the organizations Austin began to list. He listened and filed away the names for future deliberation. Certainly no one Sean had encountered would be on the list. Africa had neither the funds nor ambition for nuclear power. That left Europe and Asia. An Asian or middle-eastern source would probably target the US.

They wouldn't succeed.

An intercontinental ballistic missile would be destroyed by a kill vehicle—one missile to destroy another. The US National Missile Defense was limited, though. If North Korea deployed its full arsenal, the US didn't have the ability to counter all of them. A rogue organization with a handful of nukes couldn't pull off a successful bombing...by air.

By ground, the US had radiation monitoring in major cities. Dosimeters would detect slightly higher than background radiation. It might be possible to sneak one in, but not likely.

Sean continued to listen.

Conrad Saunders, chairman of the Joint Chiefs of Staff, spoke. "Mr. President, the USS *Marrington* is near the Gulf of Aden. We're flying a Delta Force to board and sit tight in the event we need to deploy them to retrieve the stolen weapon."

"Good." President Lawson threaded his fingers together. "What's being done to identify the culprit?"

Austin spoke. "Every agent in Europe, Asia, and the Middle East is on alert. NSA is tracking phone and internet correspondence. The mere mention of nuclear weapons in anyone's conversation, and we're investigating. We're also looking into each radical organization mentioned here today."

Sean tuned out the others as they went around the room, taking turns reassuring the president how they would retrieve the bomb when they didn't know who took it, why they took it, or where they were taking it.

*Delta Force.*

He wished he could send a Delta Force to pick up Lillian. Except, he knew exactly what she would say. He was being paranoid and domineering. He needed to speak with her, and then he would feel reassured.

———

Yu watched the young man watching her. His nervous gaze flickered from her hands to her face. He was avoiding eye contact. While this was a courtesy in her culture, she could tell he was behaving more out of anxiousness than appreciation for Korean custom.

She chopped the cucumber in thin strips with skilled precision before placing the strips in a salt-water bath. The scent of sautéing shiitake mushrooms filled the small kitchen. The aroma calmed her. Bibimbap was one of her favorite dishes.

The boy's eyes watch her hands, mesmerized. She couldn't be sure if he admired their dexterity or was morbidly fascinated by the burn scars on them. Irritation quietly rippled through her like a snake under water.

She continued chopping as she spoke to the American—the *waegukin*—whose presence she was forced to endure. "The contractor is satisfied with how things are progressing?"

The boy nodded, and she could see the top of his military haircut. Judging by his young, pink skin, she'd be surprised if he was a day over twenty-five. Either the help was getting younger or she was getting older. Probably both. She felt old. Her bones creaked. Sometimes her lower back felt like bone grinding against bone.

"Yes, ma'am. He'll be very happy with the progress of everything."

She continued chopping. She thought of pouring him a glass of Soju, but such an act would imply more respect than she truly felt for the *waegukin*. The contractor had no justification for sending such a young thing to monitor the delivery of his bomb. She had never failed to make a delivery in her entire life. This task would be no different. This one she handled with painstaking detail.

She turned off the stove, her internal clock signaling to her that the rice was done. After giving the mushrooms a quick stir, she lifted the lid on the pot of rice and watched the steam billow forth in a superheated cloud. It was not unlike the mushroom cloud that would detonate in a beautiful plume of orange and red and gray.

After spooning the rice into a bowl, she situated the vegetables in a separate bowl rather than on top of the rice, since she didn't know which he might like to eat. She set them both before the American. Turning, she set a spoon and chopsticks beside his bowls.

"Thank you."

She gave a slight tilt of her head, still thinking of the explosion. Europe would burn. She would burn. Born of fire and returned to it. The world would know pain as she had known pain.

The soldier boy ate his food, too hastily for politeness. Americans did that, though, didn't they? Gobbling down what barely passed as sustenance as though it were their last meal. She was baffled that they would eat so atrociously fast when every street corner had more of the same garbage food for sale. Perhaps the US was where they ought to be unleashing the weapon. The thought had occurred to her more than once. Yet transporting it to Europe was enough of a challenge. Besides, the man paying the bills dictated the bomb's final destination.

The contractor's boy drank from his bottle of water.

Yu's eyes fell on his bowl of rice. He had stuck his chopsticks into the rice. Her fingers curled around the culinary knife on the cutting board.

In one swift motion she thrust the knife forward into the soldier's forehead. It crunched through the soft frontal bone and buried to the hilt. A trickle of blood ran down his forehead, down his nose, along the crease of his nose, and into his gaping mouth. He fell out of his chair, dead, to the floor.

Her lip curled in disgust. If he was going to carelessly poke his chopsticks into his rice like incense sticks in a bowl at a funeral, then she might as well make it *his* funeral.

"It's good to hear your voice," Sean said.

"Must have been a rough meeting with your covert coworkers."

He could hear the sounds of a breeze through the phone and distant chirp of birds.

"You out for a walk?" he asked.

"The weather is perfect. I'm trying to shake this jet lag and be ready for the hike tomorrow. I'm going to hot springs."

Sean paced the temporary office he'd been given to work in during the nuclear crisis. "I wish I could be there with you."

"Me, too."

He rolled his shoulders. What he wanted to do was tell Lillian to come home. How selfish would that be? He would ruin her vacation because he wanted to crush her in an embrace, bury his face in her red hair, and never let her go. The angst he felt at her being so far away during a nuclear threat was his own problem to manage. He didn't want to worry her.

"Are you okay?" Her soft voice sent a wave of warmth through him.

"I'm okay. Long day. Longer days to come." He swallowed. "Tell me a story, Lillian, something bizarre or mundane. I want to hear your voice."

She hesitated, but didn't refuse. She didn't tell him he was being absurd and that they'd been apart less than two days.

She began in a soothing tone, and he could hear the smile in her voice. "I can tell you more about the Norse mythology book I read on the plane. There's enough bizarre in there to distract anyone."

"I'd like that." He settled into his chair.

"Odin was an interesting character, to say the least. Apparently, he had a thirst for wisdom and was willing to go to extreme self-sacrifice to gain knowledge. Once he hanged himself, speared himself, and fasted in order to get magical runes. Ever wonder how Odin lost one eye? He went to the Well of Urd, seeking to drink the magical waters that bestowed a wealth of cosmic knowledge. The well was guarded by the shadowy being, Mímir, who would only grant a drink if Odin sacrificed his eye. Sacrifice it he did. After he took out his own eye, he was permitted to drink."

Sean closed his eyes as he listened. The quest for wisdom. What would Sean or anyone at the CIA give for the knowledge of where the stolen nuclear bomb was now?

———

DEPARTMENT OF DEFENSE
TOP SECRET
NUCLEAR THREAT INVESTIGATION

CASE FILE: 8966B20
Deputy Director: William Austin
Re: Dr. Lillian Whyte and Agent Sean Jennings

TRANSCRIPT:
DEPARTMENT OF DEFENSE INQUIRY

DOD: Prior to more recent events, had you ever heard of the international criminal called the cook?
DR. WHYTE: No.

DOD: Were you aware that she is allegedly responsible for twenty-eight assassinations?
DR. WHYTE: No.

DOD: Were you aware that she was thought by most to be a myth?
DR. WHYTE: Sean mentioned it.

DOD: When did you learn of the cook's involvement in the theft and transport of the nuclear weapon?
DR. WHYTE: Sunday morning in Reykjavik.

DOD: When did you first see the cook?
DR. WHYTE: The following Tuesday in Paris.

DOD: When did you learn who she was conspiring with to detonate the bomb?
DR. WHYTE: After events unfolded.

# CHAPTER 6

-----

Lillian began her day with a jog around the city. She toured the pond near the city hall then headed south to the University of Iceland and past the futuristic looking Nordic House. Lastly, she jogged back north and finished her run at the harbor. She stared out at the blue water spreading under a crisp blue sky.

After her run, she bathed and slipped into khakis and hiking boots. She joined a group of tourists waiting on a minivan to take them to Reykjadalur valley. She had pre-booked the hiking tour and wasn't going to miss it even if Sean couldn't join her.

The minivan drove them to Hveragerði. From there, the group of twelve followed a burly tour guide on foot through the valley situated along the Mount Hengill volcanic range. The guide, perhaps wanting to give them the sensation of being led by a Viking, wore a long, scraggly beard with wavy, unkempt hair sprawled across his shoulders.

As he walked, he told them a story of Norse mythology. "A builder came to the gods offering to build a fortified wall in exchange for the goddess of the sun and the moon—Freyja. The gods agreed, but they didn't actually want the builder to succeed, so they stipulated that he could have no help from another person. After some deliberation, the builder decided to use his horse only. With the horse's help, he made amazing progress. It seemed as though he might meet the deadline to build the wall. If he built the wall, he would win Freyja and the sun and the moon with her. Loki, being the shape-shifter he was, turned himself into a mare and lured the builder's steed away, causing the man to miss the deadline. Sometime after the horses' frolicking, Loki —as the mare—gave birth to an eight-legged foal, given the name Sleipnir. The magnificent horse became Odin's stallion."

Lillian listened to the tale as she absorbed the tranquility and majestic landscape, lush and green and peppered with gurgling hot ponds and warm, turquoise-colored pools. Steam billowed up from the natural waterworks.

"One day, Sleipnir was galloping through the skies and stepped too close to the earth, planting a hoof directly in Iceland. If you travel north to Ásbyrgi, you'll see his hoofprint in the canyon."

Lillian took pictures of the landscape on her phone while engaging in friendly conversation with the other tourists—at least the ones who spoke English.

After a dip in one of the springs and a spring-side lunch, everyone dressed for the walk back to the van.

On the hike back, their Viking tour guide broke into a brisk song in a deep baritone.

> *"I am Thor, God of Thunder,*
> *I set mine enemies asunder.*
>
> *I bear Miölner the mighty,*
> *My hammer shall smite thee.*
>
> *From my eyes come lightning,*
> *As god of war, I am frightening.*
>
> *I am Thor, god of thunder,*
> *Hear my roar, see my wonder."*

LILLIAN SMILED AT THE TUNE. She'd bet the Icelandic tour guide would be fun on karaoke night.

The excursion felt like a great start to her adventures in Iceland. Tomorrow was a horseback tour, and the following day was a helicopter tour. Perhaps Sean would arrive in time for the latter. Although he had said he would join her, his dismal mood on their phone conversation suggested it was a slim possibility.

When Lillian arrived back in her hotel room, the sun had set. She checked her steps for the day—26,000. Time to relax. She cleaned and dressed in jeans and a sweater.

All the while, the upbeat song from earlier that day played over and over in her head.

*I am Thor, god of thunder,*
*I set mine enemies asunder.*

SEAN SPENT the afternoon being a sponge—listening, reading, and learning what he could about nuclear weapons, North Korea, and the intertwining politics of both. He grasped for comprehension of who would steal a nuclear weapon. Who *could* steal a nuclear weapon? Financing an elaborate heist would be an expensive endeavor. The list of suspects couldn't be long.

He rolled a pen between his fingers as he paced the small conference room he'd turned into his temporary office. Two laptops sat open on the table. Beside them was a mug, long-emptied of black coffee, and a legal pad on which were scribbles of his brainstorming activities.

A knock came at the door.

"Zoey, come in. I was just thinking about you."

The slim blonde entered the room. She wore a red suit and practical, one-inch heels. Her red-rimmed glasses had slipped down on her nose and a pencil was stuck behind one ear.

"You were?" She stood in the doorway.

"I assume Bill has you profiling possible culprits for the theft."

Zoey Cain was one of the CIA's best profilers.

"Yes. Deputy Director Austin has me investigating suspects."

"Well-funded suspects?"

She nodded. "I'm to pull who could financially afford to fund the theft and cross-reference it with those who might have an agenda best filled by having or detonating a nuclear weapon."

She pushed her glasses up on her nose before continuing. "But I came to say thank you."

"Thank you?"

"Eight months ago when you went to the Cayman Islands, you collected intel on the accountant. We apprehended him a few months ago because of your work."

The Cayman Islands brought memories of Lillian to the surface. He had taken her there with him—part vacation, part CIA mission. She looked amazing, basking in the sun in a swimsuit. Her hair would catch the sunlight and shimmer like liquid sunset. A sea of emerald water stretched behind her.

"You remember the accountant?" Zoey prodded. "His real name was Gabe Oleander."

"I remember. I remember he was handling the finances of bigger fish. Catching him was supposed to help uncover his clients. Any success?"

She frowned. "Not yet. But I wanted to thank you in person for your work. You rarely ever come here, to Langley, so I haven't had a chance to thank you."

"No problem."

She started to leave.

"Hey, Zoey. When you finish your list of suspects for the stolen nuke, can I take a look at it?"

"Absolutely."

As she left, Sean's phone chimed with an incoming email.

He pulled it from his pocket and blinked at the screen. The president of the United States was summoning him to the White House on Monday.

LILLIAN CHECKED HER VOICE MAIL. She had three messages—two from her assistant and one from Kelly.

She called Kelly first.

"Hello?"

"Hi, Kelly, I got your voice mail. Katie's sick?"

"Oh, how's Iceland?"

"Great. The weather's perfect, and the scenery is breathtaking."

Lillian paced outside the Hotel Borg. "What's up with Katie?" Kelly's voice mail suggested she was concerned about Katie.

"She's sick. She's coughing a lot with a runny nose. Her cough is keeping her up most of the night and she's not sleeping well. We went to the doctor, and she wouldn't prescribe antibiotics."

"Kelly, I'm not going to override your pediatrician on a patient I've never seen."

"Fine. Give me a second opinion. I see it advertised on television. Tele-something."

"Tele-health or tele-medicine?"

"Yeah, that. You get an opinion over the phone or computer or video conference."

"Okay." Lillian cleared her throat and spoke in an excessively feminine, proper voice. "Please hold while I connect you with Dr. Whyte. The first five minutes are free after that—"

"Very funny, Lily."

"Is she running a fever?" Lillian asked.

"One-oh-one in the afternoons."

"Does she pull or tug at her ears."

"No. And the doctor looked in her ears and didn't see anything wrong."

"Is she active during the day?"

"Yes, she's still playing, despite the snot getting all over everything."

"Any rash?"

"No."

"No splotches or spots on her hands or feet?"

"No."

"Well, your pediatrician probably said she has a viral infection."

"Yeah," Kelly said on an exhale.

"Sounds like it. Doesn't sound like she needs antibiotics."

"Okay. Good. Thank you so much."

Lillian could hear Katie banging metal on metal in the background.

"You're welcome. Happy to give a second opinion."

"I really appreciate it. I'm sorry to bother you on vacation."

"Not a bother. Being a concerned parent is a good thing."

She ended the call with Kelly and called her assistant, Tonya.

"Oh, Dr. Whyte, I'm so glad you called. The sepsis order set went live yesterday, and I'm getting all kinds of complaints that it isn't complete."

"What's wrong with it?"

"Something about the antibiotic section is missing."

Lillian frowned as she paced the sidewalk. Since antibiotics were a crucial part of treatment for sepsis, missing antibiotics meant missing care. Emergency room physicians were more than capable of selecting antibiotics for septic patient, but the order set would make the process smoother and offer an antibiotic selection tailored to the type of patient and type of infection suspected. After all, different pneumonias were treated differently and patients with dysfunctional immune systems were treated with different antibiotics than those with functional immune systems.

"Okay. Call Bruce Zimmerman in IT. Tell him to get with Dr. Janet Holt. She's covering for me. If they can't find the antibiotic recommendation component of the order set, there's a document in the ER shared folder." She could hear Tonya scribbling. Was it on a pink or purple sticky note? "The subfolder is 'sepsis' and the document is called 'antibiotic.'"

"Okay. I'll find it. Thank you."

"Tonya?"

"Yes, Dr. Whyte?"

"Do I have an appointment with Dr. Sumner when I return?"

"No, Dr. Whyte. I feel like he's told his assistant to brush you off because I've gone round and round with her about different dates, but he always has something already scheduled."

"Tonya, I want you to page him once a day and tag it with my name until he calls back and agrees to a meeting—day and time."

After the call, Lillian set off for Hallgrímskikja, wanting to see the church in its entire splendor, glowing with light.


Cool night air embraced Lillian as she turned to stare at the deep sapphire sky adorned with twinkling stars. She was exhausted in a content fashion. After a morning run and all day on her feet playing tourist, she would sleep well tonight.

She sat on a bench in the park near the square of Austurvöllur. A few meandering people walked the sidewalks in the distance, admiring the spectacular view of the church and its evening light.

"Dr. Whyte," a guttural voice greeted her.

Her blood turned frigid and her stomach lurched as her heart thudded against her ribcage. As long as she lived, she would never forget that deep German accent—the voice of one of her captors nine years ago in Kenya.

*The one that got away.*

She was fairly certain Ivan Kleist would have only one reason for tracking her down: revenge.

Springing from the bench seat, she lashed a leg out into his gut. She saw a brief look of surprise on his pale face before she took off in a sprint.

Why now? Nine years he had waited.

The calculating killer had waited until she was out of the United States and away from Sean to corner her. She dashed in the direction of her hotel. Would she be safe in the lobby? In her room?

She slung her purse over her shoulder. Her phone was in the outer pocket, but she would have to slow down to make a call. Not happening. She would not slow until she reached the hotel.

Could she beat him to the hotel? His legs were longer, but she was ten years younger. But he probably hadn't already logged twenty-six thousand steps for the day, as she had.

From her peripheral vision, Lillian saw an enormous object barreling toward her like a freight train. She barely had time to brace herself before Ivan plowed into her. She felt like she had been tackled by a linebacker. His large arms encircled her as she sailed to the ground. They rolled through the grass, her body encased by his.

He was so large he could probably crush the life out of her with his arms. She gasped for air. He wasn't crushing her, but his grip was immobilizing.

Grunting, he hauled her to her feet. "Settle down, *hase*. Little white rabbit."

Lillian, still dazed and sucking wind after her sprint, hardly put up a fight as he dragged her into an alley. Looking around frantically, her eyes couldn't focus long enough to see anyone within shouting distance. She clawed at his large hand blocking her mouth from screaming.

*Of course he would execute me somewhere remote.*

She would die in an alley. Would he stuff her body in a dumpster to strip her of all dignity?

"Calm down and listen to me." His hot breath spilled over her ear.

Lillian struggled uselessly to free herself.

His grip slackened. She stumbled away from him, composed herself, and spun around to face him.

Ivan's eyes roamed up and down her, appraising her fight stance.

Her heart beat wildly with fear and anger. How many times had she sparred with Sean and imagined she was fighting Ivan? Defeating Ivan. She had wanted her own retribution. He had killed soldiers, kidnapped her, and then hunted her. She had imagined showing him she was no longer afraid. She wasn't the same woman who had cowered before him in Kenya. Now, face-to-face with his frightening physique she had to summon every ounce of her resolve to not cower.

Who was she kidding? She was no match for him.

"You've had training, little rabbit." His tone held amusement.

Something appeared awkward in the way he stood, the way he readied himself. He was injured. Legs? Hips? Back? She couldn't tell precisely. The injury wasn't enough to have slowed him down chasing and tackling her, but it might be a weakness in combat.

She lunged at him with a series of swings and kicks Sean had taught her.

He blocked her blows. "I only want to talk."

She ignored him, focusing on getting closer. She needed to incapacitate him long enough to flee. At last she got a solid strike on his shoulder.

He grimaced and stumbled back from her. She had remembered where Sean had put a bullet through his shoulder in Paris.

She smirked.

His blue eyes turned to ice. "Fine. You want to fight, *hase*. We fight."

She swallowed, realizing she had accomplished little more than poking the bear.

Taking the offense again, she swung.

Ivan blocked three successive blows before managing his own strike to her left clavicle.

Blinding pain brought her to one knee. She gasped and clutched at the pain. She looked up at him through watering eyes.

Ivan gave his own smirk.

*Damn.*

Somehow he knew about her old bullet wound as well.

He stood, watching her, waiting for her next attack, but not attacking.

Why? Toying with his prey? His rabbit, as he called her?

She forced herself to stand through trembling legs, refusing to be immobilized by fear. She would not face her death on her knees.

***

DEPARTMENT OF DEFENSE
TOP SECRET

## NUCLEAR THREAT INVESTIGATION

CASE FILE: 8966B20
Deputy Director: William Austin
Re: Dr. Lillian Whyte and Agent Sean Jennings

TRANSCRIPT:
DEPARTMENT OF DEFENSE INQUIRY

DOD: According to the list you provided us here, your activities on your first full day in Iceland involved touring the island?
DR. WHYTE: Yes.

DOD: And at no point prior to Saturday night had you had any contact with Ivan Kleist?
DR. WHYTE: No.

DOD: So, the international criminal—whom you knew from Kenya—joined you on your vacation?
DR. WHYTE: It stopped being a vacation at that point.

DOD: And you expect us to believe he made no contact with you prior to finding you in Iceland?
DR. WHYTE: The last time I saw Ivan before Iceland was in the Charles de Gaulle Airport after Agent Jennings put a bullet in his shoulder.

DOD: You're on a first-name basis with the mercenary?
DR. WHYTE: I think after everything he put me through, I have a right to be.

# CHAPTER 7

----

Lillian panted, fighting the fear within her that made her want to flee from Ivan. Her shoulder throbbed with pain.

"I know what you did. For your country. For the world," he said.

She stared at him.

"Computer genius," he said with a shrug.

Taking a deep breath, she took her fight stance. This time she would let him attack and catch him off balance.

A glint of metal caught her eye. Her phone was out of her purse and cracked on the ground.

*Damn.*

"I'm not here to fight you, Dr. Whyte."

Despite her throbbing arm, she didn't let her guard slack.

"I need your help."

She blinked at him.

He looked around the alley nervously. He might not be afraid of her, but something scared him. What horrible thing would have a man like Ivan afraid?

"Let us go somewhere private."

As she straightened, she let her arms fall to her sides. "You're not serious."

He stepped closer, causing her to stiffen and brace herself.

"I can't discuss these things in public."

"These things?"

He bent over, grimaced, and picked up her phone. As he handed it to her, he put an uncharacteristically gentle hand on her elbow. He led her out of the alley.

"Nuclear weapons, Dr. Whyte," he whispered. "I cannot talk to you about nuclear weapons in public."

Her gut clenched. "What?"

"Private." He gritted his teeth, and she couldn't be certain if it was from pain or frustration.

"What's wrong with you?"

He gave a brief hostile glare before answering. "I lost a fight."

She could tell he was walking in pain. Lower back, she guessed. Now that she knew the source of his pain she could probably disable him with one accurate blow, but fight mode was replaced by physician mode as she began pondering the nature of his injuries.

She realized he was leading her back to her hotel.

"Where are we going, Ivan?"

"Your place."

"Like hell."

Holding her shoulders in large and gentle hands, he stopped and turned her toward him. "Please."

She looked away from his pleading blue eyes.

He squeezed slightly. "Please, Dr. Whyte."

She looked back into his desperation and felt her resolve melt. They continued walking. She was out of her mind trusting this cold-blooded killer even for a second.

He moved his hand down her arm and grasped her hand. "Thank you."

After they reached the hotel, Lillian walked with Ivan to the elevators. The doors closed, and they were alone.

Swallowing, she tried not to dwell on the fact that she was taking a trained killer and international criminal to her hotel room.

*Another genius lapse in judgment, Lillian.*

"Why did you come to me?"

He obviously wasn't here to kill her. Was he? Why he thought she would help him with a problem related to nuclear weapons was baffling.

Without warning, he slumped against her.

"What the—?" She slung her arms around his waist trying to keep both of them upright.

"Come on, Ivan. Stay with me. We have to make it to the end of the hall. You can do it."

She grunted under the weight of him. If he fell to the floor in the hallway, there would be no moving him.

He stayed lucid long enough for her to get them inside the hotel room before he collapsed on the one and only bed in the room. His large body occupied most of the queen-size bed.

"Are you serious?"

He didn't reply.

She peered over at his face. His eyes were closed, and he began the slow breathing of sleep.

"I should have finished kicking your ass in the alley." Except that she still would have lost.

She sighed and pulled out her phone.

*Yep. Destroyed.*

She looked back at the slumbering giant. She needed to know his injuries. She wouldn't have him die in her hotel room from some smoldering infection or internal bleeding.

Should she call an ambulance? Whatever international disaster was following him now ensnared her. His danger became her danger. She needed to know what that entailed before involving anyone else. She needed Sean's help, though she suspected that if she blurted out Ivan Kleist was on her hotel bed, Sean would have a stroke.

Well, he was CIA, so he would probably order a drone strike on Ivan and then have a stroke.

Speaking aloud, she explained to Ivan what she was about to do in case he was awake enough to hear her. "I'm taking off your clothes to assess your injuries. If you take a swing at me, I will punch you in the kidney."

Since he was face down, his kidneys were the most accessible. She watched him for a moment, but he didn't move.

Unceremoniously, she stripped him down to his boxers. He still didn't budge. Head injury?

Sitting beside him, she examined his wounds. He certainly had lost a fight. His body was like a battered eggplant—swollen and purple.

She lamented the many things she did not have—an X-ray machine, handheld ultrasound, CT scanner. She didn't even have medical gloves.

After washing her hands, she returned to the bedside and began palpating. She didn't detect any bones out of alignment. No broken ribs. His lower back was badly bruised, but anatomically intact. His right shoulder was swollen. She wondered if it had been dislocated and reset. One arm was bandaged haphazardly. Underneath the gauze was a bullet graze of jagged flesh.

On his scalp, she found no areas of bruising or bleeding. It seemed he didn't have a head injury, but he truly was beaten and exhausted.

She left Ivan sleeping in the bed and went in search of medical supplies and a new phone.

IT WAS eleven at night before Lillian had everything she needed from her shopping spree. She dropped her bags inside the hotel room and went into the bathroom. Fortunately the east coast was five hours behind Icelandic time so Sean would still be awake. She activated her new phone, and, as soon as it had a little charge, she called Sean. "Hello."

"Hey, hon."

"Sean."

"What's wrong?"

Was her voice so obviously distressed?

"Don't come to Iceland."

"What? Why?"

"I don't know if a trap is being set for you. I don't want to be bait. Don't come." Sweat broke out along her forehead. What was wrong with her? She was having a phone conversation, not performing CPR.

"Lily, what's going on?"

"Please believe me. You can help me better by staying there with the think tank."

"Are you okay?"

"Yes." She heard her own voice cracking, betraying the fact she wasn't as steadfast as she had hoped to convey.

"Tell me what's going on?"

"I don't know yet. Give me until tomorrow to figure out what's happening. I'll call you back."

"Lily." Sean's voice was pleading.

Her heart was shredding to pieces knowing she was making him worry about her. She had to convince him not to come to Iceland. If this was about nuclear weapons, then she wanted him safe. If this was a ruse, then she wouldn't have Sean lured in.

"I love you. I will call you." She hung up the phone.

Sitting on the edge of the bathtub, she breathed slowly to pull herself together. She felt bone tired. She needed to patch up her unexpected hotel room guest and get some rest.

She looked down at her hands—solid and steady. Whatever crises she faced that churned her intestines with worry, her hands never failed her.

---

THE CONTRACTOR HUNG up the phone when his assistant finished explaining the death of one of his young security detail.

*Crazy cook.*

He shook his head. The unstable psychopath who referred to

herself as the cook had killed one of his men because he had offended her and her culture. Who kills someone for such a minor offense?

The same deranged person who had no misgivings about detonating a nuclear weapon.

As he looked out the window of his private plane, he absently clinked the ice in his glass against the side. Clouds hovered beneath him. The world hovered beneath him.

The weapon wasn't only about money. The world needed a makeover. A new beginning.

James Buchanan had said, *"The test of leadership is not to put greatness into humanity, but to elicit it, for the greatness is already there."*

That was all he was doing—eliciting greatness. The country needed to be propelled into a new era of unity. The tidal wave of change that his event would incite would stop the bickering of political parties. A country divided was a country paralyzed. His actions would reset the country in motion.

As the plane descended and banked for landing, he saw tiny houses, small buildings, and cars come into view. No wonder God lived in the heavens. He could gaze down from his perch and see how his actions affected the world from a distance.

———

IVAN WOKE WITH A START. Fine streams of light shone through a window of the hotel room. He looked around for the physician, but instead found a note that she had left to pick up breakfast.

He glanced down at his lack of clothing and felt his cheeks flush. He shook off the absurd embarrassment. As a physician, she had surely seen many men wearing less than just underwear. Still, it felt oddly intimate to be nearly naked in the woman's hotel bed.

He vaguely remembered her touching him. Soft, warm hands moved carefully over his body as he drifted in and out of consciousness. It had been quite some time since a beautiful woman had touched him. Of course, Dr. Whyte was evaluating him as a physician. She didn't have to do that, not after the way he had treated her in Kenya—like an obstacle, a nuisance.

Instead of dismissing him, she had eased his pain, cleaned his cuts, and left water and anti-inflammatories on the nightstand while she fetched food. Redheaded angel. His instincts were right to seek her help. She was a rare and giving flower in a sea of Venus flytraps. She was a better person than he had ever considered striving to be.

He forced himself to sit up and take the ibuprofen. Next, he stood and ambled to the shower. The hot water would ease some of his soreness.

After plummeting down the chute in Beijing, he had escaped the cook and her minions through arduous rides on cargo planes and by bribing border patrols.

With Renni gone and the stakes high, he tried to fathom to whom he could turn. This problem was big. Bigger than stealing oil in Kenya. Bigger than hacking into weapons-storage facilities.

The cook had a reputation for ruthlessness, and he would have a bounty on his head as soon as he fled. Any number of his usual underworld contacts might turn him in or kill him themselves.

Furthermore, his family would be targeted. He had to take what he knew to authorities. But how could he reach them, being the international criminal he was, and not get shot on sight?

Indirectly.

Through the wife of an operative.

He had contacted her hospital, claiming to be a pharmaceutical representative for a high-dollar antibiotic and wanted to arrange a meeting. When he was transferred to her secretary, she explained that she couldn't arrange a meeting for two weeks because Dr. Whyte was traveling out of the country. The assistant remained tight-lipped about Dr. Whyte's location but was kind enough to divulge her departure date and return date. Traveling out of the country likely meant airfare. He hacked airline passenger lists for all major airlines traveling out of Atlanta internationally on her departure date. Viola. Iceland. She had come close to Europe when he needed her. It was inarguably a sign from God—if one believed in such frivolities.

After his shower, he put on the clean underwear and pants the physician had brought him. He drank a large glass of water and climbed under the bed covers.

He smelled her lilac scent. A soothing calm crept over him. Had she slept in the same bed beside him last night? That would have been awkward for her.


LILLIAN HAD WOKEN at six a.m. and left to pick up breakfast. When she returned to her hotel room thirty minutes later, she carried breakfast in a bag and two coffees in a cardboard holder.

Ivan appeared to have rolled over and crawled under the covers.

*Still alive, then.*

As she closed the door, she noticed through the open bathroom door, the moisture on the mirror and used towel hanging on the door.

*Good, he's mobile.*

She sat down on the small couch by the window of the hotel room, eating a slice of sour dough bread smothered in sun-dried tomato cream cheese. She stared out the window, watching the morning sun lighten the sky.

She turned her attention to motion in the bed. Ivan sat and stared at her.

"Hungry?"

He nodded.

She tossed the bag to him.

*"Danke vielmals."*

She understood the gratitude in his voice even though she didn't speak German. As she passed him a cup of coffee, she watched him devour the bread and cream cheese.

"You have a lot of bruises. You took a beating, but nothing seems displaced. No obvious rib fractures, though you probably have some contusions on your lungs. You dislocated your shoulder. Of course, you put it back, so you already knew that."

*You also have a crap-load of scars from hard living.*

She stared at him over her cup of coffee. She felt as though she was looking at a satiated tiger.

*Beware his hunger.*

He washed down the last remnants of food with his coffee.

"Your turn," she said.

His blue eyes bore into her, but she didn't back down from him.

"A nuclear weapon was stolen from North Korea. It is possessed by an international criminal known as the cook. She is working for someone—I don't know who. I think the plan is to detonate it in Eastern Europe."

"Did you steal the nuclear weapon?"

"No."

"Then you know about this plan because...?"

"I helped steal the schematics to the weapons facility."

"So, you facilitated the theft."

"Unwittingly, but that's no excuse."

"And you came to me because?"

"I need your help."

Lillian grimaced. "Doctor." She pointed a thumb at herself. "Not nuclear physicist or weapons specialist or CIA operative."

"But you are married to one."

Lillian felt the color drain from her face. Ivan knew about Sean. "You will not use me to get to my husband."

"I don't want to use you like that. I..." His cheeks reddened. "No. I don't want to use you at all. I want the CIA to intervene, but I don't want them to eliminate me in the process. You understand?"

As she drank a sip of her coffee, she noted a slight tremor in her hands. She suspected some combination of fear, anger, and fatigue had her shaking. Sleeping poorly on the small couch in the hotel room wasn't working in her favor either.

"How can someone steal a nuclear weapon?" she asked. "It can't be as simple as having the schematics and tunneling into the building."

"The cook was an assassin for the North Korean government for decades. She would know who to coerce, who to bribe, and who to blackmail. I'm sure this endeavor was months to years in planning. My part was one piece of an elaborate scheme."

Lillian kept her voice even but cold as she spoke. "You want the CIA to clean up your mess, and you want to hide behind me while they do it?"

The muscles on his bare chest rippled as he pursed his lips. "I plan to help fix my mistake."

Lillian set her cup down and bent her knees up to her chest, curling her toes into the tiny couch as she appraised him. She bit her lower lip.

So far he had accepted her criticism and admitted to making a mistake. This was not the behavior of someone intent on manipulating her.

---

DEPARTMENT OF DEFENSE
TOP SECRET
NUCLEAR THREAT INVESTIGATION

CASE FILE: 8966B20
Deputy Director: William Austin
Re: Dr. Lillian Whyte and Agent Sean Jennings

TRANSCRIPT:
DEPARTMENT OF DEFENSE INQUIRY

DOD: Your specialty is third-world-country crises, correct?
JENNINGS: It was. I retired from active field duty eight years ago.

DOD: When you met Dr. Whyte?
JENNINGS: When I married her.

DOD: With no experience in nuclear threats and not an active agent, why were you involved in discussions about a stolen nuclear weapon?

JENNINGS: President Lawson and I have a history together. I suspected, though I didn't outright ask, that he wanted a familiar face during a time of crisis.

DOD: You are referring to your history in the military together?
JENNINGS: That's correct.

DOD: You also saved President Lawson's life in Montreal?
JENNINGS: He was Senator Lawson at the time.

DOD: At that time you were also not an active field agent, yet you were involved in the international incident in Canada.
JENNINGS: I was a courier who got caught in the crosshairs. Once I was involved, I became active until the threat was neutralized.

DOD: In this instance, once you became involved, what was your purpose?
JENNINGS: My purpose was to help in any way possible to stop the nuclear threat.

DOD: But you didn't have a defined purpose until your wife became involved?
JENNINGS: Perhaps.

DOD: Once she became involved, what was your purpose?
JENNINGS: My purpose was to help in any way possible to stop the nuclear threat.

# CHAPTER 8

----

Ivan took a deep breath, feeling rested for the first time in days. For at least this moment, he wasn't running. Still, the urgency of the matter pressed upon him. He tried not to convey his desperation while the physician processed their conversation.

He eyed Dr. Whyte as she stared out the window. Her long, golden-red hair fell about her shoulders. He had to convince her and coax her without scaring her.

Entice the rabbit without spooking it. He didn't have a carrot, only a nuclear weapon threat.

He had no right to ask her to trust him, but he was asking anyway. With all she had already been through, tangling her in his mess was unfair.

So what? Life was unfair. She had the same options he did—help and have a chance to stop a nuclear weapon or hide and become its victim. Of course, either way the probability of death was high.

Although she was curled in a defensive ball, her aura pulsed with strength. She hadn't cowered from him, didn't become hysterical with the mention of nuclear weapons, and wasn't running now. Yes, he had chosen the correct person.

"We need to go to Germany. Tomorrow."

She let out a short, sharp laugh followed by a frosty stare. "You and I don't have such a good track record in Europe."

True. He had come to Paris to assassinate her, but that had been almost ten years ago. Did the woman let nothing go? "For which I already apologized."

"Did you?"

He scowled. "I apologize, Dr. Whyte."

"Lillian."

"Pardon?"

"Call me Lillian. I prefer to be on a first-name basis with those who entangle me in nuclear warfare."

He grinned, though she made no expression of amusement at her own words. "I apologize, Lillian."

He waited a long moment as she uncoiled and turned her body toward him. The light streaming through the window caressed her pale skin, giving her an angelic glow. His breath caught.

"I accept your apology." Her voice was soft and yielding.

He let out a slow breath.

"Why are you suddenly joining the good guys?"

He snorted. Ridiculous Americans. They always thought in terms of the superheroes they idolized. Good versus evil—and of course they considered themselves the good guys.

"I am a thief and a hacker. None of this means I want the world to be incinerated."

"So you want to go to Germany to stop a bomb? Seems a bit self-sacrificial for a thief-hacker. A bit out of character."

"Europe is my home. No one wants to see his home burn."

Her sapphire eyes watched him warily.

He hoped she believed him. If she traveled with him, she would see the truth. Seeing the truth was far better than having to be convinced of the truth through words.

"What terrible surprise awaits us in Germany?"

A morsel of relief tasted sweet on his tongue. She had consented.

He closed his eyes and bowed his head briefly with gratitude. "We go there, and we lead the CIA to the bomb."

LILLIAN LEFT Ivan resting in the hotel room while she went outside to call Sean and talk privately.

"What happened to your phone?"

She sighed. "It was damaged in a fight. How did you know?"

"You charged our credit card for a new phone."

"Right." He would have been investigating everything since they'd last spoken.

"Fight?"

"Someone surprised me. I was in fight or flight mode."

"I like flight better."

"Well, he's faster than he looks."

"What's going on, Lillian?"

She paced along the sidewalk of Pósthússtræti, the street outside her hotel. Deciding to tell it fast, like ripping off a Band-Aid, she said, "Ivan Kleist is here, in Iceland. He claims someone named 'the cook' confiscated a nuclear bomb from North Korea."

Sean's silence revealed he knew something of events. He wasn't acting surprised about the theft, so he must know something about the stolen bomb.

She continued, "Ivan wants to stop the bomb. He wants to lead the CIA to it."

"Ivan Kleist?"

"Yes."

"How does he know about the stolen weapon?"

"He helped steal the schematics of the North Korean weapons facility."

"How does he intend to help retrieve it?"

"I don't know. He says we need to first go to Germany. From there, he can track it somehow."

"We? As in you and him? No way. Out of the question."

She tugged a hand through her hair. "This is how it's going to go:

I'm going to work things on my end and you're going to work things on your end. Me in Europe. You at Langley. Together we'll get to the bottom of this."

She suspected Sean was fuming in his silence.

She added, "I will keep in touch. I promise."

"None of this is acceptable."

"I didn't expect you to think it was."

"You can't possibly trust him. He's using you." Sean was employing his ice-fury tone where his voice grew harder and colder, despite the anger and incredulity burning within him.

"Yes, he is. So let's make it mutual. He uses me as a shield between himself and the CIA. I use him for information. Win-win."

"My wife going to Germany with a murderer and international criminal is not a win."

She hated causing the pain she heard in his voice, but she couldn't simultaneously do what was right for the world and what would be easiest on Sean.

She softened her voice. "I'm sorry. We're leaving tomorrow. All I can do is promise to do my best and come home as soon as I can. I'm asking you to help me with all of the resources at your disposal. You can't do that if you're trying to chase after me across the pond. Stay a step ahead with intel rather than a step behind by traveling."

"Please be careful." He hung up the phone.

Lillian looked up at the sky. Dense stratus clouds floated above her against a pale gray background.

> *From my eyes comes lightning,*
> *As god of war, I am frightening.*

She shuddered once before dropping her phone in her pocket and heading back into the hotel.

---

SEAN APPROACHED Marty's desk with Zoey in tow.

Marty looked at them apprehensively. "You're an ominous looking pair with ominous looking expressions."

They gathered around his desk.

Sean leaned forward. "I need help."

"What kind of help?" Marty looked skeptically back and forth between Sean and Zoey as though the pair would start selling him life insurance or a pyramid scheme.

Zoey pushed her red-rimmed glasses up on her nose. "The discrete kind."

"Okay."

"Lillian is in Europe with Ivan Kleist," Sean said.

Marty's mouth fell open. "What?"

Zoey's expression remained grim.

Marty blinked in astonishment. "You need the cavalry, Sean. Not discrete. Is she okay? Do you have proof of life?"

Sean shook his head. "She's not kidnapped by him. She's working with him."

Marty looked to Zoey with incredulity.

The analyst bit her lip before speaking. "He's a mercenary, but personality profiling suggests he could make morally good decisions given the right scenario."

"What scenario is that?"

Sean exhaled. "Lillian and Ivan think they can track down the nuclear weapon that was stolen from North Korea."

"Ivan?"

Sean nodded. "Apparently when he discovered what he had helped steal, he grew a conscience."

Marty's eyes darted to Zoey and back to Sean. "Why?"

"I don't know. Step one is help one international criminal stop another international criminal from detonating a nuclear weapon. Step two can be capture and interrogate the first international criminal. We're still on step one."

Sean trusted his wife and her instincts, but he hated the situation and worried about the outcome. If Lillian believed Ivan, Sean felt he had no choice but to believe him also. *"Trust but verify,"* as the old

Russian proverb says.

Marty scratched at his balding head. "Okay. None of this explains the discreet part of your request."

Sean picked up a palm-size model car from Marty's desk and turned it over in his palm curiously. It had the acronym NASCAR painted on the sides.

Marty snatched it back. "Austin gave that to me."

"NASCAR?"

"Yeah. He's been taking professional driving classes and even done some amateur racing."

Sean arched an eyebrow and looked to Zoey.

She shrugged. "It's his midlife crisis hobby. Rumor has it he's pretty good."

Marty set the car back on his desk. "So, discreet?"

"The deputy director isn't going to allow the CIA to openly assist Lillian assist a criminal, regardless of whose side Ivan's currently claiming. I need you to track Lillian but not in a way that your steps can be traced. No one needs to be able to track the tracker."

"Discreet. Got it," Marty said, though his voice still held wary skepticism.

Zoey turned to gape at Sean. "You're not going to tell Deputy Director Austin?"

Sean looked at the young analyst and tried to soften his expression. "When we have something to tell him, we will do so. For now, all I know is that my wife is at the mercy of a cold-blooded killer, and I would like to keep tabs on them. *Discretely*."

"What about a team on the ground?" she asked.

Marty shook his head. "If someone is after Ivan, they can track the tracker."

Zoey frowned.

Marty swiveled in his chair back to look at Sean. "You don't have any buddies who could be on the ground and off the grid? Just answer yes or no. Don't tell me any names."

Jack. The name of Sean's old mentor popped into his head. He would trust Jack McCumsey with his life. He would trust him with his wife's life too. The man was a retired CIA operative, but he'd do a favor. This would be a tall favor to ask, especially since Sean didn't know where in Europe Lillian would end up, and Jack might spend the entire trip two steps behind her. Sean needed a dozen men on the ground to be ready, but he didn't have that many retired operatives with whom he could call in favors.

Non-operatives?

*Damn.*

He pinched the bridge of his nose. He knew of one man that would go in a heartbeat. And Sean would never hear the end of it.

———

SEAN PACED his conference room turned office, dancing his pen along his fingers, as he waited for Jack McCumsey to return his call. With his wife's life in the hands of a criminal, Sean was in need of Jack's unique skill set.

He thought of one of the missions they had conducted and developed trust and camaraderie. Their assignment had been intelligence-gathering in Sudan.

Darfur, in western Sudan, was rife with violence. Throughout the 1990s, segregation and Arab apartheid reigned supreme. Sudan's non-Arab citizens faced discrimination and ethnic cleansing. Rebel forces, including the Sudan Liberation Army (initially called the Darfur Liberation Front) and the Justice and Equality Movement, sought to reform Sudan's discriminatory practices. These forces attacked garrisons in order to fight against the oppression. But violence begot violence and the resulting genocide was atrocious.

Sean and Jack's mission had been intelligence-gathering on Sahm Majeed, who favored the apartheid. He owned land in the Melut rift basin where millions of barrels of oil reserves were located. The oil traveled a pipeline to the Port Sudan refinery. He also was rumored to smuggle gold to other markets. Sahm drove a silvery blue Aston Martin and frequented hookah bars speculated to also offer young women on the menu. In his spare time, he killed Arabs sympathetic to the anti-apartheid movement.

Jack and Sean decided to take measures beyond intelligence-gathering. What harm lay in ridding the world of an elitist and racist?

Every Wednesday night, Sahm frequented a specific hookah cafe in Khartoum. The parking lot sat next to the rectangular brick building. The best vantage point for sniper viewing of the parking lot did not afford an adequate view of the front of the building. Sean and Jack needed to be able to watch him come and go.

Jack was a superior sharpshooter, as evidenced by his Marine Expert Rifle Marksmanship badge. They found Jack an empty apartment room to squat in and wait. Sean was on ground duty. In the era of pre-Bluetooth earpieces and pocket-size mobile phones, they had small, two-way radios to attempt discreet communication.

"He's late." Sean shifted his weight in the parked car in the lot.

"He'll show. He's a creature of habit."

"And good fortune."

"Guy walks into a bar."

"Really? One of your bar jokes? Now?" Sean rolled his neck, feeling cramped in the small space of the vehicle.

"Guy walks into a bar and orders two shots."

Sean bit back a groan as he waited for the punch line.

"I only needed to give him one. Right between the eyes."

"Sniper humor," Sean said flatly. "Cute. You don't have any hookah bar jokes?"

"Hmm. I'll have to think on that one."

Sahm's pristine Aston Martin pulled into the parking lot, and a black Explorer pulled in next to it.

Sean slipped inside the bar before Sahm exited his car, and his two bodyguards from the Explorer joined him. Sean wore his Arab disguise—bronzed skin and beige thawb. He found a seat in a smoky corner, positioning himself in view of Sahm's usual table.

Sahm exchanged friendly greetings with several business partners, and they sat in plush chairs. They smoked and presumably discussed the oil business. The gold-smuggling business entailed a different set of shady characters.

As time passed, Sean watched the smoke billow and coil, yielding to air currents created by motion in the room. Since Jack was trying to quit smoking, it was better Sean was the one inside the bar.

Sahm stood and said farewell to the businessmen at his table. His bodyguards stood on either side of him.

Sean waited until Sahm's back was to him before raising the small radio to his mouth. "Target's on the move."

"Copy."

Sean rose to follow Sahm outside the Hookah bar. He blinked as his eyes adjusted to the setting sun. The last minutes of searing light would fade quickly to dusk.

Sahm reached the parking lot and shook hands with another Arab dressed in a pressed suit, sporting a Rolex. Sean recognized the young man as Sahm's cousin—another murderer, racist, and elitist.

A shot rang out, and a body fell. Screaming pedestrians fled in terror. Sahm ran for his car.

Raising the radio to his lips, Sean told Jack, "You shot the wrong villain."

"No. His cousin needed to shuffle off his mortal coil."

Sean pursed his lips. Sahm's cousin didn't have the funding Sahm had. He was a scumbag but less of a threat than Sahm. "This stakeout took weeks of planning, and now it's shot to hell."

After the Aston Martin's engine roared to life, Sahm threw the car in reverse and backed out of his parking spot. He pulled out onto Africa Drive and sped down the road.

"Not entirely," Jack said through the radio.

An explosion rocked the ground. Sean stared at Sahm's car as it lurched forward, a heap of fire and twisted metal. Black smoke billowed into the sky. The smell of rubber filled the air.

Shaking his head, Sean began walking back to his car. "Dramatic much, Jack?" When had he had time to place a car bomb?

Jack chuckled into the radio. "Now he can take his car with him to hell."

Fifteen years later, Jack McCumsey returned Sean's call.

"Jack, how are you?"

They'd had many missions together since the Darfur civil war. Most involved Jack being eccentric. Eventually, even Jack retired, and a few years later, Sean met Lillian. Life changed for the better after Lillian.

"Sean, it's good to hear your voice. You said it was urgent I call you back."

"Yes. Are you still living in Rockville? Can you meet me at Nanny O'Brien's tomorrow?"

"Yeah, sure. What time?"

"How's one p.m.?" Sean needed to keep Monday morning open since he didn't know how long his meeting with President Lawson would take.

"No problem. Say, Sean? A mushroom walks into a bar, and the bartender says, 'We don't serve mushrooms here.'"

Sean lowered his head and pinched the bridge of his nose.

Jack continued, "The mushroom says, 'Come on, why not? I'm a fungi!'"

"You're a barrel of laughs, Jack."

Jack chuckled. "All right, all right. I'll see you tomorrow."

---

DEPARTMENT OF DEFENSE
TOP SECRET
NUCLEAR THREAT INVESTIGATION

CASE FILE: 8966B20
Deputy Director: William Austin
Re: Dr. Lillian Whyte and Agent Sean Jennings

TRANSCRIPT:
DEPARTMENT OF DEFENSE INQUIRY

DOD: You accepted Mr. Kleist's assertion that he wanted to find the bomb and stop the cook even though he helped steal it?
DR. WHYTE: Yes.

DOD: You trusted a man you knew to be an international criminal?
DR. WHYTE: Not trust. I apprehensively agreed to let him prove himself.

DOD: Why didn't you notify the CIA?
DR. WHYTE: I did. I told Sean as soon as I had a vague understanding of the situation.

DOD: Your documentation mentioned Mr. Kleist had suffered injuries.
DR. WHYTE: He had multiple contusions over his body, nothing broken. He indicated they had been acquired during his escape from the cook.

DOD: Did you administer medical care to Mr. Kleist?
DR. WHYTE: Gave him two aspirin and checked on him in the morning.

DOD: Next, you left for Germany with Mr. Kleist?
DR. WHYTE: Yes.

DOD: Did he explain what it was he hoped to accomplish in Germany?
DR. WHYTE: He explained that he had resources in Germany and would be able to track the bomb.

DOD: Did you consider that he could kill you or hold you hostage and attempt to manipulate Agent Jennings into compromising national secrets.
DR. WHYTE: If he wanted to kill me, he could have done so in Reykjavik. And if he wanted to lure me into a trap, why concoct a story

about a nuclear threat? A physician would be better lured by a
medical crisis.

DOD: But you were lured anyway.
DR. WHYTE: I was convinced of Ivan's interest in tracking the bomb
and leading authorities to it.

DOD: Except things went wrong.
DR. WHYTE: Yes, they did.

# CHAPTER 9

A fter Sean spoke with Jack, he made the final decision to double down and placed a secure call to Little Rock, Arkansas. He ground his teeth in irritation at what he felt forced to do as he listened to the ringing of the phone.

"Hello?"

"Hi, Jonathan."

"Sean." The name was spoken in an exhaled breath of air. "Is Lillian okay?"

Sean and Jonathan were in-laws who tolerated each other because of their love for Lillian. In eight years of marriage together, Sean never called Jonathan for idle conversation, so he knew to be concerned about this call.

"Lillian is fine. But she is in danger. She—"

"What?" Jonathan's anger exploded through the phone. "Again? You're supposed to protect her from the dangers of your life." He unleashed a train of expletives.

Technically, this current danger wasn't Sean's fault. Lillian's connection to Ivan originated from her medical mission trip to Kenya nine years ago before he and Lillian were together.

*Except that if I'd done my job better, she never would have been kidnapped.*

Damn. It was his fault.

"Are you done with your tirade?" Sean asked. "I need your help."

Jonathan fell silent.

*Yep, never going to hear the end of this one.*

For birthday parties and holidays in the foreseeable future, Jonathan would be sure to have a few beers and start rambling about how the CIA agent needed help from the former marine.

"What do I need to do?"

And this was the reason Sean had called. He knew Jonathan would drop everything, suspend his life, and do whatever was necessary to help his sister.

"Catch up with Lillian in Europe. Keep her safe."

A knot formed in Sean's stomach. If—no, when—Lillian found out he had sent her brother into the potential blast zone of a nuclear threat, she would be outraged. If she lived through this crisis, Sean would have to deal with her hot, redheaded temper—probably for a long time. If she lived, her anger would be worth it.

"Europe? Can you be more specific?"

"Not currently. I'm working on tracking her, but it needs to be done delicately so as not to draw attention. For now, make arrangements to leave the farm and get a flight to London."

"What's the threat level?"

Sean's stomach clenched as he hesitated. "Nuclear."

Jonathan went silent again.

"We are doing everything we can at Langley to find the threat."

Quietly, Jonathan asked, "How did Lily end up in the middle of this?"

"She's with someone who involved her. Now she feels obligated to be part of the solution."

"That's absurd!"

*Agreed.*

"She doesn't know anything about nuclear weapons. Does she?"

Jonathan added his last question meekly as if afraid to know the answer and feel that he no longer knew his sister.

"No. Nothing."

"You're not going because...?"

"Because I'm more effective helping stop the situation from here." Sean rubbed the back of his neck. "She was adamant that I not follow her."

Sean could practically hear the wheels of his brother-in-law's mind turning in thought.

"She won't let you join her because she's trying to protect you?"

"Correct."

"Damn stubborn woman."

Sean agreed but didn't say so.

Jonathan huffed out a breath. "Okay. I'll make arrangements."

---

THE SECRET SERVICE escorted Sean into the Oval Office. Hours after the announced threat, Sean had received a summons to be at the White House on Monday. Although this wasn't a social visit, Sean wasn't sure exactly what it was.

Sean was escorted to the couch, but he remained standing as President Cole Lawson sat at his desk and finished a call on speakerphone.

The doors closed behind them.

A man on the line was speaking, "I'm suggesting, Mr. President, that we need to be transparent about a clear and present danger."

Cole tilted his head back and looked at the ceiling. "Robert, I'm not inciting global panic when we know very little about events surrounding the bomb."

"It'll be your downfall."

"Then, it will. Thank you for the vote of confidence."

"President Lawson—"

"I'm on my next meeting, Robert. Good-bye."

Cole hung up the phone, stood, and walked around his desk.

Sean stood and shook hands with him. "Mr. President."

Sean noticed new wrinkles at the corners of Cole's mouth and blossoming gray patches above his ears. Cole still managed a smile—bright white teeth in contrast to his dark skin.

"Who was that?"

"Senator Mull. Somehow he knows about the bomb, and I think he wants to use it to derail me. He's still bitter the country picked me over him."

Sean had never met the man who'd run against Cole in the election. On paper they had looked similar, both had military training, and both were senators. Cole, however, was far more genuine in his plans for a better America.

"Thank you for coming, Sean. How is Lillian?" Cole gestured to the couches and they took seats opposite each other.

"She's well. She's interim chair of the ER at her hospital."

*And in over her head with a nuclear threat.*

Sean hadn't seen Cole since his election campaign. After the Montreal incident, where Cole had been one of the terrorists' targets, Cole and his wife had invited Sean and Lillian to a dinner—one that didn't involve biomedical warfare and weapons.

Cole Lawson was one of the few people who knew all of the events that had transpired in Montreal. He was also one of the few who knew Lillian's role. Yet he didn't need to know her involvement in the nuclear crisis.

"She ought to be the Surgeon General."

Sean chuckled. "She wouldn't want that."

"No more than you would let me appoint you as an advisor."

Sean had declined his friend's request to join him in the White House when Cole had won the election.

"I'm the kind of man better suited to working in shadows than under public scrutiny. Always have been."

Cole gave a grim nod. "And yet here you are, summoned to advise me. Thank you for coming. I know you went through a lot of traveling and waiting to have a conversation with me."

"We're friends. I'd come even if you didn't hold your current title.

I'll be staying near Langley until this issue is resolved, so it isn't far to drive."

Cole leaned forward. "I know Korean politics and nuclear weapons are not your area of expertise. Honestly, you're the smartest and most levelheaded person I know. And you have no angles to play. I need an ally in all of this." He leaned back. "Robert Mull is eager to see me screw this up. I've got Reginald Lancaster outside my door at this very moment who, no doubt, will be pushing his antinuclear devices down the military's throat. The military is asking to expand the defense budget. I need to know if this situation can be defused."

"The military is contracting with Reginald?"

"Lancaster Defense Enterprises has a big defense contract."

Sean frowned, but turned his attention back to Cole's unasked question. "I don't have a crystal ball, Mr. President."

Cole pointed a finger at Sean. "Don't give me that conservative anything-I-say-might-be-used-against-me crap. I want your honest-to-God opinion, not a damn commitment." He relaxed his posture and crossed his legs. The irritability conveyed in his voice was still evident in his expression.

Sean knew the president was under tremendous stress. He was bound to be testy.

"I can tell you there is a team of CIA committed to ensuring we gain possession of the bomb. There is also more than one mobile team converging in Europe so as information is discovered, they can act on it." None of Sean's words seemed to bring Cole reassurance.

The president looked at him inquisitively. "Do we honestly not know the target?"

"The CIA honestly does not. I have unofficial insider information suggesting Europe."

"Can we trust this person?"

Sean chose his words carefully. "We can trust that he doesn't want a nuclear detonation in Europe any more than we do."

Lillian trusted this much of Ivan so Sean would as well.

"And the idea that Europe is the target originated from this insider?"

"That's correct."

"And his claim is not a decoy as the bomb makes its way to US soil?"

"No, sir. In my opinion."

Silence settled for a moment.

Sean leaned forward on the couch. "We will stop the bomb, Cole."

They had to succeed. Failure meant a nuclear weapon could be detonated in an area of mass casualties. Failure meant losing his wife. Both were unthinkable.

***

WITH HIS HANDS stuffed in his pockets, Sean exited the Oval Office as tumultuous feelings coursed through him. Everyone he cared about was struggling with the predicament. Lillian had hurdled herself headlong into danger—again. President Lawson faced a national crisis. Zoey and Marty were doing covert work exclusively for Sean.

He had juggled secret operations undercover for years in Africa. He could move and manipulate people like players on a chessboard to uncover information and motivations. None of those missions involved his friends and loved ones. None of those missions made him want to punch someone in frustration.

"Sean Jennings."

He looked up to see Reginald Lancaster extending a hand. Sean shook the hand—strong and beefy, but smooth and devoid of callouses. The tailored suit he wore gave the impression he was softer than he was. However, the slight stiffness of the suit betrayed the body armor sewn between its layers. Did all defense contractors worry enough about their safety to wear armored suits?

Sean knew Reginald from their Navy SEAL training. Reginald hadn't succeeded in SEAL Qualification Training, but getting as far as he had was nothing to sneer at.

"Reginald, how have you been?"

"The defense business is good."

Sean suspected a billion-dollar industry in a world with constant terrorist threats would be bountiful.

"And the family?" Sean asked casually, relaxing his posture despite feeling the urgency of needing to get out of the White House and back to work.

Reginald flashed a practiced white smile. Sean had seen the look before when the entrepreneur was flaunting his ownership of Lancaster Defenses to the media. Usually, he was flanked by body-guards, oozing a protective vibe. He always wore a red, white, and blue tie on television. An American patriot with American interests at heart.

Sean shook his pessimism. He was projecting his anger at the nuke situation on a man whose only fault was being a capitalist to the core.

"The family's good," Reginald replied. "The kids are in high school. Mandy is always planning the next charity event."

Sean suspected there was a hint of animosity at her spending his money. He didn't care for gossip, but Rachael, the president's wife, had mentioned Mandy's illicit affairs.

Reginald leaned a little closer and grinned. "You're not at the White House for a social visit, I'm sure. Is Lawson using his favorite CIA spook to diffuse the situation?"

Sean stared at him blandly. "Situation?"

Rocking back on his heels, Reginald held a twinkle in his eyes. "I don't accept a summons to the oval office without knowing why. I'm here because there is a crisis, and the United States needs Lancaster Defense Enterprises."

Sean's gaze flickered around the hallway. He wondered if Reginald were truly so enamored with himself, or thought a reporter could be eavesdropping, and Reginald wanted to make a quotable statement. Probably both.

Where had he gotten information about the crisis? Perhaps Senator Mull—the man the president was talking to earlier.

"I'm sure the president will tell you as much as you need to know," Sean assured him.

"As he did with you?"

"I'm just here for the tour."

Reginald's mouth twisted in a feral smile.

A man stood from a nearby desk. "Mr. Lancaster, the president will see you now."

Reginald wriggled his eyebrows at Sean. "Duty calls. Pleasure seeing you, Sean."

After Sean watched him turn and leave, he resumed his walk down the hallway.

*Pleasure seeing you, Sean.* Reginald's words sounded sincere. Why would that be? Perhaps seeing the president conferring with a CIA agent confirmed whatever intelligence Reginald had gathered, leading him to believe a crisis was at hand.

---

REGINALD LANCASTER DAMPENED his rising excitement as he shook hands with President Lawson. This was his moment to shine, and he didn't want to appear too eager.

"Mr. President."

"Reginald, thanks for coming."

President Lawson was the son of a renowned pacifist. Although his mother was no longer alive, her reputation survived through him. Yet Cole was no choirboy. He was military and Navy SEAL, trained with all the other cold-blooded killers—like Sean Jennings.

*History writer on a tour of the White House my ass.*

"Thank you for inviting me, Mr. President."

The president gestured to the couch. "Please, Reggie, we were in military training together. Call me Cole."

The comment stung Reginald's pride. He knew Cole meant it to be a statement of camaraderie, but to Reginald, it was a reminder of one of his failures in life. One of his few. Yet, those failures had led to his current success—like this moment where he had been invited to the White House. From here, he could help shape the course of the country—stronger, better, unified.

He unbuttoned his suit coat as he sat. "Yes, sir."

Cole sat opposite him, his face looking weary and worn. He was going to have to build his stamina if he was going to survive the presidency for another two years. By the look of him, he'd made the right decision to seek Reginald's help. This was one of the reasons the Oval Office didn't need a pacifist. It needed a pit bull.

"The world faces a crisis, Reggie."

"Tell me how I can help."

———

Lillian and Ivan took a flight from Ryekjavik to Hamburg.

Ivan had explained on the plane that he had a equipment in Germany which would enable him to work and gather more information.

He moved through the Flugafen Hamburg in determined strides, passing the rows of boarding stations within the airport terminal. "We'll rent a car and go south to Bavaria."

"Okay. Slow down." She pulled her luggage up beside her. "We got off a seven-hour flight five minutes ago. I need to go to the bathroom, stretch my legs, and eat. I'm not sitting in a car for another umpteen hours to wherever Bavaria is until I get a break."

He stopped, stared at her, and blinked. Seeming to sense her resolve, he pursed his lips. His eyes roamed the airport irritably, watching people pass them.

He extended a hand. "Hold my hand. We need to blend in better."

She looked down at his hand and then up at him. "Please."

"What?"

"'Will you *please* hold my hand, Lillian?'"

His face twisted in displeasure.

She adjusted her purse strap and stood her ground. "If we're going to work together on this and remain in close company for the next several days, you're going to be nice to me. Polite to me."

"Please."

She took his hand as they resumed walking. His grip was firm but not rough as his large, calloused hand enveloped hers. The hand-holding kept his long legs from out-pacing her.

They progressed through the airport to the rental car booth. She took her bathroom break and sent Sean a text message update while Ivan arranged for the car. When she returned, she saw him putting a fake ID card back in his wallet and withdrawing cash to pay for the rental.

Twenty minutes later they were in a black, four-door Audi.

"It's a one hour drive to a bed and breakfast I know. It's across the street from a nice pub with some walking trails nearby. We'll stop for the night, have dinner, and get you a walk."

"Thank you." She leaned back in the passenger seat and closed her eyes.


Ivan glanced at the resting redhead. They were headed toward doom, needing to focus on the nuclear threat, and she was worried about him being polite. Somehow, he grudgingly admitted, her insistence felt right. He should make an effort to be civilized since saving civilization was the point of their effort.

Holding her hand had reminded him of that—the human connection. The sensation wasn't sexual but unexpectedly comforting.

Lillian was capable of both infuriating him and grounding him. People didn't speak to him as she did—so plainly. His size and temperament meant most people avoided him or treaded lightly in his presence. Some of his friends, like Renni, could joke with him, but no one gave his manners a course correction.

For Lillian, he could slow down the pace of travel, making it less arduous. He needed to continue to build her trust since teaming up against the nuclear threat wasn't the only favor he would be asking of her.

## DEPARTMENT OF DEFENSE
## TOP SECRET
## NUCLEAR THREAT INVESTIGATION

### CASE FILE: 8966B20
Deputy Director: William Austin
Re: Dr. Lillian Whyte and Agent Sean Jennings

### TRANSCRIPT:
### DEPARTMENT OF DEFENSE INQUIRY

DOD: You knew your wife was conspiring with a known criminal, but did not inform your superior?
JENNINGS: I needed to gather more information. The deputy director had enough on his plate.

DOD: Yet you used CIA personnel and resources to track your wife?
JENNINGS: Yes.

DOD: Were you tracking her because you didn't trust her?
JENNINGS: I didn't trust Ivan.

DOD: What would make your wife consider herself qualified to join a criminal and stop a nuclear threat?
JENNINGS: History. She's proven she can handle crises.

DOD: With disregard for CIA protocol, you sent a civilian in to fetch your wife?
JENNINGS: I sent her brother to see if he could help her get home. At that point, I didn't know how dire the situation would become.

DOD: You didn't suspect a stolen bomb and nuclear threat would become dire?
JENNINGS: That situation was already dire. I didn't know my wife's situation would become worse than it already was.

# CHAPTER 10

As Sean sat at the end of the bar at Nanny O'Brien's Irish pub, he sipped a thick stout. He stared at the dark, paneled walls trying to let the dim, casual atmosphere, the chatter of patrons, and the heavy sensation of beer in his stomach ease his worry about his wife.

From his peripheral vision, Jack McCumsey entered the bar wearing jeans and a NY Yankees T-shirt. The man was as tall as Sean but had long, skinny legs and a short torso like a stork. The disproportion meant finding a comfortable vehicle was difficult but outrunning an opponent wasn't. Except he was pushing past sixty now. He wasn't doing much running these days.

Sean stood, greeting his mentor with a handshake and brief embrace where not more than their shoulders bumped.

"Thanks for coming, Jack."

Jack jutted his chin toward the other glass on the table. "Thanks for ordering me one." He took a seat.

Sean sat. They were both angled where they could see the front door. Habit.

"Bar joke?" Jack asked.

"If you insist."

"Irishman walks out of a bar."

Sean's lips betrayed the faintest grin.

"How are the kids?"

Jack shrugged. "The same. Busy working parents who resent me for time spent away from home when they were growing up. I think the older their own children get the more they understand how it's hard to keep ambitious in their careers and not make their children feel sidelined."

Sean watched sweat bead on his glass of beer. He often thought about children—thought about how fun it would be to share the love of a child with Lillian. They had room in their lives for one, but indecision had stolen time from them.

When they discussed having children, they expressed worry about a child's safety. Sean also worried about resentment. He knew the rejection Jack had faced. For years he wasn't welcome into his children's lives until they had children of their own. Since he was retired, he could offer free childcare at a time when his children were trying to pay their mortgage, pay off college, and live a middle-class life.

Could Sean and Lillian have children, keep them safe, and maintain a mutually fulfilling relationship? Maybe they were overanalyzing the situation. Maybe they would never know.

"Does the agency know you called me?" Jack took a long gulp of his beer.

"Nope."

"You've never once called in a favor since I've been retired. Must be important."

Sean locked his gaze with Jack's blue eyes. His crop of white hair was smoothly combed to one side. "It's very important."

"Does it have anything to do with North Korea?"

Sean leaned back, appraising Jack. "What do you know about North Korea?"

"I may not play the game anymore, but that doesn't mean I don't still watch it."

"Keeping up is not as easy as tuning your television to the CIA channel."

"I have my sources. I know about the missing nuke. Like I know about Montreal three years ago."

Sean grunted.

"You and your wife make quite the team."

"And it ended with her getting shot. The event is not something I want to repeat." His chest clenched at the memory of her blood on him—on everything. He took a swig of his beer without enjoying the flavor. "Which brings us to why you're here."

Jack cocked his head to one side. "Lillian's in danger?"

Sean explained the situation and Lillian's current whereabouts in Germany. As he did, his angst deepened, and he wished he had something stronger than beer to dull the dread.

Jack crossed his arms. "Stubborn and ambitious. No wonder you like her."

"Sometimes I love her. Sometimes I want to chain her up in the basement for her own good."

Jack chuckled. "Her own good? Or yours? Seems she's proven she can take care of herself."

"Not like this. Not this time. Not with me an ocean away."

"So you want me to fetch her or be her guardian angel?"

"Both. Whatever the occasion calls for."

"How come you're not going?"

Sean shook his head. "I want to go. I'm fighting every primal urge to go because I know in my gut she's right. If I work through Langley to gather intel, I can accomplish more than I can by following her around Europe."

"Hmm. And I suppose you're going to tell me how I can track her?"

"I put a tracking device on her smart watch before I gifted it to her a year ago Christmas. Yeah, I know that look. And yes, she'll be pissed when she finds out. Right now I have no regrets about it. And, no, I've never used it to spy on her."

Jack stood and stretched his long legs.

"Where are you going?"

"Clock's ticking. I need to catch a flight to Germany."

---

LILLIAN PACED the tiny motel room. She'd seen bathrooms larger than the room Ivan had rented. So much for four stars in Iceland. At least she had her own room.

A knock sounded at the door.

Lillian took five steps from one side of the room to the other and swung open the door. "What took you so long?"

He scowled. "Intelligence gathering takes time."

"Intelligence gathering is something you could have done before you helped steal a nuclear weapon."

His mouth opened but shut before any words were spoken. If his scowl were any indication, his words would have been foul. He set his laptop down on the sliver of a desk in the room and sat in the only chair.

"So this is the big reveal? The part where you tell me how we stop a nuclear weapon?"

He typed in a password without answering her.

She watched over his shoulder as he opened a file and a video feed began.

"What is that? It looks like a satellite view of earth."

"When I escaped from the cook, I contacted a Russian friend who has a satellite. I had him monitor the nuclear facility in North Korea for suspicious activity. He—"

"You have a friend who happens to have a satellite?"

"It's a hobby."

"Hobbies are collecting model cars or stamps, not owning satellites."

He turned and blinked at her. "You know any stamp collectors making five thousand Euros a day?"

Lillian's eyes widened. "You're paying this friend—what's his name—five thousand Euros a day to spy on North Korea?"

"You don't get to know his name. And, no, I'm paying him five thousand Euros a day to track a nuclear bomb stolen from North Korea."

"Why didn't you alert North Korea that the heist was planned? Why wait to track the theft after the fact?"

He rubbed his temples. "I don't have North Korean intelligence on speed dial. Do you?"

She pursed her lips.

"Are you finished with the interrogation or do you want to continue to delay the bomb relocation project?"

"Continue," she prompted.

"This is the facility. Every day my friend watches. Three trucks in. Three trucks out. Then, on this day"—he fast-forwarded the video—"an extra truck goes out. Thirty minutes later, all sorts of military vehicles rush in. My friend follows the truck. The truck connects to a train in Dandong." He sped up the video again. "Cargo from the truck is loaded on the twelfth boxcar. The train travels to Shenyang where the contents of boxcar twelve are loaded in a delivery truck. The truck ultimately stops at a remote airport. The package is loaded onto a plane. Currently, the plane is over Tajikistan somewhere. When it lands, your husband can have a team ready to intercept."

Lillian realized the painstaking process and attention to detail Ivan's friend must possess to have been able to track the bomb as it traveled across Asia. "Holy crap. You should double what you're paying your friend."

Ivan raised his eyebrows. "You're going to pitch in?"

"I don't make that kind of money."

He snorted.

"Okay. Let's call my husband, shall we?"

Ivan nodded.

Lillian paced the room as the video chat connected. She watched Sean materialize on the scene.

She rushed to the laptop. "Sean."

The look of relief on his face mirrored the relief she felt at seeing him.

"You're okay?" he asked.

"I'm okay."

He scrubbed his hands through his hair, worry etched on his face. "Can I tell you how reckless this is?"

She frowned, wanting simultaneously to scold him and kiss away his worry. "You can—or we can work on the solution."

"What solution have you and the international criminal concocted?"

Lillian looked over at Ivan. He was wisely staying out of view of the camera.

Better that way.

Sean might be clouded by his fury if he had to see the man who nabbed his wife and was taking her toward a nuclear weapon.

"Ivan has shown me what he has. We're sending it to you. He's been tracking the package since the cook stole it."

"The cook?"

"Apparently she was some type of North Korean super assassin until a forced retirement when she became an independent mercenary."

"Yes, I know who the cook is rumored to be." He hesitated, seeming to catch the irritability in his voice. He sat. "She's a super-spy myth. Like the Jackal."

"Well, Ivan met her and lived to tell about it, despite her efforts to kill him."

Sean kept silent.

Lillian continued. "Regardless of whether you choose to accept her existence or not, Ivan has tracked the stolen item—relentlessly—via satellite. It's currently in a plane over Asia. If the CIA can track it, maybe they can get a team in place to intercept it."

"I'm supposed to convince the CIA to launch a strike team based on intelligence from a criminal?"

She felt her eye twitch irritably. "I'm sure governments take offensive measures based on criminal information all the time. I believe Ivan. I'm asking you to believe me."

"Okay." His voice sounded deflated. Defeated. "Come home, Lily."

A lump formed in her throat. She wanted to go home. "Would you? Would you go home if you thought you could contribute to efforts to stop this crisis in some way?" She leaned toward the computer. "If I leave Ivan now, no one is left to hear his story. The way to get me home is to tell me the weapon is in our hands."

"Okay."

"We'll send you the satellite files."

"Okay."

"I love you."

"I love you too."

WILLIAM AUSTIN SCRATCHED his elbows before popping an antacid. He hadn't been dutifully treating his psoriasis with ultraviolet light as prescribed since it was difficult to sit under the light for twenty minutes while trying to manage a nuclear threat. In addition, his ulcer was threatening to rupture from the stress of it all.

"Jennings, I've got meetings with the Joint Chiefs of Staff and international ambassadors. This had better be worth my time."

Sean may have been a cocky pain in Austin's ass, but he didn't call unnecessary meetings. Regardless, Austin couldn't fathom how an agent—former agent, or whatever the hell he was these days—specializing in African foreign affairs would have information relevant to the nuclear crisis at hand. Since Zoey Cain was present, Sean had apparently also taken the liberty of using one of their profilers for his own agenda at a time when the CIA was all hands on deck.

"We have a contact with eyes on the nuke. He's been tracking it since the heist in North Korea."

Austin's heart thudded at the news of hope. He instantly crushed the sensation. His eyes flickered around the conference room from Sean standing at one end opposite the mounted screen on the wall and Zoey seated at the table with a laptop.

"Who's been tracking the bomb?"

"Barbara poured over the footage and authenticated the satellite videos."

"Videos from *whom*?"

"Ivan Kleist."

"We're accepting intelligence from criminals?"

"We do it all the time."

As Austin glanced at the black-and-white satellite footage onscreen, Austin pursed his lips. "Why you?" He wagged a finger at Sean. "Don't give me that smug look. Why did he send this information directly to you?"

"Perhaps he remembers me from Kenya and Paris."

"He sends satellite images to the guy who beats him up in the bathroom of Charles de Gaulle Airport? Yes, I read your report on the events following Kenya."

He glanced at Zoey, who kept her gaze fixed on her computer screen.

*What is she hiding for Sean?*

"Why he sent it to me is not as important as what he sent. Marty is tracking the plane carrying the bomb. If we get a team to the Mediterranean Sea, we can confiscate this bomb before it reaches its final destination."

"Which is where?"

"We don't know, which is why Ivan has been tracking it."

"He's helping because he suddenly turned over a new leaf?"

Zoey took her cue. "He's a mercenary, but I believe one with a conscience. A maturing conscience. Confirmed kills have been declining and contract kills have been replaced by more nonlethal theft. He thrives off government instability, but mass annihilation isn't part of his programming."

Austin considered her words. Zoey was one of his best profilers. Sean knew that. Sean had made a calculated move having her present. Convincing scheme, but Austin didn't like feeling manipulated.

"Did Ivan say who took the bomb?"

Sean sucked in a breath. "The cook."

"I knew it!" Zoey's eyes widened, surprised at her own outburst.

Austin clenched his teeth. "I asked you not to waste my time, Jennings." He turned to Zoey. "You have something to contribute?"

She pushed her red-rimmed glasses up on her nose and brushed a blond strand of hair out of her face. "I have been doing some data extrapolation on the cook. I think she exists. And she's a badass." She shrunk back at Austin's admonishing glare. "And she's unstable. Like psychologically *'I will kill you and your family for jay-walking'* unstable."

Austin sat in a chair. "You're telling me one of the world's most mythical assassins not only exists but is a fanatic transporting a nuclear weapon across Europe?"

Zoey swallowed. "Yes, sir."

He gave a long, hard look at Sean. "We'll get a Delta Force team en route to intercept. If you're wrong about this, all of our careers are over."

He hoped Sean was right. Sean's arrogance would escalate, but that would be tolerable if thousands of lives could be saved.

---

AFTER SEAN'S meeting with Austin, he reconvened at Marty's desk with Zoey by his side.

"Thank you, Zoey, for coming."

"No problem. You told me about Ivan, but you didn't tell me the cook was involved."

"I already come across far-fetched trying to explain how Ivan Kleist sent me the information out of the goodness of his heart. I didn't need to be further discredited by mentioning the boogie man. If Austin hadn't asked directly, I wasn't planning on releasing that piece of information."

Zoey lowered her voice, although no one was within earshot of their conversation. "I noticed you didn't mention Lillian's involvement."

"Austin and my wife have a love-hate relationship. He doesn't need any more emotions or confusion thrown into the mix."

Marty swiveled in his chair. "What's the next move, boss?"

"Austin has agreed to send a Delta Force team to intercept the bomb. Maybe we can glimpse what the cook looks like on their go-cams. I want to make sure all those involved are accounted for when the dust settles."

"You want facial recognition on all guilty parties?"

"Yes, I do."

---

DEPARTMENT OF DEFENSE
TOP SECRET
NUCLEAR THREAT INVESTIGATION

CASE FILE: 8966B20
Deputy Director: William Austin
Re: Dr. Lillian Whyte and Agent Sean Jennings

TRANSCRIPT:
DEPARTMENT OF DEFENSE INQUIRY

DOD: Once in Germany, what did you discover?
DR. WHYTE: Ivan had been paying someone to track the bomb via satellite. No, I don't know who.

DOD: You notified the CIA then?
DR. WHYTE: Yes, I contacted Sean and we sent him the video files as proof.

DOD: You sent the files. Why not send the CIA information on how to connect with Ivan's satellite owner and operator?
DR. WHYTE: I suspect because such a person might not be an upstanding citizen, but I didn't ask.

DOD: Then what did you do?
DR. WHYTE: Then we waited.

DOD: And while you waited, you traveled to Ivan Kleist's cabin?
DR. WHYTE: We went to his sister's cabin to wait.

DOD: With the files in CIA hands, why didn't you return to the US at that juncture?
DR. WHYTE: We had a bomb on a plane over Asia guided by a known assassin. I wasn't walking away until a US strike team had custody of it.

# CHAPTER 11

Lillian watched intently as Ivan took another swig of his beer. "Okay, Ivan, what's your motivation? Are you just a mercenary for hire? It can't be all about the money." She felt good after a long walk and a nourishing dinner. She shrugged off the confinement of hotel rooms, planes, and cars.

He regarded her carefully. "When I was a child, my mother used to lock me in the basement for days. I had to kill rats to survive. When I grew up, I kept killing rats. Only bigger ones."

She swallowed, feeling the color drain from her face. "Oh."

A wide grin spread across his face. "No. I'm messing with you. That's the American saying, yes?"

"Yes. And screw you," she said with a laugh.

He looked startled at her language, but his smile didn't falter. He raised his glass. She accepted the gesture and clinked her glass against his.

His lips flattened. "In all seriousness, most of the scum I execute are rats. They dwell in the dark and feed on carcasses. I'm glorified pest control." He considered his words and added, "Well paid pest control."

"They're still humans," Lillian said. Her tone was oddly nonjudgmental. She was genuinely curious about Ivan's motivating factors. What made this criminal tick?

"Most did very little with the life given to them. You frown at me?" He shrugged. "Perhaps you should. As I get older, I find I have less taste for murder. Reflecting back, some of them were perhaps unnecessary. I could have been more careful with collateral damage in my early career."

As Lillian downed the last of her beer, Ivan signaled the waiter for refills.

"You have regrets, *nein*?"

Lillian leaned back in her chair. "Yeah, I have regrets. Parking tickets. A few relationships. Not spending more time with my dad. But not murder."

Ivan chuckled.

She arched an eyebrow at him.

He leaned toward her, folding his arms across the table. "You have killed. You don't regret the men you have killed?"

Lillian thought about her own acts of indiscretions. Dominique Vanier had crossed an ocean to kill her. Instead she stabbed him. He died slowly and miserably and alone. She had killed him, but in self-defense. She hated that the situation had escalated to that extent, but she didn't regret defending herself. Omar Jabal, leader of a terrorist cell, had shot her, almost executed her husband, and planned to release a genetically altered, deadly disease on the world. She had no regrets about shooting him.

She crossed her arms and looked hard at Ivan. "No, but those were different."

The waiter brought two new beers.

She watched Ivan take a long drink and then set down his mug.

"Yes. It is different," he conceded lightly. "Mostly mine were for money, or because someone inconvenienced me. I certainly didn't atone for any of my behavior. Unlike you, who have spent your life helping others."

She drank her beer, and the bitter taste bit into her tastebuds. "Is that what stopping this nuclear weapon is for you? Atonement?"

He licked his lips as though he held some interesting secret of which she wasn't aware. "I'll answer that if we succeed."

He added, "What about your husband?"

The hair on the back of her neck stood on end. "What about my husband?"

"He has killed many people."

"In defense of his country. Not for money."

"And who is to say his country was not motivated by money?"

Her sharp look of reprimand eased into a soft expression of surrender. She sighed. "I have no idea if there are things he allowed himself to be manipulated or deceived into doing. If you want to philosophically propose that at least a mercenary goes at his task with eyes open and is no one's pawn, perhaps you are right. Then again, even you were deceived, and here we are."

*Teaming up against a nuclear threat.*

He eyed her sidelong. "Here we are," he agreed placidly. As he watched her, his eyes sparkled with amusement, and he grinned. "Can I say nothing to provoke you, Lillian?"

"Nine years ago, sure, you could have. Today, we're strange allies, and I find myself more curious about your life choices than judgmental about them." She studied the predator, part wariness and part fascination. Equally intriguing was having a light conversation about such a dark topic.

When she looked back down at her beer, she was surprised to see someone had drained the glass. The waiter took the empty mug and swapped it for a full one. She would have to pace herself. Other than the occasional glass of wine, her liver was ill equipped to metabolize alcohol on a mass scale.

Ivan, she suspected, could more than hold his own.

Was he testing her? He didn't seem to be. She had already proven herself by her reputation in handling herself with villains and not cowering before him.

So was this bonding? As her stomach absorbed the third beer, she stopped trying to analyze Ivan's motives.

He shared with her some of his hit-man blunders, and she described some of her more bizarre patient encounters.

IVAN WATCHED the doctor's flushed, smiling face. He had traded her beer for water after her third alcoholic beverage when he realized she was intoxicated. His intention was not to get her drunk. It had been some time since he drank with both a woman and one unaccustomed to heavy drinking.

She giggled as she told her story. "So, he tells me he slipped and fell on the shampoo bottle."

His mouth quirked. "That was his story for how the bottle got lodged?"

She slapped her hand on the table. Laughing, she wiped tears from her eyes.

"And you like this job? Where you have to retrieve objects people have lost in unsightly places?"

She punched his arm playfully. "I do more than that."

"Of course."

She glared at him with feigned malice as she sipped her water.

She was cute drunk. Pink cheeks and bright blue eyes were framed by thick, strawberry hair. Every bit still his white rabbit.

*Hase.*

Once she had been his white rabbit hiding out from him. She was no longer that timid creature. Now she was more likely to lure someone into her rabbit hole where they would be surprised to find themselves face-to-face with an aggressor and not a victim.

Early in the conversation he had tried to provoke her. She was so radiant when her temper flared. Yet, she remained unperturbed. She met his probing with the determination of a mature woman.

"At least I never shot anyone inadvertently in the ass."

He had told her the story of a botched theft. "I didn't realize the balcony was covered in a sheet of ice."

"And he was your partner, no less."

"*Ja*," he offered in a grumpy tone. He found it impossible to be irritated at her prodding when she was so delightfully giddy.

He imagined her like this in college, laughing merrily while surrounded by half a dozen fraternity boys. Then he remembered he already knew that part of her past—straight and narrow. She had been a certifiable workaholic.

Her brother, on the other hand, who had been a trained marine, had taken well into his forties before he got his work ethic on track and took over rebuilding the family farm. Neither of them had children. The end of the Whyte line. Pity. She was a remarkable woman. Ivan was curious to know what her genes would have created. Perhaps it was better she hadn't reproduced. Her number of enemies was slowly increasing, especially since he dragged her into more danger.

He felt a pang of guilt, but before he could ponder that, Lillian was standing unsteadily.

He stood and wrapped an arm around her waist.

She gave him a grateful half smile.

He startled, unsure the last time he had been on the receiving end of such an expression from anyone.

"This is embarrassing," she slurred.

He smiled, pulling out cash and tossing it onto the table. "I am the only one who knows you. You won't run into a patient or coworker here. Come. You will feel better with fresh air."

He led her out of the pub, her body tucked into his for stability.

"I think," she began, squinting into the distance as if her thoughts could be found in the night sky, "if you were a character from Norse mythology, you would be Loki."

He looked down at her quizzically.

"I'm serious. I read a book on Norse mythology before I went to Iceland."

He flexed his bicep against her. "Clearly I'm more of an Odin or Thor."

She shook her head, still leaning in to him. "You can blend in and disappear. And you look out for your own interests. Oh, don't scowl. I meant no offense. On the outside you're big like Thor, but here," she poked a finger at his chest, "Loki. He did some good things too, you know."

"Did he?" Ivan knew Norse mythology, but he was content to let Lillian's sweet voice ramble.

"He helped both gods and giants—depending on his mood. He's how Thor got his hammer, and Asgard got its protective wall around the city."

"He also tricked Hod into killing Baldur."

"I know. Crazy, right? Death by mistletoe." She chuckled.

"As punishment for his many crimes, Loki was tied down with the entrails of one of his sons while tortured with poisonous snake venom."

She crinkled her nose. "Who comes up with these dysfunctional family dynamics? Maybe my comparison was ill conceived. I wouldn't wish that on anyone."

"Perhaps. Yet, I don't possess those valued Norse virtues of honor and loyalty, so Loki and I have this in common."

Lillian fell silent. He wasn't sure if his observation made her contemplative or sad, or if she lost interest in the topic.

He was oddly content to walk, supporting her and feeling her silky hair against his arm. She smelled like warm *apfel streuselkuchen* —apples, vanilla, and sugar.

They reached the hotel and took the elevator to their rooms. Lillian remained quiet as she rested her head on his shoulder. When the doors opened, and she didn't move, he realized she was sleeping as she leaned on him.

With his free arm, he pulled out the room keycard. He bent down and scooped her gently into his arms. Her eyes remained closed and her breathing slow and steady. He carried her down the hall, unlocked and opened the door, and stepped inside the room.

The door closed behind him as he eased her into one of the beds. Reaching down, he tugged off her shoes. He pulled the covers aside then pulled them over her. She lay in peaceful sleep.

He found the situation oddly flattering—that she felt comfortable enough in his presence to let go and relax. She was understandably exhausted. From his surprise appearance in Reykjavik to learning of the nuclear threat to their travels to Germany, she'd been through an ordeal already. The average person would have crumbled under the stress. Dr. Whyte had exceptional resilience—one of the many reasons he had sought her. Recruited her. Now that the initiation was over, the real danger would begin.

―――――――

REGINALD LANCASTER PORED over the company finances. The margin was too close to the red. As soon as Cole Lawson became the likely next president of the Unites States, stocks on weapons manufacturers had plummeted. They had continued to nosedive when he took office. Lancaster Defense Enterprises did not escape unscathed.

Rather than exploit the fact that Cole Lawson had a military background with blood on his hands like everyone else, the press chose to promote the man's political agenda as if he were the next Gandhi. True to his campaign promises, Cole withdrew troops and held peace talks.

*World peace. What a crock.*

Now, Lancaster's company leaked money from every orifice, like a Black Hawk riddled with 7.62 mm armor-piercing rounds. Research and development ate its share of money. As stocks dropped, Reginald increasingly paid lobbyists to secure favors with the Senate and the House. Senator Mull was his biggest advocate, and it helped he was anti-Lawson.

His eyes wandered from the budget spreadsheet on his computer screen to the family photo on his desk. Mandy, his beautiful wife of ten years (second marriage) smiled back at him. He slammed the photo face down on his desk. She was another source of hemorrhaging funds. She was bitter that he worked all of the time and perhaps more than bitter at several indiscretions he had during some of his international travels. She didn't understand—one did not simply turn down a gift from a sheik who might buy several million dollars' worth of inventory even if the gift was a night with a young woman.

Mandy, in her classic adolescent style, sought retribution by giving away tens of thousands of dollars at charity events. She bought herself new diamond jewelry almost every time he traveled internationally. He'd been hoping she would find some more affordable hobbies. Skydiving perhaps.

Money. He needed sales and defense contracts. The meeting with the president seemed promising. President Lawson asked specific questions about kill vehicles for ballistic missiles. He was worried about nuclear warfare.

Noah, vice president of Lancaster Defense Enterprises, entered Reginald's office and set his tablet on the desk. "Page three of the paper has an article on the president meeting with the top US defense contractor a week after North Korea detonated another bomb. Social media blogs and text messaging is making this go viral. We've already seen a bump in LDE stock."

Reginald grinned. "Excellent."

*This is only the beginning.*

DEPARTMENT OF DEFENSE
TOP SECRET
NUCLEAR THREAT INVESTIGATION

CASE FILE: 8966B20
Deputy Director: William Austin
Re: Dr. Lillian Whyte and Agent Sean Jennings

TRANSCRIPT:
DEPARTMENT OF DEFENSE INQUIRY

DOD: On Monday evening, you finally told your superior about Ivan Kleist?

JENNINGS: Yes. In less than forty-eight hours after learning of Ivan's involvement, I had concrete evidence that he wanted to help in our confiscation efforts.

DOD: At this point, why didn't Dr. Whyte return home?

JENNINGS: She doesn't leave a job half done.

DOD: What did Director Austin do with the information you gave him?

JENNINGS: Verified the contents of the files and rallied a Delta Force to intercept the nuclear weapon.

DOD: What was your role by this time?

JENNINGS: The money trail. I had analysts working to pinpoint who had the funds and motives to orchestrate the theft of a nuclear weapon from North Korea.

DOD: You were already aware of the claims that the cook was orchestrating the theft?

JENNINGS: I was aware she was probably handling the logistics. I wanted to know who was paying her to do it.

DOD: Why would you suspect she wasn't fronting the operation?

JENNINGS: As a North Korean assassin, she wouldn't have the money to pay everyone involved. Furthermore, our profiler intel suggested she was never motivated by money and had previously worked alone. She wouldn't have the funds or logistical comprehension to disperse them for such an elaborate a scheme.

# CHAPTER 12

Lillian's head throbbed the next morning as Ivan drove down the highway. She had taken a few anti-inflammatories for her headache and sufficiently hydrated with water. What had she been thinking, getting drunk in a bar in Germany with Ivan? She hadn't been thinking. She had lost count of the beverages because for one brief moment she was enjoying herself and not thinking about the end of the world.

Ivan hadn't mentioned her passing out or how she had ended up in bed—clothed and shoeless and thankfully alone—in her own hotel room.

She slipped on her sunglasses and sunk low in the passenger car seat. "So we're driving to your sister's house?"

"Yes. She has a nice cabin in the woods to the south. There isn't much we can do now. We can stay there a few days and once the US has confiscated the bomb, we'll get you back home."

*Home.*

She'd been gone less than a week, but it felt longer. Home was a small apartment, and the man she loved was there. Home was her job in the emergency room. Home was near her friend Kelly and Kelly's rambunctious child.

"*I bet he would make a great dad*," Kelly had said of Sean. He undoubtedly would. Their life had room for more. What would the adventure of children be like? Was it fair to bring them into a world like this? Yet didn't the world need more love and less violence?

"You're uncharacteristically quiet."

"Hangover," she replied.

"Is that all?"

"I was thinking about home. It will be nice to be home, to be with Sean."

Lillian's phone rang. She jerked it out of her pocket and looked at the caller ID. Disappointment tugged at her when she saw it was a hospital number and not Sean.

"Hello?"

"This is Dr. Sumner."

Lillian sat up as she thought through the logistics of how the cardiologist would have gotten her number. He would have finally called Tonya back after her many pages. Then he would have demanded Lillian's number. Tonya would have told him she was on vacation. Apparently, he decided to badger her on vacation anyway.

"Hello, Dr. Sumner. This is Dr. Whyte." Since he wanted to use professional titles, so would she.

Ivan arched an eyebrow as if asking if he needed to be concerned about the call. She shook her head.

"We need to speak about your lack of professionalism in having your assistant constantly page me to set up a meeting when you're not even here." His tone was brisk and condescending.

"Tonya has been interacting with your assistant for a month and has not been able to schedule anything with you. We resorted to alternative means."

"My pager is to be used for urgent patient issues."

"This is an urgent patient issue. I need a heart failure protocol from you. We admit a dozen heart failure patients a day, and I need a protocol so patients get timely care and get routed to the right specialist."

"Draw something up, and I'll review it."

Lillian felt her temper simmering beneath the surface of her skin. "No, Dr. Sumner. I am not your assistant or your trainee. I am the chair of the emergency room. That makes you *my* subspecialist. Therefore, you can draw up a draft protocol, and the ER will see if we find it acceptable."

"I won't stand for being treated like this."

"Fine, you can sit."

"You're a real piece of work. You know that?"

"I do, thank you."

"This is horseshit, and I'll see to it that your administrative role is revoked."

She could almost envision a comical amount of spittle flying into his phone.

"Yes, you're golfing buddies with the COO. Congratulations on having political connections rather than relying on good patient care for your reputation."

"You cocky bitch."

"I want that protocol when we meet in two weeks. If I don't have it, I'll use my connections to gather data and put together a report on all of the heart failure patients over the last twelve months, including their ER wait times, time from consulting a cardiologist to when he or she actually arrived at the bedside, and whether the patient was appropriately triaged to the cardiac care unit, or if they were sent elsewhere."

"Are you threatening me?"

"No. I'm being the cocky bitch you accused me of being. We both know the care for these patients is suboptimal. I'm giving you an opportunity to fix the situation without the magnitude of the problem being put on display for the hospital administration to see. Your choice."

Silence settled over the phone before Dr. Sumner spoke. "I'll see you in two weeks, but this isn't over."

The phone disconnected. She slipped it into the back pocket of her jeans.

Ivan glanced at her as a grin spread over his face.

Lillian's pursed her lips.

Ivan burst out in a voracious laugh.

Lillian was taken aback. Was he laughing *at* her?

"You handled him, didn't you?" He laughed again. "That was wonderful. You make a good leader, *ja*?"

"I think I'm supposed to build bridges as a leader, not tell an arrogant cardiologist where he can shove his three-hundred-dollar, battery-powered stethoscope."

"Bah." He waved a hand in the air. "Sometimes you have to bulldoze a bridge to get rid of the troll under it, and then you can put up a better one."

What did Ivan know of administrative work and building bridges?

*Trolls under bridges—he might know something about those.*

"Still," Ivan continued, "he should not have called you that."

"A bitch? Well, if I hid in a corner every time an insult was hurled at me, I wouldn't be much of an ER physician." She pulled her sunglasses down and looked at him. "Why? You want to shoot him in the ass for me?"

Ivan chuckled. "Hmm. I only shoot partners in the ass."

As she leaned back in her seat, she hesitated. "Just so we're clear. We're not partners."

***

JONATHAN HOISTED his duffel bag on his shoulder. He felt good after his transatlantic flight, having taken first class. And since he was traveling this far to cover Lily's butt, she could reimburse him for the ticket later.

He took the tube and found his way to a small hotel in London. His instructions were vaguely to go to the city, though he was grateful to be starting in an English-speaking country. He was dependent on

Sean to tell him where his next stop would be—where he would cross paths with Lily.

He was also dependent on Sean for a gun when he reached his final destination. He couldn't cross borders with a concealed weapon. If Lily was in as much trouble as Sean thought—as much trouble as she often seemed to be in—then he needed to be armed.

Jonathan checked into his hotel, dropped his luggage in his room, and went for a walk. He wanted to stretch his legs, maybe grab some fish and chips at a pub and wash it down with a local beer.

He took in the bustling city and its austere contrast to his quiet farm. He was not oblivious to the many lingering looks he got from locals. Since he didn't see anyone else wearing cowboy boots and a Stetson, he figured they had a good reason to stare. He didn't mind that some of them were attractive women. Since days could pass before Sean called him and told him his next location, Jonathan had to enjoy the time somehow.

He found a pub, took a seat at the bar, and ordered food and ale. Patrons came and went. Jonathan was content to eat and drink slowly while absorbing the atmosphere.

By the time he left it was nearly eleven o'clock at night. Only a few people were walking the streets at this late hour. As he retraced his steps back to the hotel, he spotted pursuers. They weren't being terribly stealthy. When had they marked him?

They were young. Maybe in their early twenties.

He turned into the next alley to lose them. He stopped. Two more punks stood in the alley. Damn. He'd been herded like cattle.

Surveying his aggressors, he counted four punks. All were a hundred pounds lighter than him. He was outnumbered but not outmuscled. He'd been in his share of bar fights. Because he was fit from farm work, he didn't lose many of them. They wore street clothes—jeans and T-shirts with piercings and tattoos. This wasn't a hired hit. These kids had marked him, probably because he was a foreigner and wore expensive boots. They intended to rob him.

One of the boys—the largest of them—with a long, crooked nose, clicked open a switchblade as they closed in on Jonathan.

He regarded the weapon with curiosity. If he had his marine KABAR on him, he'd show these punks what a real knife looked like.

"We want your money and your boots."

*Well, they've got taste.*

"That's not gonna happen."

The leader's face registered the statement and responded with a flash of disbelief and uncertainty, followed by anger. As he approached, he seemed to appreciate Jonathan's full size. Not an easy target. Unfortunately for him, retreat in front of his followers was not an option he would likely be willing to take.

The boy's expression hardened, betraying his decision to attack. He lunged with his knife. Jonathan caught his wrist and twisted it. The boy let out a grunt as he released his grip on the weapon. Jonathan brought his knee up into his gut and let him crumple to the ground in pain.

One of the other boys rushed Jonathan, landing a punch to his jaw.

Jonathan smirked.

"Let me show you a real punch." He jabbed, making solid contact with his attacker's nose and immediately dropped to a knee before he landed a second blow to the back of his head, dropping him flat on the pavement.

Blood spewed as Jonathan turned his attention to the third boy, who was coming at him with a series of kicks and a pair of steel-toed boots.

Jonathan grabbed his ankle, spun him, and threw him into the last bloke. He stayed on the ground.

After tilting his hat ever so slightly back into position, he left his London welcoming committee bruised and battered in the alley.

---

LILLIAN STARED out the window as Ivan drove down the driveway to a cabin buried in tall pine and beech trees. A single porch light shone.

The dark, woody cabin and looming shadows gave the house an eerie look.

"Looks like something out of a Grimm's fairytale," she commented. As long as it had warm water and a place to sleep, she would be satisfied.

Ivan grunted as he parked the car.

When Lillian got out of the vehicle, she stretched. She grabbed her luggage from the trunk and followed Ivan to the front door. As the door swung open, Lillian expected to see a tall, broad *frau* with feminine resemblance to Ivan—a stern face, perhaps even sprouting hair on her chin.

Instead, a small boy, perhaps six, opened the door. He had big blue eyes and a head of untamed blond hair. Ivan's nephew, perhaps?

"Papa!" The boy leaped into Ivan's arms, his small body wrapping around the man with a vice-like grip.

Lillian turned to stare at Ivan.

"I missed you, Falco. My little *mausi*," said father to son.

"Did you bring me a book?" Falco asked.

His English was clear but with a German accent, like his father's.

*Father?* Ivan was a father.

"Of course, *mauschen*. Grab Papa's bag. It's in there." He set the boy down.

Falco ran to the car.

Lillian blinked at Ivan. "You have a son."

He nodded. "He's the love of my life. And if I hadn't led such a violent life, perhaps I would have more time to be with him. Perhaps I would be with him and not stashing him away with my sister, so that the father's sins are not suffered by the son."

Lillian watched Ivan watching his son pull the shoulder bag out of the car. The man's face held no trace of the killer she knew. His features were soft, and his eyes brimmed with adoration.

Falco ran over and deposited the bag at Ivan's feet. He panted from the hurried effort.

Ivan reached inside and pulled out a thin paperback book.

"Magic Tree House!" The boy exclaimed. He grabbed the book and hugged Ivan's leg.

"He's six, soon to be seven and reading German and English at a second grade level."

"Smart like his father, no doubt."

Ivan gave her an appreciative but doleful look. "Smarter. I hope. Maybe he'll grow up to be a doctor, like you."

Not a criminal like himself, she suspected he was thinking.

"I want to be an astronaut," Falco said. "Did you know Jupiter has sixty-seven moons?" He turned to look up at Lillian. "Who are you?"

Ivan picked up Falco. "This is my American friend, Dr. Lillian Whyte."

Falco put a gentle hand on his father's face as his expression turned serious. "I know that, Papa. You were speaking English."

He turned back to Lillian. "*Guten tag, Frau Doktor* Whyte."

"*Danke*. But I like Lily better."

His face beamed. "Lily."

"Come, *mausi*. Let's go inside. Where's your *tante*?"

"Aunty is in bed. She's not feeling good."

IVAN FELT a sense of home and comfort envelope him as he walked inside his sister's house with Falco in one arm and his bag in the other.

Lillian followed and closed the cabin door.

Ivan gave Falco one last hug before setting him down to run free.

The boy clutched his book and grabbed Lillian's shirtsleeve with his free hand. "Lily, come see my room." He pulled her down the hall.

Ivan set down his bag and walked down the hall to his sister's room. As he entered the dim room, he wrinkled his nose at the slight waft of foul odor, like decaying flesh.

"Ivan, good to see you."

He stopped at the sight of her lying in bed. She looked pale, and she had lost more weight since he had last seen her.

"Ada." He did not conceal the alarm in his voice. "Why didn't you tell me you were getting worse?"

She gave a weak smile. "You're so busy. I didn't want to bother you. Nothing can be done about it."

He sat beside her slight figure on the bed and pulled the covers up around her. "I'm so sorry, *schwester*."

"I'm sorry. Falco has been doing more taking care of me than me of him lately." She gripped his hands, her fingers skeleton-like. "I can't take care of him anymore, Ivan."

He patted her hands. "It's okay. Let's worry about you. Let's take care of you now."

He swallowed the caustic lump of guilt in his throat. He had been away too long, too many months this time. And he had done so even knowing her disease was advancing. He was always fearful of coming here, though. Fearful he would lead a trail of breadcrumbs for his pursuers. If he were ever followed by the monsters after him, his sister's cabin might indeed become a site for something gruesomely akin to a Grimm's fairytale, as Lillian had suggested.

---

DEPARTMENT OF DEFENSE
TOP SECRET
NUCLEAR THREAT INVESTIGATION


CASE FILE: 8966B20
Deputy Director: William Austin
Re: Dr. Lillian Whyte and Agent Sean Jennings
TRANSCRIPT:
DEPARTMENT OF DEFENSE INQUIRY


DOD: Mr. Whyte, you say you arrived in London on Tuesday. What did you do upon arriving?
JONATHAN WHYTE: Grabbed a pint and some fish and chips.

DOD: Did you contact anyone or make any attempt to contact your sister?

JONATHAN WHYTE: Nope. My instructions were to sit tight and await further instructions.

DOD: At this point, did you know your sister was in Germany?

JONATHAN WHYTE: No. I didn't know about Germany until Sean told me on Thursday.

DOD: What did you do for two days in London?

JONATHAN WHYTE: Sightseeing, meeting locals, making new friends.

DOD: You were sightseeing, knowing there was a nuclear weapon on the loose?

JONATHAN WHYTE: I was either going to be its victim or be getting the hell out of Europe, so sightseeing seemed like the thing to do while waiting to see how the hand was being dealt.

# CHAPTER 13

Reginald shook hands with Senator Robert Mull.

"Thank you for coming, Reginald." The bulky man looked like a former linebacker.

His background before politics had been working for his father's construction company. Mull Senior had taken a small, five-man business to five hundred in his lifetime. His son became a contractor in upstate New York before leaving the family business for the capital.

"I'm looking forward to being part of the solution," Reginald replied.

Reginald followed Bob's lead and sat when he sat. The senator's office was plain, with a single rectangular window, one desk, one lamp, and a single shelf. It appeared as though the occupant accepted his use of the space to be temporary. Not surprising, since the man still had his eye on the presidency. His campaign platform had touted how he was a blue-collar American like his father, though Reginald suspected the man had never known what life was like living paycheck to paycheck.

"What do you know about events?" Bob asked.

Reginald gave a slight shrug. "What you've told me. Based on my meeting with Cole, he's in over his head. I've offered my company's services to help diffuse the situation."

Bob's eyes twinkled with amusement. "He is in over his head. You're right about that. I told him to make a public announcement, because people are going to be outraged at a secret this big."

"Are you thinking of leaking it?"

"Perhaps. I've heard they're sending troops to reclaim the bomb as we speak. I suppose if they succeed then this will be a disaster averted, and he needn't get credit for that. We'll wait and see, but be prepared."

Reginald hadn't heard anything about the US sending troops. "A rescue mission implies they know where the bomb is."

"Yes, it does."

Reginald leaned forward. "That's good news."

"Maybe. Maybe not." The senator twisted his wedding ring on his finger.

"What is it you want our meeting to accomplish?"

Bob smiled. "Lancaster Defense Enterprises is well funded, well respected. I want you to know I was a proponent of full disclosure early in this crisis."

"Is it a crisis? If they know where the bomb is, this situation could be over by the end of the day."

"I have a feeling this situation is going to get worse before it gets better."

Reginald wondered what Senator Mull was scheming. "Well, my company is ready to support the defense of our country."

"That's what I wanted to know."

---

SEAN STOOD QUIETLY in the back corner of the observation room. The room was filled with analysts, agents, and William Austin, with all eyes fixed on the screens at the front of the room. Live before them was the Delta Force team closing in on the trucks carrying the nuclear weapon. The convoy consisted of three cargo trucks—box trucks—with the nuke in the middle.

Ivan had notified Sean that the plane had landed in a small airstrip outside Razgrad, Bulgaria. Sean turned the location over to Austin, who sent it to the Pentagon. An hour later they had satellite images of the truck trio leaving the airfield. Thirty minutes later, inbound choppers with a Delta team aboard closed in on the trucks. Ten men, two birds.

One screen revealed the satellite view of the trucks as they sped down a country highway. Another screen showed the helicopter cameras mounted for a frontal view. The two images displayed a mix of blurring trees and farmland. Another screen, partitioned into sections, showed the helmet cameras of the military personnel riding in the choppers. They wore dark camouflage uniforms with painted faces. Their hardened expressions were those of men accustomed to battle. Delta Force took on some of the most dangerous, most secretive missions for the country.

Sean felt oddly nostalgic for the many SEAL missions he'd been part of in the Middle East. Things were perhaps simpler for him then. Life had been an adventurous series of missions during that time. He had team members to look out for and a country to defend, but he never had loved ones in danger.

How much did these soldiers know about their objective? Had they been told they were apprehending a nuke? They would need to use one of their choppers to bring it to a US warship on station out in the Mediterranean.

The room was thick with tension and weighted silence as everyone listened to the pilot and mission commander's mikes.

"Five clicks out," the pilot said.

"ETA two minutes," the commander told his troops.

Their faces remained rigid.

The helicopters banked to take up a route about a kilometer ahead of the trucks before lowering over a straight stretch of road. The soldiers unloaded. Three men placed three-inch steel tire spikes over the road. From the helicopter camera, they looked like a dozen toy jacks a child would play with, except the ends were pointed instead of rounded.

As the helicopter hovered off station from the drop site over the road a hundred yards from the spikes, the Delta Force men cleared to both sides off the road.

The first truck approached the scene. The driver had a straight line of sight with the helicopter, but he didn't slow the box truck. The second helicopter flanked the rear. The standoff continued as the front helicopter hovered, and the truck bore down on it. The truck driver was calling the pilot's bluff.

The pilot turned the chopper off the road, but his distraction served its purpose. From the view of the rear helicopter, Sean saw the truck hit the tire spikes. Tire and brake fumes filled the air as the truck came to a halt on the country road. The other two trucks halted behind the lead.

The back cargo doors to the trucks rolled opened. Sean gaped at the surface-to-air missile—an SA-7 Soviet shoulder-fired weapon with infrared homing, he guessed.

The pilot screeched, "SAM! I'm pulling up! I'm pulling up!"

Seconds after the MANPADS was launched, the helicopter camera and the helmet cameras of the men on board went black.

Gasps and swearing filled the observation room.

Sean's gaze switched to the cameras of the soldiers on the ground. A dozen heavily armed men filed out of the cargo hold of each truck. The other helicopter opened fire on the first truck, the minigun chewing through man, machine, and earth.

The Delta Force trained its efforts on the rear truck, killing heavily armed insurgents. Another SAM eliminated the second chopper. The team of mercenaries—ex-Russian special forces, Spetznaz, if Sean had to guess—from the middle truck joined the fight. One by one the Delta Force men were overpowered and eliminated. The elite team eliminated half the enemy men, but lost the battle.

Sean's blood ran cold.

Austin, face pale and destitute, sank into an empty chair.

From the still activated cameras on the helmets of dead soldiers,

Sean could see the remaining insurgents loading into the middle truck. The first truck's tires were shredded, as was most of the vehicle from the helicopter's minigun. The rear truck has been destroyed by Delta Force firepower. The remaining truck was mobile, and the nuke would disappear into rural Europe in the next ten minutes.

***

IVAN QUIETLY CLOSED his sister's bedroom door to let her rest. He followed voices to the kitchen where Lillian was finding her way around to make fleischwurst sandwiches under Falco's direction.

She kept pulling out the wrong ingredients intentionally, and Falco laughingly corrected her.

"Is this the cream cheese?" She lifted an olive jar for the boy to see.

"No! The cheese is in a white case."

Ivan's heart thrummed like a well-tuned violin at the sound of Falco's giggles.

At last she found all of the ingredients—cream cheese, bologna, boiled eggs, and seasoning.

Falco sat at the counter and helped Lillian assemble the sandwiches.

"You want one?"

Ivan looked up into her radiant blue eyes and face framed in red hair. "Yes, thank you."

He busied himself setting the small wooden kitchen table. It was slightly lopsided. He had been meaning to fix that.

He grabbed a bottle of beer for himself and Lillian and poured milk for Falco.

As they ate, Falco rattled off facts about space to Lillian, who gave him her full attention in raptured fascination. Ivan was content to listen and eat.

His mind wandered, wondering if dinner every night with a family would have been this pleasant. Sitting next to a beautiful woman—well, not *that* beautiful woman. Lillian was obstinate and headstrong. And she had those damn judgmental, scrutinizing eyes. He imagined her patients caving under the weight of them and divulging their drug use or medication noncompliance.

Falco asked, "How did you meet Papa?"

Ivan's attention snapped back to the conversation.

"Well," Lillian began, "we were both working in Africa nine years ago, and we met there. Not long after that, we saw each other once in Paris. Then, a few days ago, we ran into each other in Iceland."

Ivan suppressed a chuckled since he had—quite literally—run into her.

"He never brings people here. He must like you."

She smiled. Her eyes flickered to Ivan and back to Falco. "I think we're friends."

Ivan swallowed as his eyes dropped to his plate, knowing he didn't deserve the honor.

Falco looked sad. "I would like some friends. Sometimes Aunt Ada takes me to the park, and I play with other children. Can we be friends?"

"I would love to be your friend."

Ivan wiped his hands with a napkin. He finished his beer and stood. "Come, Falco. Bedtime."

"Papa," he complained.

"No, none of that. Let's go."

Bedtime was an hour-long affair of bathing, brushing teeth, and bedtime reading.

His son reluctantly left his chair. "*Gute nacht*, Lily."

"*Gute nacht.*"


Lillian cleaned the kitchen while Ivan tucked in his son for the night.

She could hear Ivan's deep voice emanating from Falco's room. He was reading a book.

An hour later, Ivan emerged and surveyed her work. "Thank you."

She placed the last dish on the drying rack. "Was that Harry Potter you were reading him?"

He grinned. "Between my sister and me reading to him, he has heard the books about three times each. He's wanted no other bedtime books for almost a year and a half. He'll be seven soon." His voice trailed.

"What's wrong with your sister?"

He shifted his eyes to her and down to the countertop, where he picked at a chipped spot in the charcoal colored soapstone. "Breast cancer. Stage four."

"I'm sorry."

"Ada's gotten a great deal worse in the months I've been away. She can't take care of herself anymore." He walked close to her and started drying and putting away the dishes.

Lillian leaned against the counter. "Any treatment options?" She knew there would be nothing curative for advanced stage cancer, but some therapies could slow progression.

"They all made her sick. If she can't live life—shopping, walks in the park, having fun with her nephew—then what is the point?"

Lillian watched him stare at the glass as he methodically dried it.

"What are you going to do?"

His chest rose and fell with a single laborious breath. "Ideally, she would stay here, and I would take care of her during her dying days. Since we have a nuclear weapon to stop, I can't do that. There is a hospice home I can take her to."

He looked up at Lillian with an expression as though bracing himself for rejection. "I can get her there and be back here in two days. Can you watch Falco for two days? Here at the cabin?"

Lillian considered the question. The US military would soon have the bomb, if they didn't already. She could delay getting home by a day to watch Falco. "I can do that. But what happens after that?"

"I don't know. There is no one else I trust to keep him safe. I need time to think it through when I'm not so exhausted."

He put the last dish away in the cupboard and looked around the cabin. "It's a small house. Will you be okay on the couch tonight? I will sleep with Falco."

"I'll be fine."

She watched him lumber down the hall. He looked like he carried the weight of the world. Perhaps he did. Perhaps they both did.

———

SEAN WALKED to the deputy director's office. Marty had run facial recognition on the images captured from the Delta force go-cam. They identified several of the attackers. No Asian woman. No cook.

Sean planned to pour through the footage of hostiles in more detail. First, he needed to discuss with Austin the likelihood that Ivan was still tracking the bomb. He wished Ivan would call back soon to confirm, but given the escalating severity of the situation, Sean needed to be forthcoming with Austin.

As Sean entered Austin's office, he noted his boss sitting at his desk looking aged and worn. Despair was etched on his features.

"If it's not good news, Jennings, get the hell out."

Sean eased into a chair across from Austin's desk. He remained silent as Austin squeezed a hand over his forehead.

"Ten dead soldiers, and the nuclear weapon is still on the loose. Six months in my new position, and this is one screwed-up mess. Part of you must be enjoying my failure."

"Not at all, Bill. I know we don't agree on many issues, but I actually do respect you. I even advocated for your promotion."

Austin looked up from his desk.

"Yeah, surprised me, too. Don't tell anybody. I have an anti-Austin reputation to uphold."

Sean leaned back and crossed his legs. "Anyway. The bad guys are better funded than we anticipated. And yeah—good men died. Good men with families. And we're still obligated to protect those families."

Austin remained silent.

Sean continued. "The reason Ivan reached out to me is because he coerced Lillian."

Austin's face blanched as he stiffened. "Coerced?"

"Perhaps convinced is a better word."

"I like convinced better."

"He approached her, explained the situation and expressed how he wants to undo what he did. She believed him." He ran a hand through his hair. "And being the stubborn, ambitious woman she is, she decided to help him. Now they're doing god-knows-what as they traipse around Europe watching satellite feed of a nuclear weapon we can't catch."

Austin scowled. "What is it she plans to accomplish by being at ground zero of this thing? Has she taken an online course on diffusing a nuclear bomb?"

"It's her personality. She doesn't know how to do nothing during a crisis."

"I'm sorry, Sean. It can't be easy for you to be here while she's there. And with Ivan Kleist, no less."

"Thanks."

Austin straightened. "Is that why you came? You wanted to let me know your wife's enlistment into the cause?"

"No. I believe Ivan is still tracking the bomb."

"What makes you certain of that?"

"He's meticulous. He won't drop surveillance until he knows the situation is contained."

Austin grunted but didn't disagree.

"We need to be prepared to move when he calls back."

Austin frowned. "If he calls back."

"*When.*"

"Okay. When."

---

DEPARTMENT OF DEFENSE
TOP SECRET
NUCLEAR THREAT INVESTIGATION

CASE FILE: 8966B20
Deputy Director: William Austin
Re: Dr. Lillian Whyte and Agent Sean Jennings
TRANSCRIPT:
DEPARTMENT OF DEFENSE INQUIRY

DOD: Director Austin, you sanctioned the attack on the cargo that resulted in the death of ten US soldiers.
AUSTIN: Yes, I did.

DOD: Did you suspect at any time that this could have been a trap?
AUSTIN: It didn't matter. The weapon had been transferred from air to road. This was our opportunity to seize it.

DOD: After the failed attempt to secure the weapon, you learned of Dr. Whyte's involvement?
AUSTIN: That's correct.

DOD: Did it strike you as odd that a physician allowed herself to be coerced into a dangerous situation by a criminal?
AUSTIN: It didn't surprise me that Lillian Whyte agreed to help with a global crisis.

DOD: Did you suspect that Dr. Whyte could have given you false information?
AUSTIN: She would never knowingly do that. And she didn't.

DOD: What is your relationship with Dr. Whyte?
AUSTIN: She's my subordinate's wife. Does she get to read these transcripts?
DOD: No.
AUSTIN: Then I will add that she is also one of the greatest, most self-sacrificing patriots I know.

# CHAPTER 14

Lillian woke at sunrise the next morning. She grabbed her coat and went for a walk through the woods. The quiet and stillness wrapped around her like a cool, calming blanket. She was alone with the sound of the wind rustling through leaves and the scratching of squirrels in trees. It reminded her of growing up in Arkansas on her father's farm. She didn't get many quiet moments of tranquility living in Atlanta and working in an emergency room. For this reason, she and Sean had been looking at cabins in the north Georgia area.

On occasional weekends, she rented a horse to take short trail rides through a patch of woods. Those were tranquil moments.

She looked to her phone for the tenth time that morning. The signal wavered from a single bar to no service, and when she had tried to call Sean, the call wouldn't go through. She he sent Sean a text message and hoped it would transmit eventually: *Laying low, poor cell service in rural Germany. Will call in a few days when we move.*

As she tucked the phone back in her pocket, she came across a small, overgrown trail and followed it a short way. She hoped her lingering outside would give Falco time to say good-bye to his aunt.

What explanation would Ivan give his son? The boy was savvy. He knew Ada was sick, and he probably understood a little about life and death at his age.

Lillian wound her way back to the cabin and saw Ivan was helping his sister into the car. Ada was wrapped snugly in her robe with a stocking cap firmly on her head. She couldn't weigh much over a hundred pounds, judging by her sharp cheekbones and thin fingers.

Falco stood on the cabin porch, watching.

By the time Lillian reached the vehicle, Ivan had closed the passenger side door.

"Anything I can do to help?"

"Take care of Falco. I'll get her settled at the home."

Lillian's eyes flickered to the trunk of the car, wondering how he had packed so quickly. "Will they have room for her?"

"For the right price, they will make room." He looked back at his sister and then down at the gravel road.

"I'm sure they'll take good care of her."

He straightened. When his eyes met hers, he looked close to breaking. Abruptly, he pulled her into his arms. She felt as though a great grizzly bear were hugging her.

She stiffened, unsure how to handle the affection.

He fisted his hands into her hair to hold her head still as he spoke into her ear quietly. "There is a shotgun in the hall closet, up high. There's a driveway alarm that chimes inside the house if someone comes by vehicle. If something happens, there's an old trail out back that leads to a road. You head north and don't stop until you get to an abandoned barn. Three miles. I will find you there. You have my mobile number, but service isn't good out here."

He released her hair as he pulled her into an even tighter hug. After a few moments, he relaxed his hold and stepped back from her.

Lillian watched him walk around the car, climb inside, and pull away without looking back again.

After turning toward the cabin, she walked to stand next to Falco.

"Aunt Ada is going to heaven." He slipped his tiny hand into hers.

"Yes, she is."

"Papa says you'll stay with me until he comes back."

"Yeah. Is that okay with you?"

"He always comes back."

"He'll be two days." She tried to reassure him.

"He always comes back, but not always as soon as he says he will come back." Worry and sadness filled his voice.

She squeezed his hand—such a tiny, frail little thing. "Well, we'll have plenty of time to misbehave until he gets back."

He looked up at her with a skeptical grin.

She winked at him. "What should we do first?"

"Do you like games?"

"I do like games." She led Falco back into the house. As she did, she heard the chime of noise from the driveway sensor as Ivan left in the car.

"We have checkers."

"That's one of my favorites. Let's play checkers. After that, it will be nice weather for running in the woods."

His face lit up.

"Then we'll scrounge up some lunch and follow it with a nap."

He scrunched up his nose. "I'm almost seven. I don't take naps anymore."

"Well, I'm almost forty, and I love a good nap, so maybe you should tuck me in."

Falco giggled. She enjoyed the sound of his innocent child's laugh. She would have to scheme ways to keep him giggling all day. He could forget about his sickly aunt for a while, and she could forget about the nuclear weapon headed for Europe.

---

REGINALD LANCASTER STOOD as Mandy walked into his office. She wore a fitted, cream-colored dress that hugged the curve of her hips and revealed two tan, smooth legs. He loved those legs, loved the way they could make him forget about the rest of the world when they were wrapped around him.

As he walked around his desk, he extended his hands. "This is a pleasant surprise." He kissed his wife on the cheek.

His eyes caught sight of diamond earrings, probably the cost of a small car. With a forced smile, he wondered if the purpose of her visit was to flaunt them.

No matter.

When weapons sales went up due to the crisis at hand, thirty thousand dollars in jewelry would be insignificant.

"I'm here to see if you want to have lunch together." She turned away from him and walked around his room, inspecting the shelves of mock weapon prototypes behind glass cases.

He watched her backside with her firm buttocks and calves accentuated by the heels she wore. He wanted her bent over on his couch as he thrust into her. Lunch? No, he couldn't bear an hour of idle conversation while she babbled about clothes shopping or her mother. Or, God forbid, both.

He gestured to his Rolex. "I'm tied up in meetings starting in about twenty minutes."

She turned to look at him, trying to hide her disappointment behind a lipstick-laden grin that didn't reach her deep blue eyes. They expressed the disappointed words she had uttered numerous times in the past. *"You never have time for me."*

"Mandy, work is hectic and—"

She began to walk toward the door. In three quick strides, he beat her to it. He jerked her hand before it could reach the handle. She whirled on him, blond hair billowing around her and blue eyes ablaze.

This. This he had time for. Pinning her roughly against the wall, he kissed her savagely. He had no use for idle conversation and long walks on the beach, but raw sex would always lure him away from company business.

Mandy groaned hoarsely as she arched her body into him. He yanked her dress up to her hips, kneading the soft skin of her thighs and buttocks. As he pulled away, he half spun her, half shoved her onto the couch. She gasped in a mixture of surprise and arousal. He dropped his pants to his knees before plunging into her and losing himself to his needs.

When his sense returned, Reginald found himself on top of his wife on the couch with his face buried in her silky hair. He breathed the intoxicating vanilla scent. This moment. This was the moment of ecstasy when he was most vulnerable. Early in their marriage he'd bared his soul post-coitus. Later he'd shortened his emotional expression to a simple but heart-felt "*I love you.*" When Mandy transformed from a sweet to bitter woman, she stopped reciting the words back to him and started replying with "*show me.*" Her implication that his words were insufficient and hollow grated on his nerves.

In this moment, he wanted to tell her now how much he loved her. How much he needed her. How he would do everything— anything—she asked of him right now. But he knew any words he spoke would be met with skepticism. He couldn't bear a look of disdain born from years of her disappointment in him.

After events in Europe unfolded, things would be different. He would be everyone's hero.

---

JONATHAN SAT AT THE BAR, sipping his Newcastle Brown Ale. Tonight he was only a block away from his hotel, so if he did leave late, he wouldn't face another street fight.

"Monsieur Whyte?" A brunette in a navy blue pencil skirt slid into the seat next to him.

Something in her demeanor suggested she was some type of official—police or government. Her French accent suggested she would have no authority in England.

"Ma'am."

"How are you enjoying your stay in London, Monsieur Whyte?"

He turned to her, admiring a full set of lips, round hips and the curve of her calves. "Please, call me Jonathan. Let's see. I've toured a bit, had the privilege of meeting some of London's finest last night in a dark alley. And now I'm sitting next to a beautiful woman. Miss...?"

He watched her expression carefully as he spoke. Since she didn't seem to know the meaning behind his encounter last night, she was evidently not here about the street fight.

"My name is Marie Beaulieu. I am Canadian intelligence."

"You're as far away from home as I am."

"Yes and no. I was visiting family in France before I made the trip to London."

"Can I buy you a drink?"

"No, *merci*."

"Now why would you leave your vacation to come to dreary ol' London?" He tipped his head toward his empty plate. "It's not for the food."

The corners of her mouth lifted upward in an expression too faint to be called a smile. "I was asked by a friend to keep an eye on you."

He grinned. "My personal surveillance." He took a long, slow drink of his beer. "Must be an important friend."

Had Sean orchestrated this? Wouldn't it be just like the crafty agent to send Jonathan in and then add to his crew without mentioning it?

"My friend is dear to me. But I thought it would be rude to secretly watch Dr. Whyte's brother as if he were a criminal. Instead, I decided to introduce myself to the brother of the woman who saved Canada."

Jonathan's eyebrows shot up, his poker face irrevocably shattered.

Marie blinked. "I'm sorry. Evidently she didn't tell you."

"I knew my sister was involved in the terrorist attacks in Montreal. She helped somehow. I know she was shot and wouldn't tell me by whom. I know the Egyptian ambassador was killed during the attacks."

MARIE MOTIONED TO THE BARTENDER. She would take that drink after all. Once her gin and tonic arrived, she slowly sipped the beverage as she let Mr. Whyte stew in frustrated silence a little longer. He looked like an American cowboy from the movies—square jaw, fine lines around the eyes from squinting in the sun, tan skin, jeans, and even cowboy boots. Sturdy biceps protruded from his T-shirt. His cowboy hat sat on the bar beside his beer.

She decided he ought to at least know the basics. "The threat in Montreal was a biomedical weapon. Your sister eliminated the threat and shot the lead terrorist...with the help of the CIA, Canadian Intelligence, and others."

She omitted that the Egyptian politician, whom the world believed was killed by terrorists, was actually the lead terrorist. Jonathan didn't need all of the facts to appreciate his sister's heroism. Dr. Whyte might not have done it alone, but the outcome would not have been a success without her.

Marie had been involved because she was both Canadian Intelligence and had a biochemical background. Although she was part of the events that unfolded in Montreal, she had never met Dr. Whyte. By the time Marie knew of the woman's pivotal role, the physician was in a hospital ICU with a bullet wound in her shoulder.

"What do you know about current events?" His speech was slow and smooth—the way Crown Royal slides down one's pallet.

Her gaze swept the room. "I know enough to know it cannot be discussed in public."

Jonathan gave her a wry grin. "Are you inviting me somewhere private?"

Her eyes snapped to his. "Don't be stupid. I'm here to help you, not sleep with you."

His eyes roamed her face and down to her lips. "Capable woman such as yourself could probably manage both."

Were all cowboys so smug?

"I am a professional, Mr. Whyte. Perhaps you could be more respectful."

Did he know she was older than him? She scrutinized his eyes, trying to discern if he was inebriated.

"Me finding you attractive in no way implies a lack of respect. I respect you. I respect the hard work you must have endured to get where you are today. I expect you had to climb over your share of male chauvinistic assholes to get to your position within your organization. I assure you, I'm not one of 'em." He took another drink. "My sister had plenty of obstacles. She had a medical school professor tell her she didn't want to go into emergency medicine. Said it was a 'man's specialty.' Wouldn't she rather do pediatrics or dermatology? Jackass." He shook his head. "On her surgical rotation, one of the old surgeons pulled the female physicians of the group aside to explain the difference between a shotgun wound and a gunshot wound. Lillian could've out-shot, out-rode, and outrun any of those male physicians. And she had to listen to garbage like that for years. So, yeah, you have my respect, Miss Beaulieu. But you are also a beautiful woman."

She leaned in close to him, whispering, "Let's go somewhere private, Mr. Whyte, so we can discuss the nuclear threat."

***

LILLIAN SPENT the day getting giggles out of Falco. Their interaction was a nice distraction from missing Sean and wanting an update on the current status of the bomb. She had sent him a text message to let him know she would call him when they were somewhere with better cellular service. She thought the message eventually went through.

She and Falco made breakfast, played checkers, and built a fort in the small living room. It extended from the couch to the fireplace. The roof consisted of sheets and blankets slipped together with clothespins. They napped in their fort. To her surprise, he curled into her as comfortable as if she were his aunt rather than a stranger his father had brought home and deposited in his house.

In the afternoon, they played in the forest around the cabin, and he showed her his many hiding places for his valuables—rocks were stored in a specific tree trunk and sticks were stashed in a specific hole.

After a dinner of leftover beef stew, she tucked him into bed and read a chapter of Harry Potter. She said goodnight, but he drew out the process, with a trip to the bathroom followed by a request for a glass of water. Next, he pointed and told her of his many books in English, German, and French that sat on his bookshelf.

When he was tucked in and finally relaxed, she left. She busied herself cleaning the kitchen. She even ventured to clean Ivan's sister's room. She replaced the linens and tidied the disarray, avoiding moving things too much in case Ivan wanted to leave it undisturbed while he mourned.

At last, she prepared herself for sleep and lay on the couch. Quietly thinking of Sean reminded her to charge the watch he had given her. Smart as it was, it wasn't going to charge itself.

She missed Sean. She hadn't spoken with him in two days. He would be worried sick about her, and she hated to put him through such worry—his wife on a mission without him and with an international criminal at that. The alternative was unacceptable. She couldn't turn her back on the possibility she could somehow help Ivan. Stop the threat. Stop the bomb.

*Am I delusional?*

Right or wrong, she was committed now. Committed to running interference. Once the ball was in the air, there was no stopping the play.

When Ivan returned, they could drive to a place with cellular service and she could call Sean. Sean would give her the all-clear that the bomb was safe, and she could come home.

Yes. She could fall asleep dreaming that dream.

---

DEPARTMENT OF DEFENSE
TOP SECRET
NUCLEAR THREAT INVESTIGATION

CASE FILE: 8966B20
Deputy Director: William Austin

## Re: Dr. Lillian Whyte and Agent Sean Jennings

## TRANSCRIPT:
## DEPARTMENT OF DEFENSE INQUIRY

DOD: You stayed at Mr. Kleist's cabin for several days?
DR. WHYTE: That's correct.

DOD: And he left you there with his son while he took his sister to a palliative care home?
DR. WHYTE: Yes.

DOD: After four days together, he trusted you with his son, and you trusted him to come back?
DR. WHYTE: Yes.

DOD: During this time, did you have any knowledge of the whereabouts of your brother?
DR. WHYTE: No. As far as I knew, he was still in Arkansas.

DOD: During this time at the cabin, did you correspond with your husband?
DR. WHYTE: I attempted text messages, but I had poor cellular service at the cabin. Also, I assumed Sean was busy helping secure the bomb.

DOD: You weren't aware that the confiscation had failed?
DR. WHYTE: Correct. At that time, I wasn't yet aware soldiers had lost their lives.

DOD: And Mr. Kleist eventually returned to his cabin?
DR. WHYTE: He left on Wednesday morning and returned Friday evening. But he was too late for the attack.

# CHAPTER 15

---

Sean called Jonathan's cell phone. "She's in Germany. Keep sitting tight where you are."

Jonathan gave him a sarcastic reply. "Oh, hi, buddy. 'How's it going in London?' Well, Sean, it's raining and gloomy here, but thanks for asking."

Sean looked at the ceiling as though patience for dealing with Jonathan would fall from above.

Jonathan added, "I appreciate you sending the company."

"Company? What company?"

"Pretty brunette. Canadian Intelligence. Way the hell out of my league, but I think the cowboy boots are winning her over."

Sean paced the small conference room he had been working in at Langley. Since he didn't have his own office, he made one. "I didn't send you a Canadian."

"She said a friend at the CIA sent her."

"You didn't think to call me and verify a contact? You trusted she was who she claimed to be?"

*Damn amateur.*

Jonathan was lucky to still be alive, given his lack of caution.

Cowboy boots? Apparently Jonathan also wasn't making an effort to blend in with the locals.

"She passed the Whyte lie detector test," Jonathan drawled.

"Why do I sense that involves a pearly smile and a short skirt?"

Sean tuned out Jonathan since he started rambling about perceptive skills he most certainly did not possess.

The CIA sent a Canadian? The only Canadian agents Sean knew were the ones he met during the terrorist event three years ago. He didn't know any of them well enough to send them to join Jonathan.

*But Austin did.*

Sean interrupted Jonathan. "Is her name Marie Beaulieu?"

"Yeah, it is. Kinda rolls off the tongue, doesn't it?"

Sean restrained his irritation.

"So, Lily's in Germany?" Jonathan asked. "Don't suppose you can narrow that down a pinch?"

"As soon as I can, I will. For now keep your phone close. Stay in London."

"I can do that. Can you update me on the status of... well...anything?"

"We tried to confiscate the bomb. We sent an entire Delta Force team. We lost."

"Shit."

"Yeah."

"And Sean?"

"Yeah?"

"Lily still doesn't know I'm coming?"

"She doesn't know that I think she needs you. She would vehemently disagree. I don't need to add any distractions or give her something else to be pissed at me about."

When Sean hung up the phone, he forced himself to focus on the Delta Force operation. He didn't want to think about his wife spending time with Ivan. The man was a hardened criminal. The weekend sparring and monthly trips to the gun range wouldn't remotely prepare her to defend herself against a man with three decades of criminal activity under his belt.

She could outwit him, but that might not be enough. Zoey had uncovered concerning intelligence revealing a large bounty had been placed on Ivan's head. Could the man keep Lillian safe from the mercenaries who were after him? Would he bother to make the effort to do so?

She had served her purpose—gotten the CIA's attention on the matter of the nuclear weapon while Ivan remained under the radar.

Painstakingly, Sean scoured the video, watching the Delta Force team die again, one by one.

---

REGINALD TOOK a swing and felt the satisfying crunch of his glove on the headgear of his opponent. His sparring was an attempt to keep his mind from lingering on the dismal news from his project manager, Cassandra. The bomb had almost been intercepted in Bulgaria. He didn't like how close US forces had come to confiscating his nuclear weapon. He also didn't like how US soldiers had died. Nothing could tie him to the theft, but the timing of everything needed to be perfect or he would be out a great deal of money for the expense of orchestrating the event.

He took another swing, but Mitch blocked the blow. Reginald maneuvered on the mat and kicked high. Blocked again.

Thus far, the media speculation of nuclear threat in the wake of palpable tension following North Korea's bomb detonation a week ago had spurned stocks in his favor. It wasn't enough.

Mitch swung and Reginald was barely able to block the blow. Sweat from his exertion dripped off his forehead and onto the sparring mat.

He needed the full force of a nuclear weapon threat to a major city to shake the world out of its bubble. Americans needed to realize that danger was the big bad wolf blowing on their door. They had houses made of straw. They needed fortified bomb shelters, automatic weapons, and a military armed with Lancaster's weapons. He had prototypes of technologically advanced weapons and drones languishing in his research and development department because Congress cut weapons spending and President Lawson was spewing nonsense about world peace.

With a quick spin and strike, Reginald bypassed Mitch's defense and got another blow to the face.

Noah entered the gym, a complete fitness center Reginald had built in his office building. Reginald looked at the time. The forty-five minute work-out had passed quickly. Mitch bumped gloves with him and congratulated him on a good sparring match.

As Reginald walked to the water fountain and grabbed a drink, Noah gave him a brief financial report. "The stocks are better and we'll be ahead in the third quarter..."

Reginald listened as he drug a towel across his face. He took off his gloves and headgear, dropping them onto a bench.

When Noah finished his financial report, he scooped his laptop and left, closing the door behind him.

"Rosy-cheeked and innocent," Cassandra purred.

Reginald turned to look at the woman standing in the corner of his gym. She had been so quiet he'd almost forgotten she was there.

"Noah is good at his job. He's grown the company."

"So am I. So have I." She walked over to look out the window.

Reginald admired the way her suit curved nicely around her backside.

"Yes, different sides of the company."

Noah managed the legitimate side of Lancaster Defense Enterprises. Cassandra oversaw the dark side.

Cassandra circled Reginald's gym, aware of him watching her figure. He had first hired her to manage personal protection and given her the flimsy title of project manager. She vetted most of his security team. As time passed, she proved herself useful in situations requiring discretion—a competing company's tragic loss of a key executive, a scorned lover drawing attention to herself, a former Lancaster employee selling company secrets.

The body count rose over the years. Cassandra knew all of his secrets, making her an asset and a liability. She was also the only person he trusted with knowledge of his nuclear weapon plan.

"They don't have to be different, separate parts of the company. I could control it all."

He gave her a sharp look. "They need to stay separated."

He eyed her backside again. She didn't mind that he looked, but she didn't sleep with superiors, especially not when she knew the many women with whom he had slept. She had even killed a few of them. When she rose in the hierarchy of the company, it would not be because she slept with the boss.

She would soon have control. Lancaster had trusted her with back channels to fund his little nuclear escapade. His little bluff. Cassandra had already taken measures to ensure the bluff became reality.

Her boss walked over to the high bar and began doing pull-ups.

Lancaster was being short-sighted. The world was accustomed to nuclear threats. They were blunted to the shock factor it should create. Any rise in purchasing and stocks for the company would be short-lived. The world needed detonation on a major city. Only then would the company wake the sleeping titan and fulfill its destiny to become a multibillion-dollar company.

---

SEAN FOUND himself for the second time in his life sitting in the Oval Office. This time CIA Deputy Director William Austin was with him. They sat on opposite ends of the sofa.

President Lawson paced the office. "I need everything you have, even if it's speculation or off-the-record. I've got a bomb still at large and ten dead US soldiers. And I've got a senator threatening to go to the media and claim my presidency is a failure."

"Senator Mull?" Sean looked up at Cole.

"Yes." Cole turned to Sean. "Bill tells me that someone on Interpol's top ten is helping?"

Sean glanced at Austin before leaning forward, placing his elbows on his knees. "Ivan Kleist is a computer hacker and dirty-deeds-for-hire mercenary. He helped steal the schematics to the North Korean weapons facility. When he figured out that the thieves were successful in stealing a bomb, he decided it needed to be stopped. He gave us the location of the bomb, and we attacked it after an air-to-ground transfer. As you know, the Delta Force was outgunned."

"Now it's gone again?" Cole asked.

"We don't know if Ivan still has eyes on it."

"Why don't we know?"

"We're waiting for him to call back."

"Why wouldn't he have called by now, especially since we failed?"

"He has a bounty on his head after stealing the schematics. We think it's because the cook"—Sean glanced at Austin to see if he would scowl at the mention of her name—"doesn't leave witnesses. Ivan might be laying low to avoid danger."

*He might already be dead.*

That scenario was not one Sean wanted to consider, since it would mean Lillian could be caught in the crosshairs.

"Is there a way to reach out to him? What if he hasn't called because he assumes we were successful in apprehending it?"

Sean shook his head. "He's not a man to leave anything to chance."

"You sound like you trust him."

"I don't," Sean snapped.

Cole turned a curious stare on him.

Austin shifted in his seat. "Tell him about Lillian, Sean."

"Lillian? What's your wife got to do with this?"

Sean buried his head in his hands. "Nothing. Everything." He felt his throat constrict.

Austin elaborated. "Ivan knows Lillian from the Kenya fiasco. She was one of his captives when he was working for an oil profiteer. He somehow cornered her in Iceland, convinced her to help him, and whisked her away to Germany."

"*Christ*, Sean. Is she...?"

"Yes. She's still alive."

Austin turned to him. "How do you know that?"

"I got a text message from her saying she is in rural Germany. The tracking device in her smart watch confirms it."

Austin started to open his mouth.

"I can also track the heart-rate monitor in her watch. She's alive." He had instructed Marty to give him hourly text messages of her location and heart rate.

Cole sat in his desk chair. "I'm sorry, Sean. I can't imagine what you're going through."

He turned to William Austin. "I also can't believe our entire plan at this point is to wait on a phone call."

"No sir. We are monitoring internet chatter, phone, and texts. We have every agent in every major European country reaching out to contacts. We're all hands on deck, sir."

---

THE NEXT DAY, Lillian and Falco played hide-and-seek in the cabin. On round three, she couldn't find him at all. She checked under beds, in closets, in the attic, and in cabinets. She had been the reigning champion of hide-and-seek in the Whyte family, but she had been bested.

"I give up!" she called after fifteen minutes of looking.

How could the little boy—who talked nonstop about the planets, moon, and sun through a game of checkers—keep so silent during hide-and-seek?

He emerged from the hall closet.

She blinked. "I looked in there. Wait. Why are you covered in dirt?"

He grinned, part triumph at winning the game and part boyish excitement at his state of uncleanliness.

She walked over and opened the door wider, letting light from the hallway spill into the closet.

A hatch was open, leading to a crawl space under the cabin.

"Huh."

"Papa made it for me. My secret spot, he says."

She turned to him. "I solemnly swear to tell no one."

Falco smiled again.

Lillian closed the hatch. She scanned the closet and saw the double-barrel shotgun on the top shelf with a case of bullets beside it. The shelf below it had a first aid kit and a stack of linens. The bottom shelf had two backpacks.

She closed the door. "Let's get you cleaned up. Maybe we can plan a dinner for your father. What do you think he'll want to eat when he gets back?"

"Pancakes!"

Lillian laughed as she led him to the bathroom. She suspected Falco was declaring his own desires more than his father's. "Pancakes it is."

LATER THAT EVENING, Lillian surveyed the damage. The cabin kitchen looked like one of her ER bays after a trauma, except that flour and spilled milk littered the countertop and floors.

She let Falco do as much of the measuring, mixing, and pouring of the pancakes as possible, since he seemed to thoroughly enjoy the process. She didn't know the kitchen would have to be declared a disaster zone because of it. Grinning, she knew she wouldn't mind cleaning the mess if that was the price for a moment of happiness.

Falco sat at the table watching her flip the pancakes. Ivan wasn't back yet, and Falco looked sullen, staring at the dinner he had made for his father, worrying it would go unappreciated.

Then the crunch of gravel under car tires sounded. Falco perked up with pleasant surprise.

Lillian's relief turned quickly sour as a chill coursed through her. Something was wrong. She went with her instinct.

"No. Falco." Her words and tone halted him as he took a step toward the front door. "To your hiding spot, now."

His confused face paled, but he obeyed and streaked down the hall.

The hair on the back of her neck stood on end. Why was it wrong? It was nighttime and the car approached with no headlights. The driveway chime didn't sound.

The front cabin windows would have caught the headlights. Was the alarm disabled? Her heart kicked up speed as she took steps away from the kitchen window. As she grabbed her phone and purse off the edge of the counter, she took retreating steps toward the hall, watching the front door.

Bullets exploded through the windows and front door. Lillian dove for the floor as bullets peppered the wall and furniture. The bag of unused flour erupted in a cloud of white dust. The cooking oil she was using on the pancake pan spilled onto the gas stove, and the kitchen flamed to life.

Lillian crawled rapidly toward the closet. The door and hatch were open. Falco and the backpacks from earlier were gone.

Getting to her feet, she grabbed the shotgun and shells. As she closed the closet door, she heard men shouting to one another outside the cabin. She pitched the gun into the crawl space and climbed into the hole. When she pulled the hatch shut after her, darkness closed around her.

———

DEPARTMENT OF DEFENSE
TOP SECRET
NUCLEAR THREAT INVESTIGATION

CASE FILE: 8966B20
Deputy Director: William Austin
Re: Dr. Lillian Whyte and Agent Sean Jennings

TRANSCRIPT:
DEPARTMENT OF DEFENSE INQUIRY

DOD: What were you doing during the attack on the cabin?
DR. WHYTE: Running like hell.

DOD: What were you doing prior to the attack on the cabin?
DR. WHYTE: Making pancakes.

DOD: Pancakes? In a criminal's home with his son while a nuclear weapon made its way across Europe, you were making pancakes?
DR. WHYTE: Pancakes. With chocolate chips.

DOD: Do you know who attacked Mr. Kleist's cabin?
DR. WHYTE: I didn't stop to ask.

DOD: These were trained and armed men?
DR. WHYTE: Yes.

DOD: Your documentation says you believe it was the cook's men who attacked the cabin.
DR. WHYTE: Ivan thought so. She'd put a bounty on his head.

DOD: How many attackers were there?
DR. WHYTE: I didn't stop to count.

# CHAPTER 16

L illian's hand closed around the shotgun as she wormed toward the back of the cabin. The crawl space was pitch black.

"Falco?" she whispered.

A small hand touched the side of her face and grabbed hold of her ear.

"Stay here a minute, sweetie." She tried not to let her voice betray her fear.

She felt for the bullets. She broke open the shotgun, ran her hands over the barrels and loaded them. Her fingertips moved over the smooth plastic casing of the shell and harder metal end and ensured they were loaded in the correct orientation. Fortunately, shotguns were not particularly complex, and she had loaded enough of them growing up on the farm that she could do it in the dark.

She closed the gun and ran a gentle finger over the single trigger. Two shots then she'd need to reload.

"I'll get in front and lead us out." She hoped she could lead him out and not lead them in circles in the dark.

Something plastic bumped into the side of her head. Her fingers ran over the object. Straps connected two plastic cylinders. Of course. Any self-respecting uber-criminal father would give his son night-vision goggles. She tugged them on and looked around. Falco was already wearing a pair.

*No wonder he's so calm.*

She could see the way to the back porch. As she crawled, she pushed the shotgun and box of bullets ahead of her.

Weapon fire had stopped, replaced by the thumping of heavy boots in the cabin above them. Then shouting erupted.

*Feuer.*

Fire?

Fire would spread quickly. Everything in the cabin was flammable. Her heart ached for a brief moment, thinking of all of Falco's books.

When she crawled her way to the back of the house, she inspected the latticework. The woodwork that kept animals from inhabiting the crawlspace had one short section lose. Ivan's intentions, no doubt. Quietly, she slid it aside.

She rolled onto her back and looked up through the wooden slats of the back porch. She could see an armed man. Her heart thudded in her chest.

The angle was wrong to attempt to shoot at him from under the house. When she made her move to roll out and fire, the attackers would know their position, and all hell would break loose.

*Maybe they won't have night vision goggles.*

She held up a palm to Falco, indicating for him to stay put. So far, he had made less noise than she had.

He didn't nod, didn't move. His little chest rose and fell in terrified gulps of air.

*Survive today, enroll in therapy tomorrow.*

After taking a steadying breath, Lillian rolled away, out from under the cabin porch, and leaped to her feet.

The man, catching the sudden movement in his peripheral vision, turned to look.

Lillian fired. The blast rattled every bone in her body and jarred her old gunshot wound. At close range, the shotgun blast blew a hole in the man's lower abdomen, below the vest protecting his torso. He was knocked off his feet, landing immobilized and bleeding on his side.

"Let's go."

Falco crawled out, dragging two backpacks.

Lillian grabbed the bags and flung both over her left shoulder. Her shoulder protested the weight. She wondered what else Ivan had stuffed into his emergency packs.

"Bullets."

Falco grabbed the box of shotgun shells from the ground.

They ran, Falco leading the way.

The backpacks jostled on her left shoulder, and the shotgun weighted down her right arm.

She heard shouting then automatic weapon fire. Fear jolted her faster. She didn't stop to turn around, but she knew the gunmen were too far away for accuracy. With an automatic weapon, however, they need only keep firing, and the odds were in their favor.

An explosion shook the ground. Lillian pulled off her goggles and looked back toward the cabin. Half of the house was obliterated and the other half in flames. The kitchen fire had spread to something explosive. Gas line? Water heater? Propane tank?

When her gaze scanned the perimeter, she didn't see any pursuers. She looked down at Falco; his expression was a mix of fascination and devastation. She would have reached to take his hand as a gesture of reassurance but hers were occupied.

"Let's keep moving, Falco."

"The abandoned barn?" he asked as he followed her.

"That's right. That's where your father said he would meet us if anything like this ever happened."

"Papa." The name escaped Falco's lips as a whimper.

*Please, God, let Ivan be alive.*

If the hit squad had reached him first, then this was game over. Except that if they had reached Ivan first, there would have been no purpose in coming to the cabin. He must be alive.

Several minutes later as they walked the overgrown trail Lillian felt their pace slowing. Falco was tiring.

She put the bullets and night vision goggles in Ivan's backpack and put it on, wearing it backwards. She put Falco's backpack on him then hoisted him up onto her back. She kept the shotgun in her right hand.

All total, she estimated the weight was probably similar to the pack she toted along the Inca Trail when she and Sean traveled in Peru. The difference was that tonight she had no water and had depleted her adrenaline stores.

Three miles, Ivan had said. Was that three miles total from the cabin to the barn or three miles from the time they reached the road to the barn?

*Time will tell.*

IVAN DROVE IN SILENCE. He had seen to his sister's comfort at the home for the dying. She would have no pain, no suffering. The caretakers suggested that, with nutrition and care, Ada might live several more months. When the situation with the nuclear bomb was over, he'd come back to her.

He had nothing more to offer her. "I'm sorry," were words he often expressed when he saw her after spells of being gone for long stretches. They seemed a meager offering. She had raised his son since the age of eight months when his mother died. He hadn't known he was a father until the woman had overdosed and left a note claiming he was the father.

One look at the baby and Falco knew he was his son. His sister, who could not have children, leaped at the opportunity to be a parental figure. She never considered him a burden. He was a gift. Even when her cancer came back, she still wanted to keep him. She swore he did more for her spirits and her health than chemotherapy ever could.

Ivan didn't know if Falco would see Ada again, so he'd had his son say good-bye the morning Ivan took her away from the cabin.

Falco was all his now. After the nuclear threat was over, they would change identities and make a new life somewhere. He wanted to teach him to fish and play soccer.

In the distance, orange flames caught Ivan's attention. He drove nearer to the driveway. Fear ratcheted up his heart rate and seared every nerve ending in his body. His throat went dry.

When he saw a black sedan pulling onto the main road from his driveway, he pressed the gas pedal. The front end of his Audi T-boned the sedan. His airbag jettisoned. When his blurred vision cleared, he yanked off his seatbelt.

After opening his car door, he exited and approached the other car. The driver's face was covered in blood. The man was reaching feebly for a gun on the passenger seat, but he couldn't see well.

Ivan reached inside, grabbed the man's head with both of his large hands and twisted. He felt the satisfying crack of his neck breaking. Leaning over the corpse, he picked up the gun. In a quick motion, he shot the two passengers in the back seat. One was still stunned from the vehicle crash, and the other appeared half-dead from third-degree burns.

Ivan climbed back in his car, relieved it was still functional. He set the gun down on the passenger seat. As he drove down his driveway, a mixture of rage and dread pulsated through him.

A sickening pit wrenched his gut at the sight of his sister's burning cabin. After parking the car, he walked as close to the flames as he could safely get, looking for any sign of his son or Lillian.

Motion on the right caught his eye. A man was trapped under the weight of several fallen porch beams.

Ivan took several paces closer and raised the gun.

"*Warten!*" the man pleaded.

Ivan pulled the trigger. They had attacked his son; there was no mercy for them.

He listened again. The night filled with the sounds of greedy, all-consuming flames. Billows of smoke blocked the stars above. Although heat radiated from the house on fire, Ivan felt cold.

"Falco!" He yelled his name in succession again and again.

No response came.

"No, no, no, no." Despair crushed him. He fell to his knees. How had he failed so miserably? He refused to believe his son was in the fire, but he couldn't search for him until the flames subsided.

"No," he argued with himself. Falco was alive. They had rules if dangerous men came. Escape. Run to the barn. He would be at the barn.

Ivan forced himself to stand on shaky legs and get back into the car.

*He must be at the barn.*

Ivan wound his car around the road to get to the barn, wishing some shortcut existed to cut the travel time in half.

Before pulling into the dirt drive, he cut off his headlights. He exited the car quietly, observing the dilapidated wood structure under the dim moonlight. He listened a moment, but heard no sounds. After opening the barn door cautiously, he used the flashlight on his phone to pan the room.

His heart leaped at the sight of a woman sitting against the wall.

Lillian raised the shotgun with shaking hands.

"Lillian, it's me, Ivan."

The shotgun lowered. His eyes fell to his son, who lay unmoving against her. He swallowed hard.

"Sleeping," she told him.

He breathed out a sigh of relief.

She had wrapped him in the thermal blanket from his backpack.

Ivan gingerly picked up Falco and carried him to the car where the heater would warm him. He laid him in the back seat and secured the seatbelt over him.

He returned to Lillian, who still sat on the barn floor. She appeared exhausted and pale, but without any signs of injury. She was covered in dirt and sweat, but she was still his red-haired angel.

"Your night vision goggles came in handy."

He bent by her side and cupped her face in his hand. "I owe you everything."

His gratitude obviously made her uncomfortable, but he held her gaze anyway. Tears welled in her eyes.

She looked away. "I'd settle for a bottle of water and a cheeseburger."

He grinned and kissed her forehead.

She grabbed the backpack and started to stand.

When he suddenly swept her off her feet, she let out a squeal of surprise. "I can walk."

"You are my angel. Tonight, you fly." He carried her to the car, not mentioning or minding the quiet sobs she cried into his chest. She must have been terrified. Despite her fear, she had escaped and saved Falco in the process. After setting her down in the front seat of the car, he went back and grabbed both packs and the gun. When he smelled the shotgun, his gut clenched. She'd had to use it. After laying everything on the floor of the back seat, he sat in the driver's seat.

She sniffed and wiped at her eyes. Nodding toward the gnarled metal of the front of the car, she asked, "Road rage?"

"Yes. We'll get another one."

---

"Where are we?" Lillian emerged from the bathroom clean and dressed.

Ivan had bought new clothing, toothbrushes, phone chargers, and even a watch charger while she slept. He had also taken them to a hotel with internet access.

When her phone charged, she would call Sean.

Falco sat on the bed, reading a book.

"Freiburg. It's west, on the German-French border."

Her nose followed the scent of coffee. She walked to the countertop and poured some into a Styrofoam cup.

If someone had told Lillian she'd be spending her Icelandic vacation racing in terror around Europe and sharing a room with a wanted mercenary and his adorable son, she would have laughed them out of her sight.

She had a bed separate from Ivan and Falco, but that did nothing to change the strangeness of the situation. If she hadn't narrowly escaped her own execution last night, she might have demanded separate rooms. Things being as they were, she preferred to stay close to Ivan and his deadly skills.

Lillian ruffled Falco's hair and sat down on the bed next to him. "How are you holding up, kiddo?"

She sipped her coffee, wondering what sort of counseling he was going to need after being hunted by armed gunmen. He would have seen at least part of the man on the porch getting shot. When they had finally reached the barn, Falco shook and cried in her arms until he fell asleep.

"Okay," he replied, not looking up from his book.

Lillian eyed Ivan while he sat in front of his computer and entered his passcode. They needed to discuss what Falco had gone through last night.

"Are you okay?" Ivan asked.

She wasn't sure how it reflected on her character, but she didn't feel bad about firing the shotgun. Not an ounce of remorse. The few tears she shed were out of exhaustion and fear. "I took an oath to maintain the utmost respect for human life. Last night I respected mine more than the intruders'."

Ivan gave an appreciative grunt. "I thought the Hippocratic Oath was do no harm?"

"Yes, and it has the reciter swearing by Apollo and other Greek gods. No modern physician takes the Hippocratic Oath. The Declaration of Geneva replaced the Hippocratic Oath a long time ago."

"I see. Did you know that in Norse mythology, the divine healer was a goddess—a female? She was also a Valkyrie."

"I didn't know that. Didn't Valkyries take the slain to Valhalla?"

"And they were warriors. The goddess's name is Eir."

"Warrior and healer?" Lillian asked skeptically.

"I can think of someone fitting that description." He turned to her with a grin.

"Hmm. I'm a survivor, not a warrior."

"In this world, you have to be a warrior to be a survivor."

———

DEPARTMENT OF DEFENSE
TOP SECRET
NUCLEAR THREAT INVESTIGATION

CASE FILE: 8966B20
Deputy Director: William Austin
Re: Dr. Lillian Whyte and Agent Sean Jennings
TRANSCRIPT:
DEPARTMENT OF DEFENSE INQUIRY

DOD: Were you in contact with your wife following the failed Delta Force attack?
JENNINGS: No. She was in a cabin in remote Germany with poor cellular service so we were unable to converse.

DOD: You didn't send agents to secure her safety?
JENNINGS: All of our agents were searching for the bomb.

DOD: You didn't send her brother to secure her safety in Germany?
JENNINGS: No. Jonathan was in London. If I had sent him to Germany, Lillian could have been in another country by the time he got there.

DOD: Why did you meet with the president personally several times?
JENNINGS: President Lawson and I have been friends and colleagues for many years. He requested face-to-face updates on the status of the bomb.

DOD: Did he know about your wife's involvement?
JENNINGS: Austin and I briefed him on her role in helping Ivan Kleist.

DOD: Did he call into question the competency of the CIA—if it was resorting to criminal and civilian intelligence?
JENNINGS: No. President Lawson understood that all resources were presently being used to locate the bomb, and he knew we would rely on unorthodox means if it meant saving lives. He also trusted my wife.

DOD: Why would the president of the United States trust your wife?
JENNINGS: That's classified sir, but Deputy Director Austin can release that information to you if he feels it relevant.

# CHAPTER 17

———

"No. No. No," Ivan growled.

Lillian came by his side, still sipping her morning coffee. "Falco's sleeping. What's the matter?"

After glancing toward Falco in the other room, Ivan lowered his voice. "They're all dead. The military forces didn't stop the cook. They were overpowered. The bomb is on the move. Continuing west."

She pulled up a chair beside him as he sat in front of his computer. "You're saying they failed? The team sent to grab the bomb is dead?"

He rubbed his neck. "Yes. They're all dead."

She leaned toward him and laid her forehead against his shoulder. He heard her swallow—the way women did when they were trying not to cry.

The video he watched was a day old. He stared at the screen, watching the bomb get transported to a car while the bodies of the dead were left behind. Soldiers. Ivan thought of Falco in the other room. Soldiers with families.

His grandfather had been a soldier—a Nazi tool. Ivan had come to think of all soldiers as tools of the society and government that brainwashed them. The men on this mission, however, had an objective that obliterated international boundaries and economic agendas. This was the closest they would come to good versus evil.

He eased his hand into Lillian's, feeling its delicate warmth. "May they find peace in the halls of Valhalla."

Lillian sniffed and straightened, looking at the screen. "What now? You're still tracking the bomb?"

"I'm still tracking it." By which he meant he was still paying his friend to track it. "We need to let Agent Jennings know."

Ivan placed the video call.

Lillian sucked in a sharp breath and distanced herself from him. Her hand left his, taking the comfort she brought with it.

Sean Jennings' face appeared on the screen. "Just the double-crossing *sonofabitch* I wanted to talk to."

"I didn't double-cross you." Ivan was too disillusioned to conjure an angry response to Agent Jennings vehemence.

"Our entire rescue team is dead, Ivan. Dead following the lead you gave us."

"The information was accurate. The bomb was there. They had you outgunned. I couldn't have predicted that."

"What's going on, Ivan? Why haven't I heard from my wife in two days?" Sean's tone was firm.

"We had problems of our own," Ivan replied coolly.

"Lillian?"

The worry in Sean's voice had her instantly jumping into view of the camera. "I'm here. I'm okay. Ivan's cabin was ambushed last night, but we're fine."

"Were you followed?" His voice was softer addressing her.

"There wasn't anyone left to follow us," Lillian replied.

"Your wife was very brave."

Sean's gaze flickered back to Ivan and hardened. He obviously didn't approve of Ivan putting her in a predicament requiring bravery.

"Could your buddy Pico have predicted the forces protecting the bomb?"

Ivan's brow furrowed. "Pico?"

Sean aimed the camera on his laptop at another computer.

Pico Cardoza.

Ivan recognized his acquaintance from the still shot. They had performed various odd jobs together. Apparently the CIA knew this.

What was Pico doing moving a nuclear weapon? Did he know what it was? Probably not. Just as Ivan ignorantly stole a USB with schematics of a Korean nuclear weapons facility, Pico was likely ignorantly transporting a black box. When one was paid handsomely, mouths remained shut. Simultaneously, no one assumes they are a means to an end for someone's plans to annihilate a European city.

"Ivan?"

"I'm thinking." But Pico's involvement opened up a new possibility. Perhaps Ivan could get one step ahead of the bomb instead of staying one step behind it.

"Ivan?" Sean's voice grew more irritable. "Are you still tracking the bomb?"

"Yes. And I have to go." He closed the screen.

"Hey!" Lillian protested. "I would have liked to talk to my husband."

"There's no time. Pico will lead us to the bomb."

Ivan picked up his phone and found his contact list. He dialed the number.

"Pico," Ivan said.

No answer came in return, although the phone was no longer ringing.

At last, Pico Cardoza said, "I thought you were dead, my friend."

Good. Pico hadn't used his name.

"I'm harder to kill than the cook thinks."

"So it would seem. I'm glad. You'll have to share the details over a lager with me sometime. Right now, I'm busy."

"I know you're busy. I know you took down a military team after the package you're delivering. I know you're headed west." He tried to get his words out quickly before Pico disconnected the call. "I also know you're carrying a nuclear weapon."

Silence.

Ivan's stomach knotted. He'd been hoping for more surprise, more outrage. Pico could have declared his innocence and offered helped.

Pico's tone turned amused. "Okay, well. Why don't I call you back when I'm not driving? This is your number?"

"Yes."

The call disconnected.

Ivan set the phone down and tapped his index finger along the edge of it. A promise to call back was something.

He felt the physician staring at him. She had been silently watching him as he searched for Pico's number and then called him. He knew she wanted an explanation, but it was simpler to see if Pico came through rather than talk and speculate as they waited.


Lillian's phone rang.

"Kelly." She stood and checked her phone—fifty percent charge. She grabbed the room key, and left the hotel room as she put the phone to her ear.

"Hey, Lily, I wanted to let you know Katie is doing better."

Katie. Poor little thing had a cold. Although Kelly had called only a week ago, it felt longer. So much had happened.

"How are you? Are you and Sean having fun in Iceland?"

Lillian put a hand over her mouth to keep a sob from escaping. She walked out of the hotel lobby and let fresh air wash over her. She wasn't okay. She'd fled to Germany like a criminal, barely escaped death at Ivan's cabin, and shot a man dead. All of that and the bomb still wasn't in safe hands.

"Lily?"

"I'm okay. Sean wasn't able to make it to Iceland." Lillian sniffed.

"Oh, no. Is he okay?"

"He's okay."

Lillian couldn't tell Kelly about any of what was happening. Her best friend didn't even know the truth of half of the things that had happened to her.

"This was your anniversary trip." Her voice rang with a sympathy that threatened to hasten Lillian's breakdown.

Lillian looked around at the four-story hotel and surrounding woods. If a map of Germany was placed before her, and she had to pinpoint her location, she couldn't. Southwest Germany was all she knew.

"Yeah. Something came up."

"That's absurd. You want me to beat him up?"

Lillian choked back a half-sob, half-laugh.

"You want me to set Katie on him?"

Lillian chuckled.

Kelly added gently, "It'll work out. You two are an amazing couple."

Lillian blinked away a tear. "Yeah, it will work out." Would she even hold Sean again? Be wrapped in his arms? "I think I'm tired, and it's making me emotional."

"You're not pregnant, are you?"

"No, I'm not pregnant."

"Do you want to be?"

Did she? If she survived this crisis would she want to readdress the topic with Sean?

"Huh."

"What?" Lillian asked.

"That's the first time you didn't snap a no-way-in-hell response at me."

Lillian felt a bit weightless. "I guess it is."


AN HOUR LATER, Ivan picked up his phone when Pico called.

The room was silent except for the ringing phone. Lillian had voluntarily taken Falco for a walk. Before she left, she gave Ivan a long you-owe-me-an-explanation stare. Infuriating woman.

"Pico?"

"Ivan, I swear I didn't know." His voice was no longer the smooth calm it had been on the earlier call.

"I know. What's the target?"

"Europe."

"That doesn't narrow it down."

"If it's a nuclear weapon, it needn't be more specific."

"Pico."

"Paris."

Ivan stood and paced the hotel room. "You need to get out of there. Abandon the mission."

"You saved my life. That doesn't mean I walk away from a fifty-thousand Euros job."

"I'm not asking as a favor. I'm warning you as a friend. Everyone who has dealt with the cook on this mission has died. Except me." Ivan rubbed at the back of his neck. He didn't know if the statement was entirely true, but the cook had left a trail of bodies.

"She tried to have you killed? Is that why you went dark?"

"Yes. And she killed Renni."

Pico swore. After a moment, he said, "Don't worry about me. I'll be long gone before any bombs are detonated."

"Pico—" Ivan protested.

"I'll be in touch. I'll keep you notified of our progress. You got a plan once you catch up with this weapon? I may be a mercenary, but I'm not about unleashing nukes on civilians."

"Yes, I have a plan."

"I'll be in touch," he repeated.

The call ended.

Ivan kicked at the mattress on the bed—once, twice, and thrice. It didn't cool the flaming frustration he felt.

· · ·

After Lillian returned from a walk and getting snacks with Falco, Ivan hailed Sean on a video chat. As Sean's face came into view, Lillian's heart skipped a beat. She saw her husband from an angle on the screen where he couldn't see her. She eased into view, keeping her distance from Ivan.

"Where's the weapon, Ivan?"

"On its way to Paris."

William Austin appeared on screen beside Sean. "Can you be more specific?"

"Not until Pico gives me more information. When I told him he was helping transport a nuclear weapon, he agreed to keep me informed of its destination."

Austin's eyes became unfocused in contemplation. He turned to Sean. "We can get this intel up the chain. Another team can be assembled."

Austin turned back to the screen, started to speak and then stopped, staring at Lillian. "Lillian."

"Bill," she replied, acknowledging his greeting.

"You still trying to pretend you're a CIA agent?"

Her mouth quirked. "No more than you."

He pursed his lips together, though she suspected it was more to hide a grin than irritation.

Sean interrupted. "Ivan, am I right to suspect your satellite tracking ability isn't going to be ideal in Paris?"

"It's a big, congested city. Vehicles can get lost. Also, if they take any underground transportation or travel the sewage system, we will lose them."

Lillian grimaced, remembering her traipse through the sewage tunnels in Montreal. At one point, she had thought those slimy walls would be the last thing she'd ever see.

She asked, "It's big, though, right? Shouldn't it be at least a bit conspicuous?"

Ivan shook his head. "Not all nukes are created equal. Fat Boy—the bomb that detonated over Nagasaki was enormous, but most nukes can fit in a large van. Theater nukes are suitcase size."

Sean leaned closer. "We need a backup plan if the satellite loses the bomb and Pico doesn't tell us the location."

"Pico will tell me."

Sean rubbed his temples. "I'm not implying your friend is unreliable. I'm concerned that the cook could eliminate him at any point before he tells you the location. That's what she did to you, right? Once your task was complete, you were another target—another loose end to tie."

Ivan narrowed his eyes. "Okay. Backup plan is I tail the bomb in Paris."

Sean nodded slowly before looking at Lillian. "Lillian, how about you come home?"

She cocked her head to one side. "Sure. Let the men handle it?"

Sean looked at Ivan with pleading eyes.

Ivan shrugged. "She's your stubborn wife. I'm not going to have any success changing her mind."

Lillian leaned closer to the screen. "My future is at stake, too. If I can help, I'm going to help. We'll keep our distance. We'll be safe."

Sean's jaw tensed. "The blast radius is probably a mile. You cannot simultaneously keep eyes on the bomb and be safe."

"Then it's your job to make sure the team arrives before it detonates."

Sean stood and distanced himself from the computer. She watched him pace silently behind Austin.

Her intention wasn't to infuriate him or make him worry, but she wasn't going to take a back seat and watch events unfold. She had already played a pivotal role. If the cook's men had succeeded in killing or capturing Falco, Ivan would have been incapacitated and the bomb lost. Maybe her surveillance role wouldn't be critical. Maybe it would.

Ivan moved off camera, and Lillian sat in his vacant chair.

Austin moved out of view.

Sean still paced, his jaw ticking. She could see the paneled wall of a conference room behind him.

"Please don't be angry."

He turned to look at her. The anger in his eyes melted into heart-wrenching despair as he sat down solemnly.

She wanted to lean through the image and kiss away his sorrow. "I love you."

He scrubbed his hands along his face. "Why are you doing this?"

"If you were here, and I was there, what would you do if I begged you to abandon the mission and come home?"

His gaze flickered irritably from the screen to the room and back to the screen. "Please be careful." He gave a long sigh. "I love you too."

He disconnected the call.

Lillian looked to the corner of the hotel room where Falco was reading. Ivan pulled him into his lap.

"Paris, huh? You and I don't have a great track record in Paris." She leaned back in the chair and crossed her arms.

Paris had been where Ivan had tracked her down and attempted to assassinate her. Sean had been a faster draw with his weapon.

"You need to let that go," Ivan advised.

She chuckled.

"Breakfast?" she asked.

"I can't take Falco to Paris. You could stay here. Watch him for me."

Her cheeks burned. Ivan, too, was trying to bench her. "And when you don't return, I'll have to explain why I wasn't there to protect you?"

Ivan frowned.

She shook her head irritably. Grabbing her purse, she headed for the door. "I'm going with you. But right now, I'm going to go get some decent coffee." She left the hotel room.

IVAN WATCHED THE PHYSICIAN LEAVE. Truthfully, he wanted Lillian to come to Paris with him. Since coercing her to join him in Iceland, tracking the bomb felt less like a suicide mission and more like an achievable objective. He selfishly wanted to keep her for the strength and resilience she imbued. When he held her hand, he felt grounded in a reality where good people lived and strived to make the world better.

He thought of a Norse mythology poem, <u>Fjölsvinnsmál</u>, about maidens on a healing mountain—one of which was Eir.

> *"Soon aid they all who offers give*
> *On the holy altars high;*
> *And if danger they see for the sons of men,*
> *Then each day from ill do they guard."*

Thus far, Lillian had been his healing Valkyrie.

He turned to Falco, who was looking toward the door.

What life had he given his only son? One where a strange woman is brought before him. One where his belongings were lost in a fire as he fled for his life. One where he was in and out of hotels and talk of nuclear weapons took place before breakfast.

Ivan promised himself he would remedy the situation. When the crisis was over, he would settle down with Falco. He had enough money to retire, barring he didn't spend all of it tracking the damn bomb.

Ivan's outlook on life had drastically changed when he'd found out he was a father. He took less violent assignments—more theft, less murder. He had never killed families, only men in his way. Since having a son, every life he took gave him pause. Had he killed someone's father? Someone's son?

Falco closed his book. "Did you see her, Papa? She glows like an angel. She saved me at the cabin. She could save you too."

Resignation smoothed Ivan's frown. He kissed Falco on the top of his head. "She already has."

---

## DEPARTMENT OF DEFENSE

TOP SECRET
NUCLEAR THREAT INVESTIGATION

CASE FILE: 8966B20
Deputy Director: William Austin
Re: Dr. Lillian Whyte and Agent Sean Jennings
TRANSCRIPT:
DEPARTMENT OF DEFENSE INQUIRY

DOD: We were informed by Agent Jennings that President Lawson was not only aware of Dr. Whyte's involvement but had reason to trust her judgment.
AUSTIN: That's correct.

DOD: Can you elaborate on the nature of their relationship?
AUSTIN: You are aware of the Montreal incident?
DOD: We have reviewed those files, yes.
AUSTIN: Then you know that Lillian was instrumental in stopping a biomedical weapon attack. Terrorists were planning on first using the weapon against a cocktail party hosted by Cole Lawson—Senator Lawson at that time—and attended by a dozen United Nations diplomats. Cole is alive because of the actions of Agent Jennings and Dr. Whyte. The nature of their relationship is friendship.

DOD: After the Delta Force mission failed to seize the bomb, you still trusted information from Dr. Whyte and the man with whom she conspired?
AUSTIN: Lillian and Mr. Kleist's information about the bomb had been correct so far. Not knowing how heavily guarded it would be was our underestimation, not theirs.

DOD: Were you clinging to some misguided faith that a physician and a mercenary could stop a bomb?
AUSTIN: Not at all. My faith was guided by Lillian's prior actions,

and my faith was that they would be able to give us an updated, precise location of the bomb.

DOD: But it wasn't so simple?
AUSTIN: No, sir. The situation would become more dangerous—more dangerous than any of us anticipated, both in Europe and in Virginia.

# CHAPTER 18

After the videoconference disconnected, Austin took a step back from Sean as he abruptly stood. Sean gripped the edge of his chair in white-knuckled fury.

Austin calmly noted, "She looks well. Unharmed."

"Did you see where they were? She's in a fucking hotel room with that murdering asshole."

Austin hadn't seen Sean this angry since Montreal, when he had sent Sean's wife into a hostage situation to play doctor. Sean had been furious with him. At least this time, Sean's rage wasn't directed at him.

"Lillian would never intentionally hurt you or cheat on you. That was not the expression of an unfaithful woman."

Sean turned to blink at him.

"I would know," Austin added.

"Darlene?"

Austin nodded.

"I'm sorry. I didn't know." Sean's tense shoulders deflated.

"Well, then you're not spending enough time at the CIA water cooler. You're missing all the gossip."

Sean sat heavily in the chair. "I just want her back, Bill."

Austin suppressed the urge to remind Sean there was a bigger picture here—a nuclear weapon that needed stopping. "She's smart, savvy. And we both know she can take care of herself."

"I feel like this is punishment for me not going to Iceland."

"She's not the vindictive type." Austin hesitated, considering why he gave a damn about their relationship. The pair of them had been trouble for him. Trouble, but essential to the resolution of some major crises over the years. Including, it would seem, this one. "Besides, she clearly looked like she both knew and hated the pain she's putting you through. This isn't your punishment. It's just Lillian's personality. She doesn't put her trust in other's abilities. She doesn't leave a job half done."

She probably would have made a good agent.

*Except for her mouthy insubordination.*

Sean sucked in a deep breath and exhaled slowly. "Okay. Paris. Can you get the intel where it needs to go?"

"I've already sent the text."

———

Yu received news that the team she had sent to deal with Ivan had failed. It had taken an excessively long time—days—to identify his sister's home. Her spy spotted Ivan in the nearest town, which triggered mobilization of the attack as planned. Apparently, Ivan was prepared for such an attack because he had eliminated the team. No one survived.

Except Ivan.

She had never had such an elusive target. He was a *kumiho*—the nine-tailed fox of Korean folklore that could disguise itself, slinking through the night, preying on the weak. His moral ambiguity had helped her get the schematics to steal the bomb, yet she had been wrong to select him. He was too cunning. No problem. She could remedy her mistake. Once she lured him to the bomb, he would become another victim—along with the other millions.

Her inability to comprehend his actions troubled her. He knew he was a dead man. Why go to his sister's house? Why track the bomb? Her men had overheard a conversation between Ivan and his friend Pico Cardoza—ignorant Portuguese ex-commando—who thought himself clever. Was Ivan intending to stop the bomb? What does a worthless mercenary care if she detonates the bomb? Chaos only benefits the morally corrupt.

Fine. Let him tail her like the wretched *kumiho* he was.

*Come into my trap, little fox. You will not escape this time.*

Her phone rang.

"You're being tracked again," the familiar female voice said.

"Yes. This time it's Reginald." She poured a cup of *maeshil-cha.* The green plum tea was one of her favorites.

"There's a bird inbound." Cassandra's voice sounded concerned. "You're supposed to be under the radar."

"I can't explain Bulgaria, but we were prepared. You're going to keep my path clear in Paris?"

"Yes," Cassandra replied. "Any other foreseeable problems?"

"I prefer the term *challenges.* 'Problems' has such a negative connotation."

"Any other *challenges*?"

Yu thought about Ivan, about whom the contractor and Cassandra knew nothing. "No."

---

Jonathan's phone buzzed. He tossed his covers off his bare chest and grabbed the phone.

A text from Sean: *Paris.*

"Not a man of many words."

Marie rolled over in bed and slid her hand around his torso. "Who is it?"

"Sean. Lillian's headed to Paris."

He set the phone down and wrapped an arm around Marie. Her pale, silky smooth skin brushed against his. He admired how soft yet tough she was. Having never enjoyed a relationship with a woman six years older than him, now he wanted nothing less. She was not only sensual and witty, but had a maturity and self-esteem seasoned from experience.

"Does my personal surveillance cross borders?"

"*Oui.*"

He watched her fingers trail across his chest. "Could be dangerous."

"Good. All office and no play makes Marie a dull girl." Her French accent sent a thrill of desire through him.

"I might need a bodyguard." He wriggled closer to her, loving that they were still naked beneath the covers.

"I can guard this body."

He chuckled. Cupping her chin, he pulled her to him for a slow, succulent kiss. This woman mesmerized him. "You could never be dull. You're smart, funny, sexy, and beautiful. I bet you shoot good too."

"I can handle myself, cowboy."

He grinned from ear to ear as his erection pressed against her bare thigh. They had only met a few days ago and he was already wondering how he would finagle seeing her again when this rodeo ended. She would go back to Canada, and he would go back to Arkansas. The distance was unacceptable.

When their bodies merged, he sucked in a quick breath. She moved in long, slow motions. He groaned, took a fist full of her hair in his hand, and buried his face in her neck.

"How should we get to Paris? Plane? Boat?"

"Train." She rolled on top, straddling him.

Two pair of pale and pleasantly round breast situated themselves within easy reach.

"Train it is."

---

LILLIAN DREAMED of a gray horizon where a desolate land of incinerated buildings met a sky of swirling ashes.

To her left, a silvery sea churned in angry waves. An enormous serpent thrashed in and out of the water. It had the head of a dragon with green, iridescent scales, and the body of a snake. Two obsidian eyes darted around wildly, reminding her of some of the psychotic patients she had seen in her emergency room.

To her right, a black wolf as big as an elephant attacked a defenseless crowd of people. His long fangs dripped with blood and saliva. Red eyes seemed to glow in a frame of dark, matted fur.

In front of her, a beast three stories tall in the shape of a man flailed giant fists of burning fire. His body glowed and shimmered red and orange as if made of molten lava. Heat radiated from the surface of his body, and everything he touched was set on fire.

As the world danced in flames, everything sunk into a boiling sea.

Lillian woke to the sensation of vertigo. She quietly but hastily made her way through the dark hotel room to the bathroom. After splashing cold water on her face, she sat on the closed toilet, putting her head between her hands. Her temples throbbed.

Ragnarok. The end of the world. The nuclear weapon felt like the equivalent of the fire giant Surtr.

The stress of the travel and constant threat of the bomb was fraying her nerves and sending her imagination in a wild frenzy. She was starting to wish she hadn't read the Norse mythology book en route to Iceland.

LILLIAN AND IVAN stopped at a playground at Herboltzheim on the way to Strasbourg. Falco needed to run and play after a few hours of being cooped up in the car.

Lillian had been intentionally vague over the phone when she called George McClellan. She couldn't ask for a large favor over the phone, especially since it required explaining the story behind why she was with a German and his son and heading west following a nuclear weapon. This conversation needed to be in person.

Her former boss was embracing his retirement with a

prolonged European tour. Currently, his touring had him in the lovely town of Strasbourg nestled on the French-German border. He agreed to meet with her in person over brunch to discuss her urgent request.

He sounded more bemused than irritated at her intrusion into his vacation.

*Wait until he hears why I'm intruding.*

His amusement was going to morph into aggravation before nose-diving into angst.

"You had a nightmare," Ivan said.

Lillian glanced sidelong at the pale German. If they hadn't been sharing a single room with separate beds, he'd never have known. "I've been known to have those under stress."

"I'm sorry."

"I'll be fine." She bit out the words as if saying them would make them true. "It won't affect my performance."

"I have no doubts about that. Do you want to talk about it?"

She arched an eyebrow. She didn't believe Ivan made such an offer to most people he encountered. "I saw Ragnarok."

"Hmm. Annihilation of the nine realms."

"I don't want to talk about it," she said, changing her mind.

They sat silently for a moment before Ivan changed the subject. "You think your friend will agree to look after Falco for a few days?" Ivan watched Falco climbing the geometric dome as he and Lillian sat on the bench.

"He'll agree."

"And you trust him? You would trust him with your own son?"

"I trust George more than I trust myself. He raised four kids and has six grandkids."

"You protected Falco with your life. One can do no more than that." He slipped his hand into hers. "I swear on my life I will do everything I can to get you home safely to Agent Jennings."

She playfully bumped her elbow into his side, but didn't pull her hand away from his. "You swear by the Odin oath, Loki?" The Norse mythology book had claimed an Odin oath was binding and absolute. She recalled the book was now in a pile of ashes at Ivan's cabin like most of her belongings from this trip—this *vacation*.

Ivan's expression remained serious as he turned to her. "By Odin, I swear it." He lifted her hand to his lips and kissed her wedding ring.

She stared at him.

"I don't have an arm ring to swear on my life, so your diamond ring will have to suffice."

She swallowed and turned back to watch Falco playing as Ivan rested their hands back on his knee.

She hoped Paris wouldn't require the fulfillment of any blood oaths.


For the rest of the ride to Strasbourg, Lillian sat in the back seat with Falco.

"Papa says you're a doctor."

"That's right."

"Do you save people's lives?"

"Sometimes." She thought about her work as an ER physician. Maybe ten percent of the problems she managed were true life-threatening emergencies. Fifty percent were exacerbations of various chronic illnesses. Twenty percent were some form of trauma or injury. The remaining twenty percent were people who didn't have primary care providers, and so came to the ER with low acuity problems.

"So you don't save everybody?"

She frowned. "I don't save everybody." She'd seen a lot of death in nearly two decades in the medical profession—from an ER tech to medical school to residency to practicing physician.

*No one reaches the end alive.*

As she tried to think of a way to change the conversation, Ivan spoke. "To our left is the Black Forest. This is where the legend of the Grimm brothers was born."

She looked out the window at the dense evergreens.

"Around the forest you'll find the quintessential German villages.

The best to visit is Freiburg. They have museums, architectural beauties, and even a planetarium."

"Can we go there, Papa?"

"Not this trip, *mausi*. Perhaps another time."

The boy's expression saddened before he turned to Lillian, and his eyes sparkled. "Last year Papa took me to"—he leaned toward the front of the car—"what was the name of that castle, Papa?"

"Neuschwanstein."

"Yes. It was *enorm*. And we got to ride in a carriage pulled by horses. It was built in the 1800s and millions of people have visited it. It took decades to build."

"This year, Falco, we'll go to Freiburg. Maybe go there on the way back home from this trip?"

"*Ja!*"

———————————

DEPARTMENT OF DEFENSE
TOP SECRET
NUCLEAR THREAT INVESTIGATION

CASE FILE: 8966B20
Deputy Director: William Austin
Re: Dr. Lillian Whyte and Agent Sean Jennings

TRANSCRIPT:
DEPARTMENT OF DEFENSE INQUIRY

DOD: After receiving only a text message from Agent Jennings, you headed to Paris to intercept your sister?
JONATHAN WHYTE: Yes.

DOD: At this point, what did you know about the nuclear weapon, who had custody of it, and what their intentions were?
JONATHAN WHYTE: I knew that Lillian was following the bomb,

ergo it must be in or on its way to Paris. I didn't know anything about who controlled it or what his or her intentions were.

DOD: A nuclear bomb could be detonated at any moment, and you chose to put yourself within its blast proximity?
JONATHAN WHYTE: Do you have a baby sister? No. Then, you wouldn't understand.

DOD: Did you have a plan once you reached your sister?
JONATHAN WHYTE: Talk sense into her. Drag her back to safety. Maybe even save her life and cash in on favors for the next decade.

DOD: So, no plan.
JONATHAN WHYTE: A sketch of a plan subject to improvisation.

DOD: And what happened to your sketch of a plan?
JONATHAN WHYTE: All hell broke loose, and improvisation was required.

# CHAPTER 19

---

Sean found himself in the Oval Office for the third time in his life within a week. President Lawson had convened a meeting with William Austin, Reginald Lancaster, chairman of the Joint Chiefs of Staff, Conrad Saunders, the secretary of state, and the national security advisor. A transcriptionist sat off to one corner, typing on a computer.

They had already made introductions around the room. Reginald expressed his eagerness to help diffuse the situation in any way possible.

Cole paced the room while the others sat. "To summarize our situation, we have a nuke on the way to Paris after we failed to capture it in Bulgaria. We have no set of reliable eyes on the weapon, and we don't know our enemy's intentions except to say there must only be one intention—detonation."

Sean sent a quick look to Austin. Lillian's involvement need not be shared with the entire room.

"Yes, sir," Austin said.

Cole continued, "We don't know anything about who has orchestrated this catastrophe except that a Korean assassin, known as the cook, may be taking the lead. And we have no facial identification of her."

Austin replied, "We are investigating who might be behind events, but, honestly, most of our manpower is aimed at finding and stopping the bomb. We've notified the General Directorate for Internal Security that Paris is being targeted. French police are on high alert."

"What about detecting it through radiation leakage?"

Reginald shook his head. "Nukes don't leak radiation. Not enough for detection anyway."

Conrad crossed his legs. "We've got another Delta Force team en route to intercept the bomb. We're attaching a DEVGRU with them, and they'll be working with the French GIGN. What can we do to help these teams succeed?"

Sean felt a measure of relief at the extensive international forces at work. A DEVGRU—Seal Team Six—combined with the French ass-kicking antiterrorism group and Delta Force could bring the cook and her forces down.

The secretary of state looked to Reginald Lancaster. "Weren't you telling me about your drones with facial recognition?"

Reginald licked his lips. "I've got two dozen drones I can send up over the city. If you have facial recognition on anyone working with the Korean, we can upload that to the drones and spot them as soon as they surface."

Austin looked at Sean.

He took his cue. "We have an analyst who has identified a dozen men working for her."

"Let's do that," Cole said. "What else?"

Austin turned to Reginald. "Didn't you present an EMP at the weapons demo last year? If this nuke is unshelled, would it be vulnerable to an EMP?"

Sean hadn't been at the weapons demo, but he remembered hearing about high-tech electromagnetic pulse weapons in research and development and joking with Jack about how the next generation of agents would be using electromagnetic pulse "Bat-rays" like Batman instead of guns.

Reginald frowned and looked worried about disappointing the deputy director of the CIA. "An electromagnetic pulse wouldn't reliably shut it down. If the pulse cuts an external power supply without the internal supply, it could actually cause it to detonate. And most EMP shutdowns are temporary. The power supply could turn back on...and then *boom*."

Conrad grunted. "That's not an option."

President Cole summarized. "In that case, we'll plan for the special ops team to secure the weapon once Reginald's drones tell us where to find it."


When the meeting was done, Austin's mind churned through the containment and rescue plan. Sean sat quietly in the passenger seat on the way back to Langley. Austin's phone range over the Bluetooth in his car.

"Deputy Director Austin?" Zoey's voice came through crisply but tentatively.

"Yes, Zoey."

She hesitated and cleared her throat. "I know you don't care to hear about the possibility that the cook exists or could be involved, but I ran a check through our files for any mention of her. Gabe Oleander offered information on her when he was arrested several months ago. He wanted a lighter sentence in exchange, but we weren't interested in information on an espionage myth."

"The accountant?" Sean asked.

Austin recalled Sean helping the CIA identify Gabe by going to the Cayman Islands and gathering information on the man who funneled criminal money offshore.

"What if he does have valuable information?" Zoey asked.

"Where is he now?" Austin asked.

"FCC Petersburg."

Austin turned to look at Sean. "That's only a two-hour drive down 95."

"I'll go." Sean said. "My rental car is parked—"

"We'll go. You have no authority to offer anything in exchange for information."

Zoey remained silent.

"You're taking a road trip?" Sean gaped at him.

Austin shot him an irritated glance before he said, "Thank you, Zoey. I need Gabe's full file for me to review en route to the Federal Correction Center."

"Yes, sir." She disconnected the call

He pulled out his phone and started making calls to arrange an escort to the prison and for the prisoner to be ready for interrogation by the time they arrived.

———

LILLIAN, Ivan, and Falco walked to the cafe near the Cathedral de Strasbourg.

"Wait." Ivan stopped, staring in a store window.

Lillian and Falco followed him inside the store.

Wordlessly, Ivan selected a watch and tried it out on Falco, who stared in wide-eyed silence. Next, Ivan had the seller adjust the band, and he secured it on his son's wrist. The watch head looked a bit large on the boy's small wrist, but the craftsmanship was exquisite. The circular face was gold, with visible gears churning behind the glass frame. The band was made of soft, brown leather.

Ivan stayed bent down on one knee. "Do you like it?"

"Yes, Papa." Falco hugged his father.

"I'm sorry you lost so many things in the fire. Objects are replaceable. People are not. *Ja?*"

"*Ja.*"

He ruffled the boy's hair as he stood.

Lillian gave Ivan a smile.

He scowled at her appreciation of his sentimental side. "Okay, Let's go. Out."

As they walked, Falco skipped between them, holding both of their hands. Lillian knew that to onlookers, they looked like a family.

She didn't care what her relationship with Falco appeared to be. For a moment in time, Falco had his father and tranquility.

Later today, Ivan would depart to chase a bomb, leaving Falco with strangers in Strasbourg. The boy didn't know if his father would return from Paris. When this was over, they would all need therapy.

"Lillian."

She looked up to see George at the cafe waving at her. She waved back at him.

Lillian, Ivan, and Falco walked into the cafe and wound around tables and chairs to join George and Angie on the street side of the cafe, which was encircled by a decorative fence.

"George and Angie McClellan, this is Ivan Kleist and his son, Falco."

Everyone shook hands.

George leaned down to Falco. "I've a grandson your age. I bet you like planes and trains and trucks."

"Yes. And space. And books."

George smiled with a sparkle in his eye. "And hot chocolate?"

Falco's eyes widened.

"They have good hot chocolate here, if it's okay with your father."

Falco looked up at Ivan, who nodded.

"His English is wonderful," George noted.

"Thank you." Ivan gave a slight smile.

They sat around the table. Lillian sat between George and Falco.

George snapped his napkin in his lap and turned toward Lillian. "I was pleasantly surprised to get your call, though I imagined it would be you and Sean dropping in."

George had met Sean at holiday work parties for the ER staff. He knew Sean as most of the rest of the world did—a history professor.

"He's helping a friend with a project, so I'm traveling without him this time."

He was helping his friend—President Lawson—with the threat of nuclear warfare. So she hadn't lied.

Angie pushed a strand of gray hair from her face before trailing her fingers down to her pearl necklace. "How did you and Ivan meet?"

Lillian had already planned how to answer the inevitable question. She would keep the same basic story she had told Falco. "We met on my medical mission to Africa. We reconnected on my trip to Iceland."

Angie shuddered. "Africa was a frightening time." She turned to Ivan. "We were informed by the Red Cross that Lillian's entire camp in Kenya was destroyed. Military personnel..." She stopped herself and glanced at Falco who was inspecting the menu. She lowered her voice. "They couldn't tell us for weeks if she was alive."

"Very frightening," Ivan concurred.

"But you survived, also. Are you a physician as well?"

Lillian took a sip of water. She was going to let Ivan sink or swim on his own with this line of questioning.

"No. I'm a computer programmer."

The waiter arrived and took drink orders.

George asked Ivan, "Do you know Lillian's husband, Sean?"

Lillian turned in her seat to give Ivan an amused look.

He blinked at her.

She smiled sweetly in return.

"I've had the pleasure of meeting Dr. Jennings twice." He turned to look at George. "Very impressive. He has published history books and is a professor."

Lillian realized Ivan must have been keeping tabs on Sean as much as her.

They placed food orders. When brunch arrived, conversation turned into discussions that included Falco. The boy divulged space trivia facts and revealed his love of Harry Potter books.

"One day, I want to see Harry Potter World and drink butter beer."

Angie smiled, a warm grandmotherly smile. "Well, for now would you settle for the Strasbourg Cathedral? It's lopsided, you know. They can't even finish the other tower or the whole structure might collapse."

With that, Angie, Ivan, and Falco left to see the cathedral.

Lillian set down her silverware and turned to her friend and former boss. "Thank you for orchestrating time for us to talk."

"Well, something in your tone suggested this was more than a social call in Alsace. Is it about the job? The chair position?"

"No. The job is fine. And temporary."

"It doesn't have to be temporary. If you want full chair of the ER, you have enough support for it."

Did she? She hadn't thought so.

"I'll sort out the leadership role. This is a bigger problem. Ivan has been tracking a bomb in the hands of"—*what are they? Terrorists? Anarchists? Annilihists?*—"people who intend to detonate it. We just learned the target is Paris. We need to get there and track it until a team can confiscate it."

George gaped at her. "Do you hear yourself? You're telling me you are passing through Strasbourg on your way to Paris, tracking a bomb. Why are *you* doing this?"

"I made CIA contacts with everything that happened in Africa. Since then, I've occasionally been a...resource. Ivan knows this and asked me to help."

"Okay. Let's say I believe all of that because you're the most rational and honest person I know. Why aren't government agencies handling this?"

"They tried." Lillian averted her eyes and stared at the empty dishes on the table. "A ten-man Delta team tried to intercept the bomb in Bulgaria. They were all killed."

George ran a hand through his thin, gray hair. "That's awful."

"The next combined special ops team is en route to Paris, but they need eyes on the ground to track it."

"Your eyes?" His voice was skeptical again.

"Mine and Ivan's."

"And I'm in the picture...I'm involved because? Lillian." His last world snapped like a whip. "You want me to take Falco? Are you mad? I would be an American babysitting a German national in France." He dropped his voice. "Somebody is bound to arrest me."

"Would you rather I take the kid to Paris? To the bomb? A weapon so heavily guarded a Delta Force team was slaughtered when they tried to grab it?"

He glared at her. She knew that look well. As her former boss, he had to deal with fallout from her actions—an angry parent she had chastised for child neglect; the head of another department calling because she complained about one of their subspecialists delaying care; a resident who took offense when she suggested he go back to medical school and learn how to interpret an arterial blood gas.

George's expression had managed to capture both a sense of exasperation at her management of the situation and inability to declare her statements false. She suspected part of him liked how she challenged people to perform better and raise expectations of themselves. Simultaneously, he would have preferred the waves she made to be little capillary waves rather than tsunamis.

"Doesn't he have other relatives?"

"Falco doesn't have any other family."

She wanted to tell George she wouldn't be asking him to help if he did, but finesse was going to persuade better than sass. "His aunt was just put in a palliative care home for stage-four breast cancer."

He leaned back and crossed his arms. "Well, Angie is going to love this. As you can tell, she loves children. He'll be spoiled by the end of his visit. Which is when, exactly?"

"Not more than a few days."

He pursed his lips. "Anything I need to know—special diet, allergies, medications, night terrors?"

She pondered his questions. They were logical for a parent of four kids and grandparent of six kids. Having no children of her own, she had watched Falco and never thought to ask those important questions.

"Not that I know. We'll double check with Ivan. Also, he hasn't shown any signs, but I think PTSD is a possibility."

"Why would a six year-old have post-traumatic stress disorder?"

Lillian felt reluctant to share an abundance of detail, but George needed to know what Falco had been through. She explained the attack on Ivan's cabin and how Falco would have seen—at least partly through the porch wood slats—Lillian shoot one of the attackers.

"Good God. You shot someone? Are they coming after Falco again?"

Lillian shook her head. "They were after Ivan. You won't be in danger after we leave."

"*You* will be. Lillian, what if neither of you return from this?"

"We're just going to help track it. In the unlikely event that something happens, Sean will know what to do."

"Sean?"

"Yes."

"Who—judging by your unspoken words—is as wrapped up in this as you?"

"Yes."

"Okay. Okay. Can you call me daily? Let me know you're okay?"

"I will do that."

"This is one heck of a retirement vacation. It's going to be hard to top this for Angie on our next trip."

"Thank you."

---

IVAN KNELT DOWN, face-to-face with Falco—the greatest gift the world had given him. A gift he didn't deserve. He felt like a vice was closing in around his heart.

"You are my pride and joy. This trip is important. I wouldn't leave you otherwise."

"I know, Papa."

"I promise to replace all of your books and clothes burned in the fire." He stared at the boy's smooth skin, stormy blue eyes, and long, light lashes.

Falco's little brow furrowed. "Where are you going?"

"To Paris."

"With Lillian?"

"That's correct."

"That makes me feel better. She'll protect you."

Ivan gave him a quizzical look.

"She protected me."

"Yes, she did."

"When will you be back, Papa?"

"A few days." He pulled Falco into a hug.

"But I don't know these people."

"Neither do I. But we trust Lillian, don't we? They are friends of hers. If she trusts them, I trust them."

"*Ja.*"

"Besides, they are plump with big smiles, which means they have big hearts and will probably spoil you with treats."

Falco's smile made Ivan's heart lift and ache in one swift motion. Ivan touched the watch on his son's wrist. "I'm with you even if you can't see me."

Lillian approached and knelt with them. "Bye, kiddo."

"Will I see you again?"

She looked at Ivan and back to Falco. "I'd like that. Maybe your dad can give us another play date."

Falco gave a lopsided grin.

Ivan nodded appreciatively at Lillian.

"Come here, you." She pulled Falco into a half hug, half-tickling embrace.

Giggles erupted.

Ivan stood. Leaving Falco was difficult. It always was. If he hadn't stupidly taken the job with the cook, he might not be in this predicament and hoping it wasn't his last good-bye.

———

DEPARTMENT OF DEFENSE
TOP SECRET
NUCLEAR THREAT INVESTIGATION


CASE FILE: 8966B20

Deputy Director: William Austin
Re: Dr. Lillian Whyte and Agent Sean Jennings

## TRANSCRIPT:
## DEPARTMENT OF DEFENSE INQUIRY

DOD: You were aware that the cook had eliminated every obstacle she had encountered thus far, including a Delta Force, yet you continued to follow Ivan?
DR. WHYTE: Yes.

DOD: At this point, you only knew the bomb was heading to Paris with no more specifics, yet you continued to follow Ivan?
DR. WHYTE: Yes.

DOD: Despite insistence from your husband—endorsed by the deputy director of the CIA—you chose to remain with Mr. Kleist?
DR. WHYTE: I chose to remain part of the surveillance team.

DOD: Your plan was only for surveillance?
DR. WHYTE: Yes. We discussed trying to tag the bomb with a tracking device, but if a Delta Force team was unable to get within ten feet of it, neither would we.

DOD: At this point did you know that the cook planned to trap Ivan?
DR. WHYTE: I did not.

DOD: And you didn't know about the cook's parallel plan?
DR. WHYTE: No.

# CHAPTER 20

On the road to Petersburg Federal Correction Complex, Austin took a call through his car's Bluetooth.

"Bill, this is Conrad."

"What news?"

"I updated the president. Lancaster's drones picked up a couple insurgents. We've got eyes on truck. In the nick of time too. The nuke went underground at an old World War II revetment site turned park in the Paris suburbs. Our special ops team is planning their attack as we speak."

Austin felt a swell of relief. "Great news, Conrad. Have you got identification from the facial recognition on the terrorists?"

"Mostly ex-Spetznaz."

"Any Korean women?"

"No cook."

Austin tempered his disappointment. Between what they were about to learn from Gabe Oleander—hopefully—and what Ivan would supply them later about the cook, they should have enough information to find her with the help of Interpol.

A half hour after the call ended, Sean and Austin arrived at the Petersburg Federal Correction Complex. After supplying their identification, they were led through multiple checkpoints to a stark and sterile room with a table and two empty chairs. Austin noted the camera in one corner.

Gabe Oleander, a plump man with a receding hairline sat in a brown jumpsuit. Crinkling his nose, he sniffed the air. "Feds?"

"CIA," Austin replied.

Gabe grunted. "You all smell the same to me."

"I hope that means we smell like opportunity," Sean said. He took a seat in the chair, ignoring the way Austin glared at him for taking the lead.

"We need information on the cook."

A crooked smile curved along Gabe's lips. "I was told you didn't want to hear about mythical creatures."

"Now we do."

"What's it worth to you?"

"Your freedom."

"Sean," Austin warned.

Gabe leaned back. "Could be I know who's been funding her."

"Who?"

"What's she doing with all that money, anyway? Ten million dollars is a hefty sum to pay an assassin."

"She's trying to kill a lot of people."

"She probably could."

"Who's paying her ten million dollars?"

Gabe leaned forward and linked his fingers. "First of all, you're not gonna believe me. Secondly, I need more than freedom. I need protection."

"Protection from whom?"

"The biggest arms manufacturer in the US."

"What? Who?"

"He's an all-American icon. I need protection."

Sean leaned back in his chair. "Reginald Lancaster?"

Gabe cackled. "Look at your face. I told you, you wouldn't believe me."

"This is absurd." Austin started to walk toward the door.

"Wait," Sean said over his shoulder.

Shocked that Sean would take this guy seriously, Austin's mind raced with questions. Why would a weapons manufacturer steal a nuclear weapon? What did Reginald stand to gain by detonating a bomb in Paris?

He remembered Reginald in the meeting with the president and secretary of state. The man wanted to sell more weapons. Austin remembered the cook's mercenaries using a Stinger missile manufactured by Lancaster Defense Enterprises to take out the Delta Force helicopters—a fact that they only noticed after Sean and Marty scrutinized the video feed. A nuclear detonation in a major city meant every country would buy more weapons. Lancaster's weapons. Would Reginald do such a thing for profit? What about the cook's motivation? Also for the money?

Sean stood and walked over to Austin. "This is plausible."

Austin lowered his voice. "Jeez, Sean, you were in the SEALs with Lancaster."

"Yeah, and if you were the country's largest weapon's manufacturers in a world where one of the biggest industrialized nations recently elected a pacifist, you'd be facing financial disaster. What better way to boost sales?"

Austin shook his head even though he saw the plausibility. "Nuclear warfare is too extreme. He's not a fanatic."

"He might be a man with a financial agenda."

Gabe's face lit with anticipation. "She really did it, didn't she? She stole a nuke?" His eyes went wide. "Is she bringing it here?"

Austin glared at Gabe. "What do you know?"

He shrugged. "Rumors, man. Just rumors."

Sean turned back to Austin. "We need your best analysts scouring Reginald's finances. If so much as a penny is out of place, we bring him in for questioning."

Austin scratched an elbow. He couldn't afford not to follow every lead, no matter how outlandish.

"Wait," Gabe called. "What about my protection?"

Austin turned to look at him. "We'll send someone back in to collect more details. Anything you know about Lancaster's off-shore money movement will help us apprehend him. Our defusing the situation is your protection plan."

Gabe gave them a pitying look. "Then I guess I'll be here awhile, because once the cook sets her mind to something, it happens."

Austin hesitated at the door and crossed his arms. "What aren't you telling us?"

"She always has two methods of operation. You either never know she's coming, or you're watching the right fake when she knocks you out with her left hook."

LILLIAN LOOKED DOWN at her patient on the cot. The air inside the tent was stifling hot and suffused with the smell of sweat and blood.

She held a large syringe and needle in her hands aimed at an acute angle toward his chest. *Toward his chest.* What was she doing? Then it occurred to her—cardiac tamponade. The patient had fluid around his heart, and she needed to remove the fluid to relieve the pressure.

Sweat dripped down her cheek and onto her face. Her hands felt moist under her gloves.

She inserted the needle and started to aspirate, distractedly wondering why she was in a hot tent and not in her emergency room. She hadn't treated patients inside a tent since her medical mission trip to Africa.

When she finished her procedure, she set the needle and syringe aside. "Can you check another blood pressure?" She looked around, realizing she was alone in the tent with the patient.

She pulled off her gloves and walked outside, her shoes kicking up dry, reddish-brown dirt with every step. A slight but welcomed breeze touched her skin as she blinked her eyes to adjust to the sun. Vast, flat desert spread out in every direction. The ground at her feet was dry, cracked dirt. The patient in the tent had been the only sign of life.

"Lillian!" Sean ran toward her, fear and panic in his wide-eyed expression.

Her heart thumped wildly in her chest, but her feet refused to carry her toward him. Her voice to call back to him failed her as her throat constricted.

Behind Sean a huge mushroom cloud filled the sky. The ground shook as the explosion billowed into the sky in a plume of brilliant orange and yellow. The blast stretched horizontal, sweeping dust and light and suffocating heat toward her. Sean vanished in the explosion. Heat seared her body in agonizing pain.

Lillian awoke, struggling in a panic. She flailed wildly, trying to free herself from the sheets, trying to get her bearings in the dark room. She gulped in air.

Massive arms closed around her. "Lillian. Lillian." A deep, gentle, and familiar voice grounded her.

As she remembered she was safe in a hotel room, she relaxed in Ivan's arms. Her breathing slowed from panting to controlled deep breaths. "I...I haven't had nightmares like this since Kenya."

She tried to sit up, but Ivan kept his arm secured around her.

"Shhh. Take a few deep breaths. Your heart is racing, little *hase*."

She leaned back into him and took a deep breath. "I'm okay." She assured herself as much as him.

He rubbed his hand along her back and massaged his thumb in small circles over the tense muscles.

Lillian tentatively closed her eyes, relieved to see only black and not a nuclear explosion waiting for her behind her eyelids.

As she let her relax into the sensation of safety, she slipped back into sleep.

<hr>

REGINALD WATCHED the video feed from a command center in the White House. The room was filled with secretaries and military generals. Lancaster drones were front and center, leading troops to the nuclear threat. They had found the bomb using facial recognition taken from the attack in Bulgaria. Of course, he had known where to send the drones to ensure their success in a timely fashion.

Since Paris was six hours ahead and the attack was occurring in the dead of a dark French night, the images were dim with a black and green hue. Soldiers moved with stealth and unleashed deadly force on the mercenaries. Even through the dizzying effect of dozens of cameras and flashes of light, he could tell the good guys were winning.

And the good guys would remember how Lancaster drones helped save the day. His full cooperation and unwavering patriotism would earn him the respect and international reputation he deserved.

In thirty minutes, the on-scene commander reported all insurgents were down, and they had control of the nuke.

Looking around the room of delighted and relieved faces, Reginald met the thumbs-up with a smile and a nod. *Just like this*, he told himself. Tomorrow morning he would smile and nod before the adoring media just like this. Stock shares would soar. They might even call him a hero. America's patriotic defense contractor. If the country were enamored with him, he might even run for the presidency and deny Cole a second term.

America...a car in every garage, a chicken in every pot, a 9 mm under every pillow, and an Uzi in every neighborhood watch.

<hr>

IVAN AND LILLIAN sat across the table from each other at a cafe off the Rue de Babylone. They hadn't spoken most of the morning. She had been shaken by another dream, worse than the last one, but didn't elaborate on it.

Ivan had begun the night sleeping in his own bed, but when she wrestled her nightmare, he chanced holding her. She could have attacked him, fought against him, or feared his intrusion. Instead she had trusted him.

He tried to grasp what it meant to have earned the trust of a woman like her. She trusted him to keep her safe even when she slept. A strange sense of accomplishment lifted his feet off the ground all morning.

"Do you ever think about having children?"

She blinked at him.

"Is that something you and your husband ever wanted?"

"We've talked about it," she answered slowly. She sipped her coffee. "I think part of us both want children, but our hesitation has been in exposing a child to the violence of the world. The violence in our lives."

"You would make a good mother—loving and giving, but not curling."

"Curling?"

"Yes, curling. You know, like the Olympics." He put his hands together as if holding a handle and shook them back and forth. "Curling children like Olympic athletes curl the stone."

Lillian chuckled. "Like creating the exact trajectory you want your child to follow?"

"Yes, curling."

"I like the analogy. And you're right. I don't design anyone's future. I couldn't imagine doing it for a child."

Ivan's phone rang, and he was briefly grateful that something broke the silence between him and the physician. "Pico."

"No, Mr. Kleist. I think Mr. Cardoza has helped you quit enough at my expense." The cook's English was carefully and slowly pronounced.

Ivan sucked in a breath as he shot Lillian a look of dismay. He pinched the bridge of his nose. Pico was dead. Another friend lost. Pico should have escaped when Ivan warned him.

Now, Ivan was in Paris—at ground zero—with no way of knowing where the bomb would be set. He stared down at his half-eaten crepe.

Lillian's warm hand gripped his. Looking around the cafe, he saw that no one was in earshot of their table. He set the phone down and switched it to speaker, but kept the volume low. He put one finger to his lips.

Lillian pursed her lips.

"You have been very persistent, Mr. Kleist," the cook continued.

He heard a delicate clink as though a spoon had hit the edge of a porcelain cup.

She continued. "One might even begin to mistake you for delusional—thinking yourself capable of thwarting my plans."

His stomach twisted in knots. He forced himself to keep an even tone. "I've been called ambitious."

"I was thinking foolish."

"I've been called that as well. Yet here I am, outliving all your attempts on my life."

"Yes. And I have the reward you seek."

He waited. He had no one else she could reach or hurt. She had no threats that could break his resolve.

"The bomb will be detonated at the Eiffel Tower at three o'clock today."

"Why would you tell me this?"

"You think you can stop me. I disagree. I have nothing to lose by telling you. Not now. Not when the detonation is so close, and all of my pieces are in their place. Come. Meet your maker."

The cold conviction in her voice sent a chill down his spine.

The call disconnected.

He stared at Lillian, squeezing her hand in some small effort to garner her strength. The cook hadn't mentioned Falco. If she had wanted to truly scare him, she need only threaten his son.

*She still doesn't know about him.*

At least he had succeeded in keeping Falco a secret.

"Sounds like a trap," Lillian said. "I need to let Sean know. I don't know if whatever agents they have are close enough to intervene."

The waiter came by the table and Ivan presented cash to cover the meal.

"I need to stop her."

"Remember the part about a trap?"

"Hmmm. Her soldiers will be expecting a lone blond man. They will not be expecting a couple." He looked into her eyes. Once again he needed her help. Once again he felt fortunate to have her.

She arched an eyebrow. "Couple?"

"For pretend."

"Do you even know what a doting man does with his sweetheart in Paris?"

He felt his ears burn as he withdrew his hand. "I know how to be affectionate."

"I'm not trying to embarrass you, but a lot is at stake here. If you waltz out there dragging me by the hand behind you as you look around with your scowling pair of eyes, then your disguise is pretty thin. I'm brazen, but I don't do suicide missions."

He stood and she followed suit. Instead of leaving the table, he stepped close and towered over her. She tried to take a defensive step back, but he pinned an arm behind her back and thrust her body close to his.

As he brought his face close to hers, he spoke in a low rumble, "Then I will need to imagine you are a beautiful, intelligent woman whom I fell in love with on a mission to stop a nuclear weapon. I will need to imagine you have all of the elements of a Valkyrie—strength, determination, and heroism."

His heart thudded against his rib cage, and he was surprised at the huskiness of his own voice.

Lillian's cheeks flared red.

As he leaned closer, looking from her red hair to her red lips, concern flashed in her eyes. He could feel her panting breaths as her chest rose and fell against his. Arousal or fear? Both, he decided.

When he released her, she took a step back from him. He walked away from the table and out of the cafe.

She followed after him. "Where are you going?"

As he stared at the concrete beneath his feet, he took long, determined strides. "To the hotel to take a cold shower."

---

DEPARTMENT OF DEFENSE
TOP SECRET
NUCLEAR THREAT INVESTIGATION

CASE FILE: 8966B20
Deputy Director: William Austin
Re: Dr. Lillian Whyte and Agent Sean Jennings

TRANSCRIPT:
DEPARTMENT OF DEFENSE INQUIRY

DOD: At that point the president approved a combined special ops team?
JENNINGS: Yes.

DOD: And they succeeded in stopping the bomb?
JENNINGS: One of the bombs.

DOD: At what point did you learn of Reginald Lancaster's involvement in the nuclear threat?
JENNINGS: Deputy Director Austin and I traveled to obtain information about the cook from a prisoner at the Federal Correctional Center in Petersburg. He suggested Lancaster was involved.

DOD: What did Zoey Cain's investigation uncover?
JENNINGS: Mr. Lancaster had funneled large sums of money to

international accounts in the last several months. Those accounts couldn't be linked to his standard business partners.

DOD: Then, you decided to apprehend a public figure in a public forum with civilians present?
JENNINGS: No. First we broke the fourth amendment and eavesdropped on a call between Mr. Lancaster and the cook about the package delivery, and then we apprehended Mr. Lancaster in public.

# CHAPTER 21

---

Sean woke abruptly to his phone ringing. "Lillian?"

"It's me."

"Are you okay?" He looked at his watch. She was six hours ahead of him, so it was mid morning in Paris. He had stayed up until he learned the good news and then decided to rest for a few hours before calling Lillian. Since this fiasco began he'd been sleeping only a few hours at a time and living off black coffee and stale vending machine sandwiches.

"Yes."

"I've got good news, hon. The special ops force has custody of the bomb."

"Since when?" she snapped. The tone was not the relief he expected, and her alarm jolted him awake like a shot of espresso.

"Since four hours ago. I saw the entire thing on go-cams. We have the bomb. You can come home."

"Was the cook apprehended?"

"No, she wasn't there."

"Sean, the cook called Ivan and told him the bomb would be at the Eiffel Tower at three today."

"Why would she tell Ivan exactly where the bomb is?"

"He thinks she underestimates his ability to stop her. But if our soldiers have the bomb, how can she detonate a bomb she doesn't have?"

Sean's stomach lurched at the memory of Gabe Oleander's warning. "It's her left hook."

"What?"

"There's a second bomb. We missed something. Lillian, please get out of there. If you leave now, you can go back to Strasbourg and be out of the blast range."

"No, you're going to have Bill notify special ops and have them come to the Eiffel Tower, right?"

Sean looked at his watch and did the mental calculations. The Delta Force team would have already loaded the bomb on a bird and be back to the naval ship in the Mediterranean. The GIGN might still be close enough. "I'll let Bill know about the Eiffel Tower. Let them take it from here."

"When US troops or French troops have bomb in hand, I'll back off. We're not in control of the situation yet. I think I can help."

"What aren't you telling me?"

"I'm telling you everything. I want this bomb stopped as much as you do, and I'm not quitting. I'm helping Ivan."

Sean ground his teeth together. She was hiding something. Why would she truly believe she was essential to stopping events? Ivan must have convinced her to help him get close to the cook. He was the only one who could identify the Korean assassin. Yet she could identify Ivan. Shit. Lillian would be his cover. The cook would be looking for a lone German, not a man with a beautiful redhead. A couple.

He clenched his fist, wishing he could put it through Ivan's face. If she survived the cook's forces, Lillian could be a casualty of friendly fire when friendlies arrived to seize the bomb.

"Sean?"

"I'm here. I want updates on your status and the status of the bomb. Call me or text me." He hung up the phone. If she wanted to act like an agent, he could treat her like one.

*And agents needed backup.*

He dialed Jack's number.

"Jack's VIP lounge, how can I help you?"

"You have eyes on Lillian?"

"Yep. Your watch tracker works right nice. As of two hours ago, I'm outside her hotel room."

"We have custody of the first bomb, but there's a second. Eiffel tower. Three o'clock."

"What—are the nukes multiplying? I'm guessing from your tone that your wife is attending this shindig?"

"Up close and personal."

"I hear your worry, and I sense your anger, but would you have this handy information without her involvement?"

"She could be less involved, and we'd still have this information."

"I see. And how goes the rest of the investigation?"

"We might have an origin of the funds. It's not good."

"Oh?"

"US origins." Sean had spoken with Zoey when she completed her dig into Reginald Lancaster's finances. He looked guilty. Now, they needed to prove it.

"Oh damn."

Sean rubbed his neck. "Please, Jack. Tell me you'll look out for Lillian."

"I'll watch her back."

---

Yu dialed the contractor's number. "Mr. Lancaster."

"No names, remember?"

"I think I can call you by name when you deliberately helped the US secure the nuclear weapon I worked so hard to steal from North Korea."

"Watch your language."

She was intentionally using plain descriptors in the likelihood that the call was being traced. "I would have been killed by their attack if I had been there."

"But you're alive and well paid, so what is the issue?"

"Your plan all along was to have Lancaster Defense Enterprises save the day. You never intended to let me have my explosion. My day of reckoning."

"Don't be ridiculous. Your job was sloppy, and the Pentagon was on to you way back in Bulgaria. It was only a matter of time before they caught up to you again. The only way to turn this into a profit was to be helpful."

She smiled at his blatant lie as she gazed out her balcony window, tea in hand. She had a nice view of the Eiffel Tower—such a hideous tower of molded metal. But not for long.

"Do you know, Mr. Lancaster, that a separate second North Korean facility was robbed?"

"What are you talking about?"

"There is a weapons' development facility outside Pyongyang where they are developing suitcase nukes. Big punch, little package." She looked over her shoulder at the bomb on the bed. It wouldn't level Paris, but the crater in the middle would be quite the new tourist spot...once the radiation had cleared.

"Are you out of your mind?"

The words sliced into her, and her teacup slipped from her hand as a sudden feeling of her hand burning—again—seared her. When the sensation passed, she disconnected the phone and bent over to clean her mess.

She called Cassandra. "He knows."

"What? Why? He'll try to stop you."

"Can you turn the drones against the team that confiscated the first bomb?"

She heard the sound of Cassandra's fingernails clicking on a wooden desk. "Yes. I can do that."

"Then we don't have a problem."

---

LILLIAN EXHALED DEEPLY with her eyes closed, ignoring the click of the hotel door opening.

"What are you doing?" Ivan asked.

As she felt the stretch deep in her hamstring, she replied, "Yoga."

"Now?" He slung a black backpack onto the bed.

"Yes, now. The stress of everything is consuming me. I'm having nightmares again. I need to get this tension out of my system so I don't curl up into a ball and cry."

His expression softened—as soft as it could for a man who'd lived hard and dangerous all his life.

"Easy there, big guy. I'm not going to break." She stretched into mountain pose. "I need yoga. A massage wouldn't hurt either. I should definitely get one of those when this is over."

"I know what will make you feel better." He dumped the contents of his backpack on the bed.

Lillian stared at the guns and clips before lunging into warrior pose. "No, guns never make me feel better."

Ivan's lower lip protruded as he methodically arranged his arsenal. "They always make me feel better."

He straightened out a piece of red fabric. "Perhaps this will make you feel better."

"What is it?"

He held up a sleeveless red dress. "Your disguise to help my disguise."

Lillian shook her head. "Is it bulletproof?"

He scowled.

"Fine. Disguise. Got it."

Lillian twisted into another pose. "So, we have a plan?"

"Same as when the cook called. Kill the assassin. Disable the bomb."

"Do you know how to disable a nuclear weapon?"

He shrugged. "I watched an online video."

She gaped at him, trying to discern if he was serious or joking with her. His expression betrayed nothing.

"You realize that your plan is heavily reliant on you. If anything happens to you. I'm dust in the wind."

"Yes, the fate of the world rests in the hands of Loki. No tricks, doctor. I don't want a nuclear explosion. You could try to at least sound as though you have a morsel of faith in my ability."

"Considering you've been an international criminal at large for twenty years and escaped one of the world's most notorious assassins, I think you've proven you're more than capable. I wouldn't have followed you this far if I didn't have faith."

He gave her a bow of his head. "Okay. Now. Which gun do you want?"

"And where in that red dress am I supposed to hide a gun?"

———

AUSTIN SAT, gazing at a menu, as Reginald Lancaster entered the dining room of the restaurant and walked toward his table near the window. The weapons manufacturer and current public enemy number one sauntered to the table.

The scent of eggs and bacon filled the air, reminding Austin of the food he had forcibly forsaken to better his cholesterol.

When Reginald was a few steps away from the table, he faltered. His smug expression was replaced by confusion and irritation. "You're not the secretary of defense."

Austin lowered his menu and stroked his hand along his blue satin tie. His pristine charcoal suit was in contrast to the distressing week he'd been having. His gaze shifted from side to side, observing the bodyguards on either side of Reginald.

The deputy director of the CIA stood. "No, but we've met. We have questions for you, Mr. Lancaster."

On cue, Sean materialized beside Austin from a corner table.

As recognition of Sean crossed Reginald's expression, his scowl deepened. They had lured him out of his security-laden office and into a public restaurant. Austin could see Reginald's mind churning, probably deciding if he wanted to risk a public fiasco by trying to escape.

"We'd like you to go quietly," Austin said in a tone that suggested Reginald's apprehension wasn't contingent upon his cooperation.

Reginald's gaze flickered around the room. Guests at the restaurant were starting to stare at the five-man standoff. Whether he knew it or not, Reginald was surrounded. Five plainclothes FBI were seated at various tables. Three government vehicles and ten more agents, both FBI and CIA, waited outside the restaurant.

Reginald's jaw tensed. "Let's go."

As Austin moved toward Reginald and around the table, Reginald's men flexed. Austin raised his eyebrows, and Reginald signaled his men to stand down with a shake of his head.

They escorted Reginald to the middle vehicle parked on the curb, a black, all-wheel-drive Yukon XLS with tactical reinforced steel doors and bulletproof windows. It was flanked by matching SUVs in front and behind.

Before he entered the back seat, his hands were secured with electronic handcuffs—the latest in tamper-proof design. The mix of electronics and mechanics meant that the lock couldn't be picked with standard cuff keys, paperclips, hairpins, or metal chards. The matching key transmitted a code to disengage the electronic lock from the mechanical lock. Then, the key could be turned to manually open the cuffs.

Austin watched two agents close the door and climb in the front of the middle vehicle. When Sean and Austin were seated inside the back of the lead vehicle, Austin signaled the driver to go.

Tension eased from Austin's chest slightly as they drove away from the curb. They would take Reginald to a "black house" for interrogation. He was a public figure, so they needed to manage their investigation carefully. He was also a master of weaponry with an arsenal at his disposal. It was important they take him to an undisclosed location.

"That went better than expected," Austin commented.

"I told you he's more politician than military specialist these days. He won't risk his reputation with an incriminating public display."

"It was risky." Austin had trusted Sean's judgment to lure Reginald into public with the anticipation of a meeting with the secretary of defense. Given Reginald's ego and the current undisclosed global crisis, the weapons tycoon wouldn't refuse. If he had resisted being taken into custody, however, civilian lives would have been at risk.

"How far are you seeing this thing through?" Sean asked.

The deputy director of the CIA didn't engage in ground missions, but Austin fully intended to micromanage a situation involving the threat of nuclear warfare. "We have a bomb to find. I'm part of this until it's done."

***

Cassandra had watched a video feed of the drones that helped the special ops team locate the bomb. The soldiers—American and French—had impressively overpowered the few Spetznaz left to guard the large nuclear warhead. One weapon was down while the other remained undetected.

As the victorious team reclaimed the bomb, she observed through the drones the loading and transport of the bomb away from Paris. The French anti-terrorism group looked more than relieved to see the bomb depart French soil. With the American soldiers gone, that left only the French, who could potentially disrupt the planned detonation at the Eiffel Tower. They didn't know about the second bomb, but one couldn't be too careful.

She sat at the console and maneuvered the drones to target the remaining helicopters and military trucks. Lancaster had an array of drones armed with grenades, semiautomatic weapons, or EMPs. These particular drones had internal bombs containing C4. She positioned one each under the two helicopters and two trucks, and activated their self-destruct mode. The cameras went black. The entire military team was now cut off from any rescue attempt of the other bomb. Truthfully, she had done them a favor. The men were out of the one-mile blast range of the smaller nuke.

Cassandra received the text from Lancaster's security detail that he'd been taken into CIA custody. She needed to play this carefully. Lancaster's men were fiercely loyal. She may have been the one to have hired most of them, but he had been the one who cultivated loyalty by getting them out of their own predicaments—DUIs, assault charges, gambling debts.

If he was behind bars, she could help manage more of the company, but his men wouldn't stand for Lancaster being jailed without an attempted rescue. She couldn't *not* send a team. Yet, she needed to pick the right team. If she chose a small group and under-resourced them, they might fail, and Lancaster's fate would be sealed behind bars. Such a ploy would appear obvious to his men. She would have to send the full cavalry. Even if they succeeded, and Lancaster was freed, he'd be a man on the run. Jail or at large, either worked in her favor.

After giving instructions for Lancaster's rescue, she opened her laptop and logged in. She wouldn't be on the rescue mission because she needed to ensure the bomb was detonated. The cook had a specific time in mind, and Cassandra could respect a death with personal meaning. However, if the assassin failed to detonate the bomb, Cassandra would do it herself.

Yu sat in the Champ de Mars, facing north. To her right was the Louvre, further north was the Arc de Triumphe. South were the Paris catacombs. To her left was the Hippodrome. Four targets. The center show was the Eiffel Tower. The grand finale.

The other small car bombs would serve as distractions. Paris police were on high alert, searching bags. No one had searched her stroller, but she wasn't close to the Eiffel Tower yet. Once the distraction bombs detonated, she could walk to the Eiffel Tower and plant the stroller, which of course had a bomb and not a baby.

She had a nice view of the iconic structure. A front-row seat. Tourists frolicked in every direction. Families. Lovers. And the peddlers vying for their attention and their Euros.

One couple moved closely together, embracing and caressing fingers and bodies intermittently entwined. The woman's red dress swirled around the man's black slacks, face disappearing beneath his fedora as he leaned into her red hair. Quintessential Paris love.

Yu's small group of soldiers waited in a tourist bus hiding out of sight of Paris police. Her men were adequate with weapons, but they wouldn't blend into a crowd. They had instructions to stay hidden unless needed. They might have declined to participate regardless of the promised money if they knew they had been hired to protect a nuclear weapon.

Since Cassandra used Reginald's drones to paralyze the French counter-terrorism unit, the only remaining threat was Ivan. One man. One very pale, broad, and easily identifiable man. He was also the only adversary who could reliably identify her.

Her eyes had scanned the passersby over and over. Ivan wasn't here. Perhaps he had grown wiser and recognized his limitations. He could be in the trees, but sniper work wasn't his mode of operation. His assassinations were up close. Even if he managed to get near enough to kill her, there was no stopping the bomb. Detonation was certain.

Yu had given Cassandra access to the computer for remote detonation.

It was time for her to move closer. In five minutes, the other bombs would donate, creating her window of opportunity.

---

R EGINALD STEWED in silence in the FBI transport vehicle. Where had his error been? Had they tracked his communications? His finances?

He had tried to be so careful. Only one answer was feasible—the cook had betrayed him.

She was also planning to detonate a second, smaller bomb. He could warn the CIA, since they surrounded him, but that would require admitting conspiracy and would eliminate any hope of him being a hero in this scenario. He certainly never intended an actual nuclear weapon to be detonated, but stopping it to fully expose himself was extreme. And yet, the CIA was one car away.

Why was Sean Jennings part of his apprehension? Reginald's blood boiled to think a former colleague could have discovered him. Why else had the spook been to see the president and then been at the restaurant? Reginald half expected a gloating expression from Sean, but his face had been impassive.

Unfortunately, Reginald had no leverage over Sean. Not for lack of trying. Sean's presence at the White House several days ago concerned Reginald enough to dig deeper. Apparently, the man still worked for the CIA. He had a wife—an emergency room physician. Neither of them were public figures, and their lives seemed unimpressive. She treated drunks and drug addicts in urban Atlanta, and he wrote history books.

Reginald had decided to take precautions and position his men close to Sean's wife. This way, if Reginald's hunch that Sean was working with the CIA to uncover information about the nuclear weapon was correct, persuasive measures to deter Sean could be implemented. Reginald was surprised to discover Sean's wife was vacationing alone in Iceland. He flew a team of men out to the tiny island, but she had already disappeared.

According to the state department, her passport dinged in Hamburg, but that was the last trace of her. No credit card use. She hadn't registered under her name at any major hotels. Why the cloak and dagger? Had she been tipped off of the danger? Was she running from something else? Was she an ER physician or was that another front?

In any case, his endeavor to find her had been unfruitful. Now he was in government custody with no leverage. But he didn't possess a million dollars in liquid assets and two homes in undisclosed locations with no extradition agreements with the US so that he could sit in a federal prison. He didn't have an elite ex-military team at his beck and call for no reason. Reginald Lancaster would not be contained.

# CHAPTER 22

Sean strummed his fingers on the car door as he stared out the window. The Virginia countryside sped past them. Beside him, Austin loosened his tie.

"Too easy?" Austin asked.

They had gotten Reginald in the convoy and stripped him of his bullet-resistant blazer, his high-tech watch, which probably also had a tracking device, and his Italian leather shoes, which probably also had a tracking device. The peaceful scene outside the window was in stark contrast to the turmoil Sean felt within him.

"It's not over yet." He turned to look at Austin. "I can't predict if he'll retaliate with force or millions of dollars in legal representation, but it's not over."

Austin carefully removed his suit coat and tie and laid them on the seat. "Don't give me that look. This is a five-hundred-dollar suit. I don't want it to get damaged."

Sean heard radio communication from the front of the vehicle. They would turn off the highway at the next right and be at their first stop in ten minutes.

Austin pulled his phone out of his jacket pocket. "Austin."

He listened for a moment, before cursing.

When he hung up the phone, Sean stared at him.

Austin's expression was grim and worry etched the lines of his face. "That was the defense secretary. Reginald's drones took out GIGNs helos. They're scrambling for vehicles, but they won't make it to the Eiffel Tower in time."

Sean called Lillian, but got no answer. He called Marty next and got an update on her location. Then he called Jack.

When he hung up the phone, a small drone flew above them close enough they could hear the buzz of the engine.

"That looks ominous," Austin said.

Sean tried to follow the small object as it looped back toward the three-car convoy.

"Anybody else see that drone?" One of the drivers said over the radio.

The driver of Sean's car answered. "Copy. Keep your distance and check—"

An explosion thundered behind them. Looking through the back window, Sean could see the rear vehicle in flames.

Sean felt and heard the engine of their car stop.

"What the hell?" The agent in the front pushed the ignition button, but nothing happened as the car coasted to a stop.

"Bat-Ray." Sean's words escaped as a breath exhaled with dread.

"What?" Austin was looking out the window as the SUV behind them also slowed.

"Zoey said Reginald had a prototype EMPs. The suicide drone must have been coupled with an EMP." Sean unbuckled his seatbelt.

Austin pulled out his cell phone and stared at the black screen in disbelief.

Leaning forward toward the front cab, Sean talked to the FBI agent. "Put it in park and try to restart it. EMPs usually don't fry the electronics, only shut them down temporarily."

Sean reached for the door handle.

"Where are you going?" Austin asked.

"To see if they can get Lancaster's transport restarted. If not and a latch-up occurred in the electronics, momentarily disconnecting and reconnecting the battery might work."

"We're sitting ducks here."

Austin was right. With farmland on either side, there was no place for cover. Despite the tank-like appearance, their vehicles were technically bullet-resistant, not bulletproof. Bullets from handguns or automatic weapons could eventually weaken and pierce the glass or the reinforced steel doors. And obviously another kamikaze drone could penetrate the armor.

The engine of their car roared to life.

Sean jogged back to the second Yukon. The driver was trying to restart the car without success.

In the distance another car approached, a blue Cadillac. Civilian or threat? He needed to assume threat, especially since it didn't appear to be slowing at the sight of a burning SUV.

"Forget it. You two go to the wreck site and help your colleagues. Agent Arbor, you're on prisoner transfer. Pile in the other car." He yanked open the rear cab.

Agent Arbor filed out with a firm grip on Reginald's arm. The other two rushed to the burning vehicle.

Reginald jerked an elbow up into the unsuspecting FBI agent's face. Agent Arbor recoiled back as Reginald pounced, taking them both down to the asphalt. Sean spun and kicked a leg into Reginald's side. He let out an *oomph* as he rolled off the agent and into a ball on the ground.

As he reached out a hand to the agent, Sean said, "You okay, agent?"

"Yes, sir." The young man looked like he'd taken more of a blow to his ego than a physical insult. He got to his feet and secured his prisoner before leading him into the Yukon.

Sean opened the driver's side door and addressed the agent. "I need you in the back."

Austin climbed out of the car and stood beside Sean. "What are you doing?"

The driver scowled. "We have orders—"

"You have at least two heavily armed vehicles approaching to take a prisoner this country can't afford to lose. They've already used deadly force. You want to drive or want a man who's studied with NASCAR trainers to drive?"

Austin gaped at him.

As the agent reluctantly got in the back seat, Sean turned to Austin. "You're up, Bill."

Austin climbed in the driver's seat as Sean took the shotgun. Sean pulled out his phone and tapped his foot anxiously as it powered back on. He was relieved the EMP hadn't destroyed it, and he needed an update from Johnathan, Jack, Lillian—somebody.

---

LILLIAN SPUN in Ivan's arms. He moved lightly, drawing her near and far. When he pulled her closer, he would adjust his hat and lean in saying, "I am whispering sweet nothings to you."

She laughed. Even knowing he was moving her closer to his target, she laughed. Who was this suddenly charismatic man? How was he able to feign affection so well?

She tried to discreetly discern who he had marked since she had never seen this villain named the cook.

She saw mostly couples and families, groups moving together at a leisurely pace. One father of an American family tapped his watch irritably as his children ran through the Champ de Mars on the way to the Eiffel Tower. "We're burning daylight here," the father snapped. A few individuals walked their pets. One woman pushed a stroller. The scene in no way suggested nuclear detonation was imminent. Perhaps there were several policemen lurking about, but she assumed they would normally be in such a public place.

Since Sean knew the Eiffel Tower was the target, she repeatedly and inadvertently looked to the sky as if expecting a dozen Black Hawks to descend and take control of the situation.

As Ivan made his next motion to draw her near, his lips touched her cheek. Before she could scowl at him for the kiss, he spun her away from him. Her red dress flared around her, and she had to catch her balance so as not to stumble in her heels.

When she looked back toward Ivan, he had pulled his gun. The shot was loud as the bullet went through the back of a woman's head, presumably the cook. She was a small, unimposing woman in a black dress. Burn scars marred her hands.

Lillian stood in stunned silence like the rest of the onlookers as Ivan moved toward the stroller.

"Move!" Ivan shouted at her. Gone was the playful man she'd held hands with moments ago.

With her ears still ringing from the shot, Lillian obeyed.

He holstered his gun as she came beside him. He stepped aside, letting her push the stroller. She looked down. No baby. Something bulky and heavy was under the blue blanket.

*It's not a boy.*

People screamed and ran or stood looking around in confusion.

"Two o'clock," Ivan said.

Lillian snapped her head to the right to see armed men filing out of a tour bus parked on the Avenue Gustave Eiffel. Even if they hadn't seen Ivan shoot the cook, they could still identify the stroller.

Lillian and Ivan had no cover in the park. Behind them was open grass. On either side were narrow strips of trees. Their only possible cover was the Eiffel Tower. A dozen thugs moved to intercept them.

Explosions erupted in every direction. The ground quaked, but the blasts were distant. More panicked screaming filled the park.

Lillian's nerves frayed, but she reminded herself whatever those explosions were, they were not *the explosion.*

Ivan put a hand to her back. "Keep moving. Those are distractions."

Ivan's hand was on his gun as they burst into a sprint toward the Eiffel Tower. Lillian pushed the heavy stroller as Ivan ran beside her.

She saw that the cook's men were on track to intercept them. They had no cover in the open.

Then police began shouting and fired weapons at the cook's soldiers. They were forced to duck behind the row of tourist buses, enabling Lillian and Ivan to dart past them.

"Ticket booth," Ivan barked.

Lillian followed Ivan's orders, took a sharp turn, and came to a sliding halt at the L-shaped ticket booth.

Tourists and workers shrieked and ran at the sight of Ivan's gun. Lillian heard distant firing, but they were now surrounded on three sides by concrete.

All the mercenaries needed to do was launch a frontal attack and overpower them.

---

Jonathan and Marie sat in the Paris taxi both painfully aware of the precious seconds ticking by as traffic kept them from getting to the Eiffel Tower.

Sean had texted Jonathan to expedite getting there, but the roads were jammed. They sat, unmoving, on the Rue Saint Honore a few blocks from the Louvre.

An explosion reverberated outside the taxi.

"*Merde*," Marie swore.

Jonathan's breath hitched until he realized that if that had been *the* explosion, he wouldn't be around to wonder about it.

He stepped out of the idling taxi and looked around at the surrounding buildings. Smoke billowed in the distance to the southeast, near the Louvre. Further from him to the northwest, another stream of smoke crept toward the sky.

He pulled out his phone.

"Sean, I'm trapped downtown. We've got multiple explosions."

Sean swore. "Decoys. You need to get to Lillian. Now! She's directly under the Eiffel Tower. She's not answering her phone."

"It's gridlock here."

"Find a way, dammit. You're a cowboy. Go off-road."

Jonathan hung up and pocketed his phone. He scanned his surroundings again. Jewelry shop. Leather store. Art gallery. Curb-to-curb cars. Pedestrians. Bikes. He could steal a bike. Pedal to the rescue.

Screw that.

Where was a nice motorcycle he could steal when needed?

Then his gaze fell on the corner of the Rue Saint Honore and Rue Royale. A beautiful chestnut mare with white stocking feet stood on the sidewalk.

*Hello, gorgeous.*

Her mount wore navy slacks, a light blue, collared shirt, and a helmet. In addition, a bulletproof vest was strapped around his torso, and he wore a gun on his waist.

As Jonathan walked toward the mounted policeman, he hoped he wouldn't be shot later for horse thieving. The policeman dismounted to talk to a group of pedestrians.

"Where are you going?" Marie was jogging beside him, trying to keep pace.

He looked down at her legs.

*Good thing she wore pants today.*

"Can you ride?"

"What?"

"Can you ride a horse?"

"No."

"Then you can stay here or hold on tight."

She pursed her lips. "I think I will need to stay here and do damage control."

He reached the policeman who was crowded by several pedestrians asking about the commotion—at least he assumed they were asking about the commotion and not the weather, but it was all in French.

"Howdy."

The policeman spoke angrily in response. Jonathan suspected his proximity made the man nervous.

In a quick motion, Jonathan grabbed the reins and pulled the horse in a sharp turn that disrupted the policeman's balance. He lunged for Jonathan while reaching for his weapon. The crowd backed away with surprised shouts. Jonathan kicked at the man's hand, preventing the policeman's attempt to draw his gun.

The policeman let out a grunt. Marie stepped between the men, flashing her identification and yelling in French. She went nose-to-nose with the angry Frenchman.

As Jonathan hoisted himself in the saddle, she handed him her SIG. He signaled the horse into a gallop. Surprised pedestrians gasped and darted aside.

The small, synthetic saddle had a different feel than his leather, western seat, but he knew this was better for the speed he needed. He charged south on Rue Royale. He needed to cross the Seine and then travel east along the river toward the thousand-foot iron monstrosity.

His little sister's life was in danger.

***

Austin felt a sense of impending doom as he gunned the SUV down the highway. Rocks settled in his stomach, knowing the pursuit wasn't finished. Since Reginald had made the decision to buck his detainment and commit to being a fugitive, he would unleash his full arsenal to achieve his goal. If the ruthless weapons maker eliminated the entire team apprehending him, he would be free to escape—perhaps even free to invent his own story about the attack on the transit team.

Sean glanced in the rearview mirror before turning to Austin. "We have to lose this tail before we go to the safe house." Tension rippled through Sean's face and muscles.

Since the man wasn't easily rattled, Austin felt even more alarmed.

"Working on it." Austin approached a bystander vehicle and quickly veered around it. The blue Cadillac behind him did the same.

Sean was right. If they stopped, and Reginald's men knew where they were, they would be ambushed. How did they know how to find them?

"Is he wearing a tracker?"

"We disabled his phone and searched him," Agent Arbor said.

Austin's hands were starting to perspire, and he wished he had his driving gloves to help keep his grip on the steering wheel.

When Sean turned in his seat toward the back, all hell broke loose.

"The cuffs are off!" one of the FBI agents hollered.

Sean launched himself into the back seat as someone fired a shot, then another. A struggle ensued, but Austin couldn't safely take his eyes off the road to see who was shot and who was fighting.

How had the son of a bitch wormed out of his cuffs? Damn. Must have been the EMP. The electronic portion of the cuffs probably shut down. After that, they could be unlocked mechanically. Reginald could have picked the lock the old-fashioned way.

In front of him, a barricade of two Cadillacs blocked the road. Steep ditches on either side made an off-road venture impossible.

Another shot exploded inside the vehicle, this one close to Austin's head and the bullet struck the dashboard.

"*Christ*. Sean?" His ear rang and he was certain the concussive blast had ruptured an eardrum.

"Working on it," Sean replied. His voice was strained.

Austin heard the snapping of bone, and a man screamed.

"Barricade!" Slamming on the brakes, Austin spun the car in a full 180-degree turn, but not before the occupants of the Cadillacs threw themselves away from the vehicle.

*That'll slow them down.*

In the back seat, a thunk of bodies against the side of the vehicle reverberated.

Austin pressed the accelerator, and they were headed back down the highway. He had traded a collision with a stationary car for a potential head-on collision with the blue Cadillac speeding toward them.

He saw a small paved road ahead on his left. "Hold on!" He hit the brakes and fishtailed onto the side road.

The Cadillac attempted the same move, but took the turn too sharply and slammed into the ditch on the side of the road.

The paved road quickly deteriorated to a pothole-ridden blowout waiting to happen. Austin swerved as best he could to avoid the gouged portions of asphalt.

The men in the back seat continued to fight, jostling Austin's seat as they threw one another around. The smell of sweat and blood filled the vehicle. Sean was taking an inordinate amount of time restraining Reginald, making Austin wonder if Sean were injured.

Someone slammed into the back of Austin's seat. It jarred him and disrupted his reaction time. The right front tire dipped into a pothole. The vehicle lurched and spun, the wheel jerking against Austin's grip. Before Austin could gain control again, the SUV nose-dived into a ditch and fell on its side. White-hot heat and blinding pain hit Austin as his airbag exploded.


SEAN BLINKED and fought a wave of nausea as he struggled to remember where he was. Around him was broken glass, the smell of oil, gunpowder, and tangled bodies. Dead bodies smelling of excrement and blood. His eyes focused on Reginald as he pushed himself away from the side of the vehicle that had landed in dirt. Reginald's eyes were open and his pupils fixed. His neck lay at an unnatural angle between the door and the driver's side seat.

Beside him was one of the FBI agent. Reginald had escaped his cuffs, pulled the man's gun, and shot him. Agent Arbor, dazed, was scrambling out of the vehicle. He reached the dirt and vomited.

"Bill!" Sean could see Austin slumped in the driver's seat but still breathing. Sean climbed to the front of the car, even though his left armed throbbed with pain. "Bill, we gotta move."

Austin reached for his seatbelt. As he unbuckled it, he gazed around the car, dazed.

"Let's go, Bill."

Steam billowed from under the hood of the SUV. Sean reached across Austin and pressed the button on the door to release the trunk. He grabbed the shotgun. They climbed out the back of the SUV and half jumped, half tumbled into the field on the opposite side of the ditch.

"You're bleeding." Austin jutted his chin toward Sean's left arm.

"Yeah. So are you."

Austin reached up and winced as he touched a gash on his scalp. Blood had dripped down one side of his face and was already drying.

"Keep moving. We need to get out of sight."

"Lancaster?"

"Dead. If we're lucky, his rescue party will find him and give up."

As the three men moved deeper into a cornfield, Sean felt the many aches in his body. When he'd finally wrestled the gun from the maniac, Reginald had tried to gouge his face with his handcuffs. Sean had blocked his arm and caught the blow. He had struggled to restrain Reginald without killing him. They still needed information on the second bomb. The car accident had killed him anyway. When the car had tumbled, Sean's knee had jammed into something or someone now it pulsed with pain.

After a hundred yards, they both slumped into the dirt between the rows of corn. Sean pulled out his phone,

"How'd you know about NASCAR?" Austin asked.

"CIA water cooler."

"What did Reginald say?"

"What?" Sean looked up at Austin.

"He said something when you all were fighting. I was too busy driving to pay attention."

Sean pressed the button to call Lillian and spoke with Austin as he waited to connect. "He asked me if the nuke was stopped. I told him we were working on it. He said he only wanted the threat of a nuke, not an explosion, but things got out of hand."

"How could he think they wouldn't get out of hand with the people and weapons he involved?"

"I don't know, Bill."

The call to Lillian went to voice mail.

Sean called Marty. "Give me an update."

"She's under the Eiffel Tower. She's got a pulse, but it's racing like a rabbit, man."

Sean put his hands on his head and his head on his knees.

# CHAPTER 23

Lillian crouched by the stroller and pulled off the blanket. Ivan sat on the ground behind her, leaning against the wall.

She looked at the cylindrical metal object within a square metal box. The bomb was smaller than she expected, but stripped of the need for a fuel and propulsion system, she supposed the bomb itself didn't have to be large to inflict the intended damage. It essentially needed only a polonium-beryllium core within plutonium, surrounded by uranium and encased in explosives with detonators.

Well, she had apparently absorbed some of Ivan's teaching about nuclear bombs during their long car rides.

She heard additional gunfire. She looked around the corner briefly before scooting back to safety. "Looks like some police are slowing down the cook's men."

"Not for long. I hear rifle fire. There's a sniper out there."

She looked at Ivan. "Now what? Oh, shit. You've been shot."

He had his gun in his right hand and, with his left, held pressure over his abdomen. Lillian took note of the location—right upper quadrant. Ivan's liver would ooze, and he would slowly bleed to death without a trauma surgeon. He was already looking paler than usual.

She snatched the blanket and crawled over to help him.

He took the blanket from her, but waved her away from him. "No. No. Stop the bomb first."

"I have to fix you so *you* can stop the bomb."

"We both know you can't fix me outside of a hospital, Lillian." He jutted his chin toward the stroller. "Tell me what you see?"

She looked inside again. "Bomb. Wires. Computer. The wires go to the bomb and to the computer. There's also a cell phone. There's no timer. Aren't these things supposed to have a red digital timer so we know how much time we have?"

"This is not a Hollywood movie." He grimaced as he applied pressure with the blanket.

"So what do we do? You're the computer programmer. The computer *genius*. Can you disarm it by unlocking the computer?"

"I don't know her passcode."

"I need solutions here, Ivan."

"I'm thinking."

Her mouth went dry. "What the hell are we doing here if you don't know how to disarm it?"

"I hoped we could reach it before it was rigged."

"Well, it's rigged, genius. But she didn't get a chance to detonate it, so are we good? Do we have a bomb that's not set to go off?"

"She probably planned to do it herself, but she would also have a contingency plan."

"Like a remote detonator?"

"Yes, someone could remotely log onto the computer and trigger the bomb."

"So somebody in Timbuktu could blow us to smithereens right now?"

"Theoretically. Probably. Yes."

"How do we stop the perpetrator?"

His brow furrowed in concentration again.

She continued talking, "Okay. I've got all black wires. Do you have scissors? A pocketknife? Do I find the red wire and cut it?"

"For God sake's woman, don't cut any wires. The engineers of the bomb would have provided an internal power supply. Cutting power from the main power supply externally can trigger the bomb from the internal power supply."

"Well, the computer triggers the detonation, so I can power off the computer, right?" She leaned closer to look at the computer.

"No," he snapped.

Lillian froze, her finger inches from the computer's power button. Her stomach quivered.

Ivan grimaced. "She would have installed a failsafe so that an interruption between the computer and the power supply would trigger the bomb." He lifted his weapon and fired, hitting an incoming assailant.

Lillian cringed as the gunfire rattled her eardrums. "Okay. You said whoever is the backup detonator could remotely log onto the computer?"

"Yes."

"For someone to do that, the computer must have internet access."

"Yes."

"What's the hot spot for internet access for her computer?"

"It has to be the phone."

"So, I turn off the phone. No phone, no hotspot. No hotspot, no access. No access, no boom."

Ivan was quiet for several heartbeats. "Is the phone wired to anything?"

She looked down. "No."

"Turn off the phone."

As Lillian powered off the phone, Ivan shot another advancing gunman.

She knelt beside Ivan. They didn't have much time. The cook's remaining soldiers were closing in on them. Surely, if they knew the

Korean's plans involved a nuclear weapon they would be running away from the Eiffel Tower rather than toward it.

Ivan grew pale and his eyelids drooped. *Not long for this world.*

They huddled together, reminding Lillian of the painting she had seen at Cafe Loki—a man and a woman trapped between a wolf and a snake, crawling on a sea of bodies with spewing volcanoes in the distance. She cradled Ivan and stroked his hair. "You did it, Ivan. You saved Paris."

*But I can't save you.*

He gave her a weak grin as he slipped one of his hands into hers. "You'll take care of Falco?"

The fragility in his voice broke her heart. She sniffed. "By Odin I swear it shall be done."

His chuckle turned into a grimace. "I did fall in love with you. My Valkeryie. My Eir." His breaths became more rapid and shallow. His eyes glazed and fixed, looking up at the underside of the Eiffel Tower.

She leaned down and kissed his forehead.

His eyes closed, and his breathing slowed to a halt. His grip on her hand slackened.

Tears streamed down her cheeks. "Go and be celebrated in Valhalla."

Lillian situated the blanket over Ivan's body as the cook's forces continued to advance toward her.

She checked the clip. Four bullets. She had stopped the remote detonation of the bomb, but any of the men bearing down on her could pull a wire and trigger the detonation.

A cold sweat trickled down her neck. Sean had been right. She should have stayed in Strasbourg or hopped on a flight back to the states. She hadn't changed the outcome of the bomb, and only succeeded in putting herself in the path of bullets.

She took aim at the approaching gunmen.

*Come closer.*

She was no superstar when it came to aim. With only four bullets, she couldn't afford to randomly fire, even though fear and adrenaline were urging her to squeeze the trigger.

A shot rang out and the nearest assailant fell.

*Sniper.*

Her heart leaped at the thought of an ally. Sean was covering her —somehow. He had sent protection for her.

The men approaching her took more caution and cover. Another one fell under a sniper bullet. From her vantage, she couldn't tell how many were remaining.

A shot sounded, and the concrete wall beside her splintered. She screamed, rolled, and crouched to fire. Her shots missed and the gun clicked empty. With his weapon in hand the gunman ran toward her, aiming at her chest.

Time slowed in the seconds before her death. She wished she could see Sean one last time. The last words he shared were in anger and frustration toward her recklessness. He'd been right to be furious with her. She wished she could hold Falco's hand and make him giggle. She wished she had spent more time with her brother.

Behind the approaching assailant, she heard the distinct clip-clop of iron horse hooves striking concrete. The cowboy riding the horse fired a bullet through the gunman. The man fell dead.

Lillian looked up in surprise. "Jonathan!"

He dismounted and ran to her, hugging her fiercely. "As best I can tell, that was the last of them. I took out three. Sean's sniper took the rest."

"Sean sent the sniper."

"And me."

"Oh." She realized that made odd sense.

Jonathan began inspecting her.

"Not my blood." She jerked her head in Ivan's direction but didn't turn around to look at her dead friend.

"Baby carriage?"

"The bomb."

Jonathan frowned. "Is it still live?"

"No, but don't sneeze near it all the same."

"Thank God for that."

He looked back at her again, part scorn and part amusement. "Why is it I always see you in dresses in the midst of a global crisis."

She punched him in the shoulder.

He chuckled.

"Thank you for coming."

"I was fairly incredulous at you thinking you could affect the outcome of a nuclear explosion. Guess I was wrong."

"Thanks, I think."

"A red dress, though? If you're going to gun down bad guys, you need to learn to dress appropriately."

She eyed his jeans, boots, and cowboy hat. "And you're dressed appropriately?"

"Seein' as how I rode on a horse to rescue your ass, I believe I was."

She laughed.

Figures approached in the distance.

"Police are coming. Better put that down." She gestured toward Jonathan's gun.

"I suppose we'll be spending time in jail until the authorities sort things out." Jonathan set down the gun and kicked it away from him.

Together they knelt on the concrete floor beneath the Eiffel Tower.

"Sitting in one spot doing nothing sounds like a vacation compared to my last week."

They raised their hands high in surrender.

"Sean will bail us out though, right?"

"Eventually."

———

CASSANDRA STARED at the live news footage on the seventy-two inch television screen in Lancaster's office. Paris was in crisis. Four separate car bombs had the city in a state of panic and chaos. Cameras covered each bombsite as well as a helicopter with a more distant view of downtown Paris.

Citizens were urged to stay indoors and not use public transportation. The police were trying to curb vandalism and hunt the terrorists responsible.

Cassandra sat before her computer screen as she watched the larger wall-mounted television screen. She had logged in, remotely connected, and was prepared to detonate the nuclear weapon. The cook had apparently failed. She wondered if she had lost her nerve or was somehow killed. She didn't seem like someone who would lose her nerve. Neither was Cassandra.

She would have to detonate the bomb herself. She turned her attention back to her computer. Her heart thumped with excitement. As her fingers reached for the keyboard, the remote login window flickered. The wording changed from CONNECTED TO HOST to CONNECTION FAILED.

Had the cook disconnected her? She looked at the news footage again. No detonation. She clenched her fists in frustration.

Her phone buzzed with a text message, *Rescue mission failed. Lancaster is dead.*

Dead.

She had been hoping for jailed, but dead would definitely work. If she played her position right, she could pin the bombings and the nuclear threat on both Reginald and Noah. After all, who would believe that the vice president of a company didn't know what the president of the company was doing? A lowly project manager could rise in the ranks and save the company.

This could work out nicely.

---

SEAN'S PHONE RANG. "Jack, give me good news."

"Lillian's safe. Her brother is with her. They're both being arrested by French police. The bomb squad parked on the Avenue Gustave Eiffel."

Sean felt the vice around his chest loosen.

"Was it bad?"

"Pretty bad. Quite the showdown. Ivan is dead. I took out several goons, though I wasn't in a perfect position to get them all. I was rooftop on some law offices on the Avenue Charles Floquet. There were busses and police and tourists all obscuring my view. At least with the chaos of the gunfight and panic on the ground, no one of authority noticed a few intermittent sniper shots. Jonathan shot two or three as best I could tell. Damn if he isn't a real cowboy. Rode a horse to the Eiffel Tower."

"Huh."

"Cowboy walks into a bar wearing nothing but paper."

Sean tilted his head back and closed his eyes to the blinding sun as he waited for Jack to tell his joke.

"Gets arrested for rustling."

"Cute."

"What are you up to?"

Sean looked around at the dirt and corn stalks surrounding him. "Relaxing, catching some sun."

Austin was watching him carefully, obviously trying to discern with whom he was speaking.

"Thanks for your help, Jack. Take a vacation. I owe you one."

"I'll be back in DC. You can buy me another beer."

When Sean ended the call, Austin spoke. "Jack? As in Jack McCumsey? Former CIA agent? Did he help Lillian?"

"Yeah, I had him watching her back in Paris. Is that going to be a problem?"

"No problem."

Sean looked over his boss who was covered in dirt and blood.

"That was some good driving."

"Thanks."

Austin added, "So, Lillian's okay? And the bomb?"

Sean took notice that Austin asked about Lillian before he asked about the nuclear bomb. He lay back on the dirt as he suppressed a smile. "Parisian bomb squad is on it. Lillian and Jonathan are in police custody."

Sean breathed deeply, relaxing for the first time in over a week.

He felt aches from the car crash, but the throbbing in his head was subsiding. As he sat on the ground, he didn't care if the team they'd called to pick them up took ten minutes or two hours.

"I guess I have another international incident to smooth over."

"I guess you do."

———

LILLIAN LAY side-by-side with Jonathan on the cold concrete floor.

Jonathan strummed his fingers on his chest. "Well, this is phenomenal. My helping you lands me in a French prison. Good thing they tore down the Bastille a long time ago because judging by the French police's furious expressions, they would've liked to throw us in a dungeon." Jonathan turned and stared at his sister with an expression of incredulity on his face. "Did you actually disarm a nuclear weapon by turning off the mobile phone?"

"Technically, it wasn't armed yet, so I disabled it rather than disarmed it."

"Semantics. Accept the fact that your brother thinks you're pretty badass. It won't last forever."

"I accept."

She turned her head to look at him. "What did you tell the police when they interrogated you?"

"That I was in Paris enjoying the company of a lovely Canadian woman when I inconveniently had to rush to my sister's aid."

"Canadian woman?"

"Yeah. Someone in the CIA sent me my personal guardian angel."

Lillian's eyebrows shot to her scalp line. Bill was full of surprises. Sean had sent someone to protect her, the sniper who saved her life, while Bill had sent an agent to help Jonathan. Did he send a woman to protect Jonathan or keep him out of trouble? Perhaps both.

"She's smart, she's pretty, she's—"

"Don't finish that sentence." She feared he was about to say *was good in bed,* and Lillian wanted no details about her brother's intimate life. "You're smitten. I get it."

She bent her knees to take the pressure off her lower back. All of the stressful events at the Eiffel tower were settling into her muscles. Every part of her body ached, but pain meant she was alive. "But, to the police, you didn't mention—"

"That you were helping an international criminal diffuse a nuclear threat without the consent of any national authority, including your husband's CIA?"

"Yeah, that."

"Nope. You?"

"Nope."

"What did you tell them?"

"They need to get all of their answers from William Austin, Deputy Director of the CIA."

"That must have driven them *bastillistic*."

Lillian chuckled. "Yep." They had made red-faced, unveiled threats about her spending life in prison. Their hostility was so fervent she wanted to toss oral sedatives into their foaming mouths. She had been too exhausted to feel intimidated or to fight back, so she had sunk into comfortable silence.

"You know there's going to be a big inquisition? CIA, Homeland Security, Department of Defense—they're all going to want every granular detail."

"Wonderful. More paperwork."

"How long will it take Sean to get us out of here?" Jonathan asked.

"Guess it depends on whether or not he's still mad at me for going on a dangerous mission without him."

"So...we're going to be here for a while."

# CHAPTER 24

Lillian watched Falco sit in his aunt's arms as they waited for Sean to de-board the plane. Ada's color looked better and skin less waxy. She still had some good months left in her. She and Lillian had arranged for her to stay in an apartment in Heilbronn and have home health nursing help. Lillian ruffled Falco's soft, blond hair. His resilience had amazed her.

Jonathan sat on a bench reading *How to be a Canadian* by Will and Ian Ferguson.

After the police interrogation, she and Jonathan were interviewed by French intelligence through the office of General Directorate for External Security. Finally, Austin achieved their release, and they went to Strasbourg to retrieve Falco.

When George had let her into their hotel room, Falco ran into her arms and hugged her. She absorbed the embrace, her throat constricting and eyes burning.

After a few seconds, Falco backed away from her. "Where's Papa?"

She had held his small hand in hers. "I'm so sorry." She swallowed. "I couldn't save him." Tears welled in her eyes despite how she had sworn she would keep herself together when she saw Ivan's son.

She had waited for a reprimand or a tongue-lashing or a scolding glare or a reproachful glance. Instead, Falco walked back into her and wrapped his thin arms around her neck. Her heart ached for him as she hugged him again.

"I think you did," Falco said before breaking down in sobs.

On the drive to where his Aunt Ada was staying, Lillian had explained—in vague, nonviolent terms—how Ivan had died a hero.

After they picked up his aunt and worked on housing arrangements, Ada had brought up the topic of adoption and solicited Falco's opinion about staying with Lillian.

"When you go to heaven?" he had asked.

"When I go to heaven," Ada assured him.

He turned to Lillian. "If I stay with you, are you gone a lot?"

"I work weekdays. I attend two medical conferences per year that last about three days each. My husband and I usually go on a couple of vacations a year. You could come with us."

She had mentioned the possibility to Sean over the phone who didn't balk at the idea of adoption. Sean would adore Falco after spending a little time with him.

"Where do you take holidays?" Falco had asked.

"Usually beaches or pretty cities."

"Disney World?"

"We haven't done that one yet. We probably should."

"What about school. I'm supposed to start kindergarten."

"We would help you find a good school." She gave a nervous smile, feeling like she was being interviewed for the position of motherhood. The truth was she had no idea how to be a mother and would probably need to read more than one manual on the subject. But she loved Falco and that had to count for something on an otherwise sparse resume.

"Does your husband like children?"

"He does. Sean and I talked about having children. And we'd be happy to be your parents. We can't replace your father, but we can give you a good home."

"I like playgrounds."

"We can find playgrounds."

Any moment he would ask her to prepare a peanut butter sandwich to see if her culinary skills were adequate for raising a child.

"I like trampolines."

She cringed. "Yeah. I have to draw the line there. I'm an emergency room doctor and I see far too many childhood injuries from trampolines."

He narrowed his eyes at her in disapproval, but after a few moments seemed to find her response appropriately parental. "Okay. I will live with you."

She pulled him into a hug.

Falco sniffed. "Can you replace my Harry Potter books?"

"You bet."

Now, three days later, at the security checkpoint, she saw Sean walking toward her. He wheeled a small suitcase behind him and carried a satchel.

Lillian ran into Sean's arms as Falco hung back with his aunt. Sean's embrace was powerful and wonderfully crushing, shattering the agonizing distance and days of worry that had separated them.

"I'm sorry," she said. Sorry for the pain she had caused him. Sorry for going on a mission without him.

He kissed her before hugging her again. "I missed you." When she had insisted on staying to make sure Ivan's sister and Falco were situated before she flew back to the states, Sean had flown to her.

When they finally pulled away from each other, Sean looked over at Falco. He walked over to him and gave a tentative smile. As he bent down, he pulled a book out of his satchel. He walked over and extended it to Falco. "I have the other six in my suitcase for you."

Falco accepted the book with a gasp and wide-eyed stare.

Sean knelt on one knee and extended his right hand. "I'm Sean."

With a grin, Falco shook his hand. "Falco. *Guten tag.*"

Sean winked. "*Freut mich dich kennen zu lernen.*" *Pleased to meet you.*

———

LILLIAN EASED around the wooden table at the bar. The DOD hearings had been long and tiresome, but were over. At least she hoped they were over. They had pointed out how she had broken international laws and what repercussions might be expected.

She looked around the table—Sean, Jonathan, Austin, Jack (whom she learned was the sniper who saved her life), Zoey (whom she'd met during the Montreal incident), and Marty.

Everyone had assembled at the bar to decompress after the interrogation.

Lillian hugged her brother and Zoey.

Then she hugged Jack. "Thank you for what you did."

"Thank you. Without you I'd have been French barbeque."

Jonathan removed his hat and shook hands with Jack. "So you knew Sean back when he was a rookie agent, still green?"

"That's right."

"I bet you've got some good stories on when Mr. Perfect here was less than perfect."

"I suppose I do."

Jonathan winked. "We'll talk later."

Jack took a seat at the large table where he could see the entrance.

Jonathan extended his hand to Austin, "Deputy Director Austin, pleasure to meet you."

Austin pursed his lips. "You might as well call me Bill. Your sister does."

"I owe you a thank-you, Bill."

Austin gave him a puzzled look.

"Marie Beaulieu was very helpful in getting me safely from London to Paris."

Lillian leaned forward with a mischievous grin. "And since you're dating her, it seems she was helpful in more ways than one."

Austin raised a hand. "I don't want to know any of that."

Lillian chuckled.

Sean began ordering beers and appetizers for the table.

There were few patrons in the bar as it was still midafternoon, and the evening crowd wasn't off work. The bar had a cozy, dim atmosphere and the right mixed scent of beer and greasy fries.

Austin turned to Lillian. "I hear congratulations are in order for your position as chair."

She bowed her head slightly. "Thank you." Austin smirked. "Now you'll experience the joys of insubordinate employees amid the pressures of higher administration and public opinion."

She arched an eyebrow. "Guess I'll have to put on my big-boy pants."

Austin shook his head as he took a seat at the table.

She was excited for the position and had already made strides in meeting with the Cardiology chair to affect change on the ER-consultant relationship. Tonya had more than pulled her weight, and Lillian had managed to get the woman a pay raise starting next quarter. Lillian had let her know by writing on a pink post-it note and handing it to her. The woman had squealed and hugged Lillian as she fumigated her with the scent of her hairspray.

By the time drinks arrived, everyone was making small talk. Marie was flying in later to spend a few days in DC with Jonathan; Austin had a race this Saturday; and Jack would be spending the weekend with his grandchildren.

"Hey, Sean," Jack called over the chatter of conversation. "President walks into a bar."

Sean smiled and raised his glass. "Sure, another bar joke. Why not?"

"No. Seriously. President walks into a bar."

The table followed Jack's gaze toward the bar entrance.

President Lawson entered the room. "Please, don't get up. I can't stay long. Secret Service is outside and none too pleased with my detour."

Everyone stood anyway.

Cole walked around the table, shaking hands. "I know not all of the men and women heroes of Europe's ordeal are represented here, but all of you were instrumental in stopping the nuclear bomb. Thank you to each and every one of you."

He reached Lillian, and they hugged. "Good to see you again, Cole."

"Always good to see you, Lillian. You keep Sean in his place, got it?"

She grinned.

Jonathan blinked at her before whispering, "You failed to mention you're on a first-name basis with the president."

"I'm full of surprises."

# EPILOGUE

———————————

TEN MONTHS LATER

Jonathan pulled Marie by the pant waist toward him. Dinner was delicious, but he was ready for dessert.

"*C'est quoi ça?*" she asked.

He kissed her slowly, savoring the moment. Her lips parted, accepting him without reservation.

He broke off the kiss before it swelled into something more. "I've liked seeing you over the last several months." He looked down at her lovely face and flushed cheeks.

"And I you."

"Trouble is," he wriggled his hips closer to hers, "each time I see you, I want more." They had been meeting in different cities over the last ten months to spend time together.

She smiled before she pursed her lips together.

He didn't like the expression, so he waited for her to explain.

"I have my work in Canada and you have your ranch."

"I can give up the ranch."

"*Non*, it's your home."

He ran his hands along her back. "It was my father's home. I've got no family there anymore."

"You have friends."

"I'll make new ones"—he kissed a smooth spot of skin above her clavicle and relished the way her body quivered in response—"in Canada."

She placed a hand on his chest. "You would do that to be with me? You would leave your home?"

"Home's where the heart is honey, and mine's been with you since we met."

"*D'accord*." This time her smile didn't fade.

"Canada, here I come." He picked her up, intending to carry her into the hotel bedroom when his phone rang.

He cursed under his breath. The ring tone was Lillian's, and he knew he had to answer the call. He set Marie down and dug the phone out of his back pocket.

"Hello? Yeah. Okay. Got it."

He turned to Marie. "I need to get to Atlanta. My niece is on the way."

---

"Mom, I want to go with you."

Lillian breathed through another contraction as she zipped up her hospital bag. Sean waited anxiously, shifting Falco's overnight luggage from one hand to the other.

She couldn't bend down to kiss Falco, so she ruffled his hair. "I need you to stay with George Pops until Rose is born." George McClellan had become like a grandfather to Falco, and sometime during their bonding they had agreed to a silly nickname that stuck.

"Why?"

"Because we don't know if this will take twenty minutes or twenty hours." She made her way down the stairs, feeling like a hippo trying to walk on stilts. They had bought a two-story home in Alpharetta when they found out Lillian was expecting. "And you don't need to sit around a hospital waiting room."

The boy's shoulder's sagged.

Outside, George's SUV idled on the curb as he patiently waited in the driver's seat. Kelly's car was parked behind him. She bounced with a bright smile as the Jennings family approached.

Lillian hugged Falco to her leg briefly. "Love you, pumpkin."

"Love you, Mom." He followed Sean to George's car and climbed inside the back seat.

Sean strapped him in, put the luggage in, and thanked George. Sean leaned in the back seat and kissed Falco on the top of his head.

Kelly was still bouncing. "This is so exciting."

Another wave of contractions hit Lillian as she struggled to climb in the back of Kelly's car. At what point had she outgrown the back of a sedan?

She gritted her teeth. "Six months of nausea"—her morning sickness had been longer than normal—"followed by weekly doctor's visits"—she was forty and thus considered high risk—"followed by sleep deprivation for the last month since finding a comfortable position with a bowling ball for a belly is impossible. None of this prepares one to be in the right frame of mind for labor."

She strapped the seatbelt and pushed her head back against the seat while breathing.

"Whatever." Kelly hopped in the driver seat. "You're jumping for joy on the inside. When this part is done, you'll be holding that sweet baby girl in your arms."

Lillian smiled at that.

Sean climbed into the car beside Lillian.

As Kelly pulled away from the curb, Sean leaned over to Lillian. "You're doing great."

She gripped his hand. "Falco's okay?"

"He's good. He's going to make Rose a birthday card."

Lillian choked back tears. Heavens. She could cry at the score of a melancholy movie trailer with these ridiculous hormones.

She looked over at Sean. "You ready for this?"

He kissed her on the lips. "I'm always ready for another adventure with you."

QUICK NOTE FROM THE AUTHOR:

If you enjoyed this book and want to know about future releases by CB Samet you can CLICK HERE to sign up for my mailing list or go to www.cbsamet.com!

Also, check out my *SAMET Suspense Sampler* which contains a Lillian Whyte adventure novella, *Red Threat*. The sampler is four novellas for just 99c.

# DEAR READER

If you enjoyed this book and want to know about future releases by CB Samet you can CLICK HERE to sign up for my mailing list or go to www.cbsamet.com!

I promise I won't spam you. I only send an email when I have a new book released, giveaways, or special discounts. And I'll never sell your information. You can also unsubscribe at any time.

If you enjoyed *Gray Horizon*, I recommend *Whyte Knight* next. It will take you back to Lillian's last adventure, and then you can finish off with *Black Gold* which is a little more of a slow burn thriller compared to *Gray Horizon* and *Whyte Knight*.

Also, as an independent author, I rely heavily on readers to spread the word about books they've read. If you enjoyed this story, kindly let others know by posing a brief comment on social media or leave a review where you purchased it.

Follow me on Bookbub!

Thank you for reading,
*CB Samet*

# OTHER BOOKS BY CB SAMET

---

**The Dr. Whyte Adventure Novels**

Black Gold

Whyte Knight

Gray Horizon

---

**The Rider Files Suspense Novels**

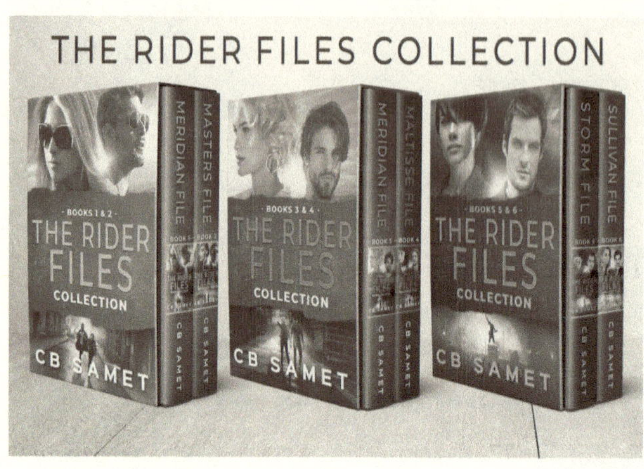



Meridian File / Masters File / Box Set 1

McMillan File / Maltisse File / Box Set 2

Storm File / Sullivan File / Box Set 3

Sharp File

---

**The Shadow Guardians**

Join the Thoren sisters in this fast paced urban fantasy series as they join the Shadow Guardians and reach their full potential as Valkyries to defeat the growing forces of darkness. Sign up for my newsletter and get Raven's Flight, a prequel novella for FREE.

**Raine Down, Book 1**

Rosalyn's Run, novella

**Storm Surge, Book 2**

Thalia's Orb, novella

**Sky Fall, Book 3**

———————————

**Love action/adventure and strong female leads in a fantasy world? Check out my other genre:**

**The Avant Champion Fantasy Series**

The Avant Champion: Rising

Malakai: An Avant Champion Origin of Malos Story (prequel)

The Avant Champion: Honor

The Avant Champion: Ashes

Brothers' Bond: An Avant Champion Malakai Story

The Avant Champion: Conquest

Isabel: An Avant Champion novelette

The Avant Champion: Redeem